C000181713

CHARITY BEGINS

Christine Williams

Pen Press Publishers Ltd

© Christine Williams 2007

All rights reserved. No part of this publication
may be reproduced, stored in a retrieval system,
or transmitted in any form or by any means, without
the prior permission in writing of the publisher,
nor be otherwise circulated in any form of binding or cover
other than that in which it is published and without a similar
condition including this condition being imposed on
the subsequent purchaser.

First published in Great Britain by
Pen Press Publishers Ltd
25 Eastern Place
Brighton
BN2 1GJ

ISBN 978-1-905621-81-1

Printed and bound in the UK

A catalogue record of this book is available from
the British Library

Cover design by Jacqueline Abromeit

Contents

1-	Like a Lamb	1
2-	Collision Course	17
3-	Sweet Caroline	36
4-	Part Time	55
5-	Headache and Headroom	77
6-	Loose Ends	97
7-	Monday Mayhem	115
8-	On Tour	133
9-	Broken Dreams	150
10-	Spin	168
11-	Endings and Renewals	184
12-	Past Forward	200
13-	Epilogue	219

CHARITY BEGINS

With all best wishes
to Eileen. Enjoy!
Christine
1st July 2007

Re- dedicated
to Sandra
May 2016
Eileen

-1-
Like a lamb...

Eight-thirty, Monday morning. New job, with a grand title: Area Manager. Well, sort of grand anyway. Better than so-and-so's assistant or such-and-such a supervisor. New office over the shop. Not the flagship store, that's true, but charity shops aren't often described in terms of 'flag-ship' or 'jewel in the crown'. New company car too! Well, newish; new to me at least. The colour of the front passenger door didn't quite match the rest of the bodywork and the driver's seat was a bit squishier and grubbier than the others but the paintwork was shiny and clean and, joy of joys, I didn't have to pay for the tax and insurance.

High optimism, less-than-high confidence. Just for a heartbeat I wondered if I shouldn't try for high on both, if I was going to succeed. 'Show them you know what you're doing even if you don't,' someone had said to me years ago. 'It works every time if you do it with style!' Did I have the style to carry it off, though (that was the crucial question), or would they all realise that I'd never done this sort of thing before as soon as they clapped eyes on me?

'Just be yourself' seemed an even dafter piece of advice since it was 'myself' that was having a crisis of confidence. It had all seemed so easy when, four months earlier, I'd sent off the job application in a haze of enthusiasm and determination. Eager for a change of focus, I'd been absolutely convinced I could do this job standing on my head. Now, facing this first day, it didn't seem so simple.

Oh Lord, where were the keys? Rain was dripping down the back of my neck as I stood at the door of the shop fumbling around in the bottom of my bag. Standing outside in the rain looking like an idiot wasn't the kind of first meeting I'd planned, but there was someone who looked as though she knew what she was doing, striding purposefully towards me as I searched for keys I was sure I'd had in my hand when I'd got out of the car two minutes ago. Didn't I?

1

Sigh of relief. She was dangling a set of keys from one finger. She was obviously one of the 'seniors' I'd been told about, a long-serving (or long-suffering, they might say) volunteer who opened the shop when the manager had missed the bus/couldn't find junior's football kit/threw a 'sicky'.

Lord, what was I thinking of! How could I possibly even imagine that any one of my dedicated team of trained, motivated, enthusiastic staff would do such a thing? Well, nobody's perfect, as I'd said to my manager the previous week after reporting back half an hour late for our review meeting following a gruelling two-week training programme. She'd given me a pained look and changed the subject.

Anyhow, today was the first day at my own desk, in my own office and on my own patch. I felt worn out already, after two weeks of shadowing experienced staff around like a baby duckling follows its mum – trusting, naïve and completely clueless! It seemed as though the more I learned, the more confused I felt. No doubt I'd soon find out all the down-side things that people had so carefully, but incompletely, hidden from me during those hectic days.

The induction training had paired me up, 'buddy'-style, with experienced Area Managers in other parts of the country. Nice idea, except I'd first found myself in Kilburn (London, that is) among the pubs, markets and chaotic multitude of languages that spoke of new immigrant populations, and then to the wilds of north Derbyshire – in March! Wet, cold, bleak and with winds that had been gathering speed since leaving the Ural Mountains, both were totally alien environments for a gently reared child of soft, rolling countryside and a bucolic lifestyle like myself.

Still, it was all useful stuff, I supposed, and designed to show me that this was no tin-pot organisation but a large, highly sophisticated, profitable company to which I was expected to make a significant – and worthwhile – contribution. Who was I to argue? I was the new girl, the innocent, and I kept my mouth shut and my eyes and ears open. Everyone was friendly, helpful and… had I detected a little sympathy in their patronage? I couldn't quite figure out why that should be, but no doubt all would become clear in good time.

'Good Morning!' I said brightly to the senior volunteer

approaching me. Rats, was that too bright? She looked me straight in the eyes, a slight frown on her face and with her jaw jutted out determinedly. Attila the Hun in a woolly hat and ear muffs.

'I suppose,' she said grudgingly. 'And who are you then?' I heard the bump as my fragile optimism hit bottom and shattered.

'I'm the new Area Manager,' I said, not quite so brightly but holding out my hand in a friendly gesture of greeting. 'My name's Gillian and I'm pleased to meet you.'

'Hum,' she said, ignoring my outstretched hand, 'another one!' And with no lifting of the frown, she pushed aside bags and boxes left on the doorstep and reached across, key in hand, to let us both in.

Taking my courage in both hands, having reclaimed the one she'd ignored, I asked her: 'Have there been many, then?' as we picked up two bags apiece and walked through the unlit, cluttered shop to the stockroom at the back. It was pitch black and I narrowly avoided falling over the bag she dropped at my feet so she could free a hand for the light switch.

'Um,' she said with exaggerated thoughtfulness, gazing at the ceiling for inspiration. 'Three in the last three years – if you don't count the one 'oo never turned up at all or the one who went sick at the end of the first week and didn't come back.' She paused and I was lost for words, struggling to think of something to say that didn't sound like mindless, gibbering bravado. 'Course,' she continued, 'if they'd been reasonable we wouldn't have had to discourage 'em, would we?' She fixed me with her gimlet gaze.

For a moment we were both still a statues, gazes locked. Hers spoke of ownership and confidence in her unassailable right to discourage the Lord God Almighty if she saw fit, whereas mine was – well, just pleading, really.

'Shall I put the kettle on, then?' I squeaked, then bolted, with as much dignity as I could muster (which wasn't enough to be noticeable, I suspected) for the stairs.

Upstairs I was faced with three doors. I tried them all and found them locked. More scrambling in the bottom of a much-too-large-bag containing almost everything I might need for an assault on Everest, should I decide to take off and do that on the spur of the moment. Actually, I thought, that was quite a tempting prospect.

This time, however, I found the keys almost immediately and tried the first one in the door on my left. Bingo! Right first time. The hinges of the door creaked and all I could see was pitch black in the room beyond.

Gradually my eyes adjusted to the gloom and I could just make out a small, narrow room lined with laden shelves. There was an overpowering smell of dust, damp and decay. Carefully I stepped inside and peered into the gloom, swiping away cobwebs that tangled in my hair and stuck to my face. I could just make out boxes with yellowing labels, brown paper packets tied with string and piles of what looked like magazines and newspapers. The room was cold. Clammy, actually, which was odd because this was an upstairs room with a party wall to the building next door. Still, it was only April and a damp one at that, and there appeared to be no heating or ventilation. Imagination took over as I took a pace backwards. Was that a foetid breath on my cheek? If I peered more closely into that far corner, would I see ancient, bloodshot eyes glaring back? Just as carefully, with the hairs on the back of my neck standing on end and being careful not to turn around to present my back to the room, I stepped out onto the landing again and slowly closed the door.

What on earth was that all about? I asked myself, feeling foolish. Too much imagination, too little common sense and nerves so stretched they pinged in a light breeze! Not to mention a horror movie on the box at midnight before bed last night. Hardly the most soothing way to cure insomnia. I gave myself a mental shaking and told myself to snap out of it.

Next I tried the door labelled with a faded, crooked sign that proclaimed 'Area Manager' and – success! I was in my new domain. I took in a large space with several filing cabinets, two desks, two tables, assorted chairs, some wall mounted shelves and an ancient, rather grubby photocopier. There was a telephone on each desk, an answerphone of about the same vintage as the photocopier and dozens of filing trays all piled high with mountains of files and pieces of paper. On one of the desks, the larger of the two, sat a computer that looked so old I wondered if it was steam-driven. Everything was overlaid with a delicate layer of dust which, in the draught created by the open door, began to dance merrily in the sunlight filtering bravely through windows that obviously hadn't seen a shammy leather for goodness knows how long. Everything looked as though it had been sleeping since before the Great Exhibition and I half expected to see a picture of HRH – Victoria, that is – on the wall.

Nerveless fingers let my bags drop to the floor. What had I done? Thrown over a job I knew inside out, with people I liked and respected, is what I'd done, and for this? OK, so it had been dull as ditch water and about as rewarding as filing my tax return, but at least I got to work in an office that somebody dusted occasionally.

I was overwhelmed with a need to sit down and put my head in my hands, the classic gesture of despair (my mother used to say I had a strong sense of the dramatic), but realised my smart new suit would probably never recover from contact with these chair seats or desk tops. Perhaps that cup of tea might help?

There were more sounds coming from downstairs now. I could hear a disembodied voice saying, 'Is she 'ere, then?' and another replied 'Yup, she's putting the kettle on', to which a third said, 'Well, at least she's got her priorities right, ent she?' Laughter all round and I was heartened to think that it didn't sound too unkind. Oh, how we can find a crumb of solace in a hostile world when we're in despair!

One of the other keys on the ring opened the door to the kitchen. For a moment I was absolutely stunned. A small but beautifully kept kitchen-cum-staff room sparkled and gleamed with diamond-like twinkles from the stainless steel kettle, the taps at the sink and the pipes from the water heater. A comfortingly large boiler, presumably for the central heating and hot water, hung on the wall, the two exposed sides decorated with transfers of woodland and garden flowers. There were spotlessly white tea and hand towels, a fine array of cleaning fluids and powders stacked neatly in a plastic pot, and a formica-topped table dressed with a lace cloth and a pretty crystal vase.

A voice behind me breathed in a stage whisper, 'Don't let Marjorie see you in 'ere without asking 'er permission first!' and my frayed nerves betrayed me as I jumped and gasped at the unexpectedly close proximity of the voice. I was acutely and painfully aware of my lack of preparedness for this morning. It was turning out to be not at all what I'd expected. Where were the jolly, friendly, welcoming lady volunteers? Those stalwart, charity workers who made everyone feel warmly welcome and thought only of the greater good? Smiling faces and permed, blue-rinsed hair? 'In your imagination,' said a little voice inside my head and I wondered if St John's Wort really did work, or whether I should go straight to super-strength Prozac.

I turned around, conjuring up a lopsided smile from somewhere. 'Who's Marjorie?' I asked in what I hoped was a friendly but firm and confident voice.

'She's been 'ere 12 years, she 'as,' my informant said, happily. 'Was the very first volunteer they recruited for this shop. Seen off nine shop managers and all your lot.' Nine managers! My lot? Does she mean other Area Managers or all the charity's management representatives from me right up to the Board of Trustees? Probably the latter, from the look of glee on the face now grinning at my obvious discomfort.

'Marjorie's collected everythin' in 'ere. All of it's donated stuff, o' course, 'asn't cost us a penny. She washes and polishes everything every time she comes in. Real whirlwind, she is. Obsessed, if you ask me but it makes a change from the mess downstairs so we don't complain when she gets all hyper-active, like. Whoa betides anybody that spills their tea, mind, or don't sweep up their crumbs!' The woman moved across to a little wall cupboard with shiny white painted doors and dainty glass knobs. 'Tea and coffee and stuff in 'ere,' she said, yanking open a door with a force that brought my heart into my mouth, given what she'd just been saying, 'and cups and stuff down 'ere' – pointing to the not-quite-matching but scrubbed and polished base unit underneath. 'The list of what everybody has is 'ere' – she pointed to a neat notice, handwritten in copperplate, taped to the wall – 'and you'll soon learn 'oo we all are.'

She looked at me properly for the first time and her expression softened a little. There was even the suggestion of a wry smile. 'Don't worry, pet,' she soothed, 'we're not that bad. And if we are you can always leave, like all the rest!' She chuckled merrily and I just knew my smile looked like a rictus.

'My name's Iris,' she said cheerily, 'and I've bin 'ere for over five years. You want to know anything about this place and all of us, then you just ask me. I know 'em all, and most of the customers as well. Can't do wivout me, they can't!'

'Hello, Iris, nice to meet you. And thanks, I'll remember your offer. Since you've mentioned it, though, do you know about that cupboard across the landing? It looks as though it's been like that since MafeKing.'

She fixed me again with that same look she'd given me with at the shop door, leaning forward slightly as though she was going to tell me some universal truth.

'I remember my Great Uncle Hubert telling me about Mafeking,' she said. ''E were just a bit of a lad when 'e went out there. Got caught with Baden Powell's mob at Mafeking and thought he were done for. He weren't, o' course, 'e came through it OK and came back here about… Ooo… it must o' bin between the wars. Came back with a black woman, he did. Said 'e'd married 'er! Well, it's no great shakes nowadays, is it? 'appens all the time, nobody turns an 'air but then – oh dear me! What a fuss! Anyway, she didn't like it 'ere, too cold for 'er, it were, and she went 'ome again. Near killed poor Hubert, it did, that fond of 'er, 'e were. I couldn't figure out why 'e didn't go with 'er, 'e didn't want to be back 'ere any more 'n she did. It were years later that me Dad said summat about a British Army Major and his wife and a scandal, and Great Uncle Hubert not being welcome any more, specially since 'e upped and married one of the locals, like. I were just a little 'un, yer see. I didn't know all these things then, I just listened to stories.' She paused a moment, lost in thought, then came back to life just as I thought I should attract her attention again to the matter in hand. ''E could tell some stories, I can tell you! 'E were quite old, like, when I knew 'im, but I remember the one…'

''Er, Iris,' I interrupted, before she could went into full flow, 'the cupboard?'

'Oh. Yeah. Sorry. Got carried away there,' she said. 'Right, the cupboard. 'Aven't a clue, ducks!'

We both turned in unison at the sound of footsteps clumping up the stairs and a voice calling 'Hiya! Sorry I'm a bit late, that bus driver 'ates me – it's the second time 'e's driven straight past me since I asked 'im what he was playing at, bein' late every day!'

A tiny scrap of a girl with a mass of red, curly hair and a face made up in classic 'punk' style breezed into the room behind us. This must be Kylie, the shop manager, I thought. I had imagined the description my manager had given me was an exaggeration but I could see it wasn't. Kylie looked like a 12-year-old who'd been in her mother's make-up box. Her black-rimmed eyes, pale, pale face and mouth covered in several layers of shiny red lipstick would have been intimidating if she had looked older but, as it was, she looked about as frightening as Andy Pandy.

I'd been told that she was 23, a single Mum, almost terminally cheerful and habitually late. I also knew that her volunteers were fiercely loyal, treated her like a wayward daughter and ignored her instructions completely. After all, it was their shop, wasn't it; what slip of a girl was going to tell them how to run it?

'You made it, then,' she said to me with a cheery grin, 'sorry I weren't 'ere when you popped in last week for a butchers but I 'ad to see Charlie's teacher.' Charlie must be her son, then. 'Little bleeder only—' She giggled and checked herself. 'Sorry, forgot where I was for a minute! Little beggar only kicked the teacher, didn't 'e? They was going to exclude 'im! I ask you, a six-year-old! What next?! Wotcha, Iris,' she said, 'stick the kettle on will you, love, while I gives the new boss 'ere a guided? Thanks a bunch.' And she took my arm, steered me out of the kitchen and back towards the stairs. I went, meekly of course, what else?

'Follow me, and I'll show yer what we do 'ere. I should say,' she turned bright blue eyes up to my face for the full, artless impact, 'we do fings a bit different 'ere but it works, see, and we makes pots o' money!' she added proudly. 'This,' she said as we reached the bottom of the stairs, 'is me stock room.' We gazed around, me with the right degree (I hoped) of interest to show that I was impressed and she with a proprietorial air. She waved her hands over the chaos. 'Over there is kid's stuff, that's ladies, that's gents, that's books and bric-a-brac, that's toys and that's Lucy's.' Her hands swept expressively across her crowded domain.

'Lucy's?' I asked

'Yeh. Lucy fancies 'erself as a bit of a expert on old stuff. She gets a mate of hers to look at it and says wever it's wurf more than we'd 'ave asked in the shop, like.' She looked up at me again, a picture of injured innocence. 'Some folk won't pay, you know,' she said seriously, 'even if somink's really valuable they won't pay what it's wurf 'cos we're a charity shop. Reckons we gets it all for nuffink so we shouldn't charge much. Can you beat that, then? Mingy bastards! Oops, sorry, naughty word. Shouldn't use 'em here, should I?'

I was on slightly safer ground now. 'Better not,' I said, 'we don't want to upset anyone, do we? Especially the customers. Some of them would be offended and might take their business elsewhere. What's your routine then?'

'Routine?' she said, puzzled. 'Oh, I get yer! Ginger brings the stuff in at the back door, dumps it over there in the corner, and we picks over it to see what kind o' fings 'e's brought us. Then we hangs up the clothes and bedding, like, chucks the shoes and books and records and fings in the corner and piles china and glass and fancy stuff on them shelves. Easy peasy!'

I doubted that. I'd seen what happened in the shops I'd visited over the past two weeks and knew there was much, much more to it than that. No doubt Kylie was making light of it, trying to impress.

On the wall, in the space between an overflowing bookcase and an even more overflowing filing cabinet, an ancient and yellowed poster proclaiming the virtues of Health and Safety in the workplace sagged, defeated. I got the picture. Upstairs a phone rang. 'That's yours,' said Kylie. 'Ent you going to get it, then?' I was galvanised into action and leapt up the stairs in over-coiled, over-wrought reaction. I'd already reached across the desk and picked up the phone before I remembered the dust and quietly mourned my lovely suit as I said brightly, 'Area Manager's office, Gillian speaking, how can I help you?'

'Gillian? Who the hell's Gillian!' said a voice that clearly belonged to someone who wasn't in the best of tempers. 'Oh, yeh, course, it's your first day today, isn't it? Sorry, it's this bloody mobile, tried to ring three times and bloody thing keeps cutting out on me! Are you still there?' The voice was very loud and its owner was shouting. I held the phone away from an ear which was, apparently, permanently damaged into tinnitus, and said, 'Yes, I'm still here, how can I help you?'

'It's Cyril, the rag man!' he yelled. 'I'm running late today but will be with you this afternoon, about three if that's alright? We can talk prices then. Have the kettle on when I get there, there's a good girl.' And he was gone.

I looked at the phone in my hand and just knew I had a vacant expression on my face. Cyril? Prices? Good girl? I hadn't even had a cup of tea of my own on my first morning here yet! How could I talk about rag prices, let alone negotiate them, on my first day? I stored away the 'good girl' for another, less fraught, time. I understood the system well enough – it was basically very simple, which was just as well, really, given the way the day was shaping up. People donate possessions they don't want to charity shops all over the country where staffs of mainly volunteers sort through it, decide what they can re-sell to raise funds and discard what they can't. The 'can't' covers a wide range of reasons. Books might be too battered, glass and china cracked, toys broken. Clothing and fabrics might be torn, faded, have buttons missing or zips broken or maybe are just too out of date. The costs of repairs and cleaning would be enormous and the returns doubtful. So anything made out of fabric was sold on to specialist merchants, who bought tons of 'rags' and siphoned them off into all kinds of reclamation projects. One way or another, a charity shop is a sophisticated recycling machine.

Still, the volume of donations that weren't saleable was enormous. As I'd come to realise just how much there was during my two-week induction, I'd wondered if charity supporters might think twice about donating at all if they saw what happened to a good proportion of their prized possessions. It seemed to me that everybody who donated a sackful of cast-offs wanted to think that their own unwanted bits and bobs would sell for veritable fortunes and were, therefore, absolutely indispensable to any charity worth its name. Some would be aghast if they could see the apparently cavalier way some of their donations were dealt with.

It was the sheer quantity of donations that made the whole thing work so brilliantly. Large amounts and lots of variety meant there was always enough that could be sold on and that we could select for quality, and price for sale accordingly. Turnaround time was short, with goods staying on the shop floor for only two or three weeks at the most, to be replaced with something else if they didn't sell. This method attracted new customers as well as frequent return trips by avid charity shop fans attracted to the constant stream of bargains. The 'rag' merchants paid for what they took away, so unwanted goods earned revenue even when they didn't make it to the shop floor.

But understanding how the system worked was a far cry from negotiating the price with an experienced and no doubt wily merchant, and I wasn't even sure if I had the authority to discuss it at all, let alone negotiate! Was there a contract? Where would I find it in all this dust-covered stuff anyway? Oooo beam me up, Scotty, please!

'Yer tea's in the kitchen!' hollered a rather disgruntled voice, whose owner was disappearing down the stairs. Iris, I thought. We hadn't got away to a very good start. A sigh escaped me. Not only had I disrupted Kylie's 'guided' by taking the phone call, but I'd failed to make the tea as well. Chin up, I thought and squared my shoulders. At least there was a cup of tea waiting for me in the kitchen.

I sat down at the little table with its lace and flower vase, and raised the cup to my lips. From below I heard another round of voices raised in greeting, this time with undeniable joy and, I was sure, girlish flirtation. 'Yo, ladies!' sang one voice and, 'Yo, Damian!' chorused the rest, fan-club style.

Damian was my assistant and I hadn't met him yet, but I'd been briefed. He was in his mid-fifties, film star handsome, a hypochondriac and gay as carnival bunting. He was also deeply committed to the charity, although no-one knew why, and worked as a volunteer for 16 hours a week. He diverted any attempt to find out the reason for his dedication with firm but charming determination. Everyone knew (somehow) that he was financially comfortable and didn't need to earn a living but he'd never said anything about his source of income either. However, his love life and current boyfriend, whom he seemed to change like most people change their underwear, was the subject of avid discussion, much angst and not a little envy.

Light footsteps ran up the stairs and a tall, slim figure in leather jeans and what looked like an expensive Paul Smith shirt hove into view at the kitchen door. 'Gillian!' he trilled in a voice like warm honey, both arms outstretched. 'How *lovely* to meet you at last! We've heard *so* much about you and it's *wonderful* to have you with us, on our little team!' I could almost see the exclamation marks on his lips. It was like being on the set of a soap opera. He gripped my upper arms lightly and leant forward for the continental, two-cheek air kiss. Fortunately I'd spent quite a lot of time in the company of people who did this (that's a whole other story!), so his move didn't catch me unawares and I joined in, charmed in spite of myself, by his genial welcome and good looks. After all, it isn't every day I was kissed by such a stunning looking man, gay or straight or anything in between. As he drew away I thought I saw a little gleam of surprise and his smile indicated that I'd passed some kind of test. First success of the day!

'Ah, tea!' he said as he turned away from me slightly and I had the chance to study him while he poured himself a cup from the pretty, floral china teapot. He was just a shade under six foot tall, slim as a boy with iron grey, professionally styled hair. His clothes looked new, his boots were as shiny as those of a guardsman and he wore discreet but expensive gold jewellery, including a tiny gold earring. I wondered what on earth he was doing here, in this kind of place doing this kind of work. He wouldn't have looked out of place on the catwalk during Paris fashion week.

'Come on then,' he said as, cup in one hand and my wrist in the other, he left the kitchen and turned towards the office. 'I have to show you our little haven!' Next door he stopped just short of going base-over-apex. My bags were just where I dropped them and he moved them out of the way with just a little touch of drama in every movement, and put down his cup on one of the desks.

'This one's *mine*,' he said, 'and that one's *yours*. I use the computer, you see, and *you* don't need to, which is why my desk is *bigger*. Besides, you'll be out most of the time, travelling around your empire, won't you?' It wasn't a question, more a statement which took in the whole office and implied 'and this is *my* empire, ducky!' with infinite sweetness laced with just a dash of bitter lemon. For the first time I noticed that his desk was free of dust, in stark contrast with the rest of the room.

I took a deep breath, thought to myself 'Start as you mean to go on' and plunged into the deep end. 'You're quite right, Damian...'

''Scuse me?' a little voice said at the back of my brain. 'What's this "you're quite right stuff" then?' Oh, Lord, I thought, he's back! My own personal guardian devil who lived on my shoulder just behind my right ear. No guardian angel for me, just the opposite. A little companion whose aim was to get me into as much trouble, often of the most deliciously wicked kind, as possible. I'd thought I'd got rid of him when my counsellor said he was sure everything would be all right now. Can you sue a counsellor for failure? Perhaps not. Still, I had to admit that life had been a bit tedious without my alter-ego stirring things up sometimes, making sure my well conditioned, goody-two-shoes, Pollyanna self didn't get too boring and complaisant.

'Go away, I haven't finished yet.' I projected withering thoughts and said out loud to Damian, 'Quite right, this is your empire. I'm assuming you know where everything is? Excellent! Cyril is calling in this afternoon at three so I'll need the rag contract, please and while you're at it, can I have the sales figures for each shop, against target, for the last 12 months and their targets for the current quarter? Since it's Monday morning, and you'll need to call the shops to collect last week's sales figures, I think around lunchtime will do. It's 9.20 now, will that give you enough time?' He opened his mouth but not a lot came out except the flash of a gold filling and I plunged on before he had a chance to collect himself. 'Good. That's fine then. I'll be downstairs with Kylie finishing off her guided.' And I turned tail and fled, leaving Damian speechless and stunned, and myself with a guilty feeling hovering around my conscience.

Arriving in the stock room at the foot of the stairs, red-faced, adrenaline pumping and new suit looking the worse for wear after its encounter with the desk during Cyril's call, I came face to face with another new body. Just in time I pulled up, feeling a bit like the coyote in those old Roadrunner cartoons. Didn't he always end up rushing everywhere, only to meet his nemesis?

'You've been in my kitchen!' the body said, and her words were akimbo even if her arms weren't.

'Hello,' I replied, adrenalin fuelling a return of over-the-top brightness, 'you must be Marjorie. I've heard such a lot about you this morning. How do you manage to keep such a beautifully clean and pretty kitchen in the midst of all this?' And I waved my hand vaguely around the stock room.

'Oy!' said a disembodied voice from behind an overloaded clothes rail. 'That's my stock room you're talking about!' Kylie's head appeared from between the legs of a pair of men's trousers. She was smiling, though. 'Still, I see what yer mean,' she said cheerfully, 'dump, innit?' And her face disappeared again.

I turned back to Marjorie. 'With great difficulty,' she said frostily, 'especially when people just help themselves and leave all the clearing up for someone else to do.' She didn't quite huff and puff but I could see a remarkable relationship with the big, bad wolf in the story of the three little pigs.

'You're quite right,' I agreed, 'my Mum always used to say that everything should have its own home and when you've finished using it, you should put it away again. That way everything's always tidy.' Marjorie was thawing out in front of my eyes so I plunged on while I seemed to be ahead. 'I was just trying to find the office, you see, and didn't see the sign on the door until I'd unlocked the kitchen by mistake. I was so impressed. I'll bet you have a beautiful home too.' The smile disappeared and I thought I'd gone too far but no, after a little wobble it came back again.

'Well,' she said, 'I expect just this once won't harm. You weren't to know, I suppose.' I thought it best not to say that I hadn't actually made the tea anyway. It seemed better just to let things carry on, since we were doing OK. Then, after a brief pause and a re-arrangement of shoulders previously tensed for battle, she said, 'I'd better go and set it all to rights again.' With that she was gone, leaving me feeling hugely relieved.

Kylie appeared again from behind the rail holding something that looked suspiciously like a jock-strap in her hand. She looked serious and checked that Marjorie had disappeared before she whispered, 'Marjorie don't have a home of her own. 'Er 'usband buggered off three years ago. She didn't know about his scams and debts till the bleedin' bailiffs turned up. They does that, yer know,' she said seriously, and I wondered if I had heard the tinge of a personal experience in her voice. 'She lives wiv 'er sister now, nowhere else to go, see, and they don't get on. That's one o' the reasons she's 'ere every day, it's somewhere for 'er to go. We need volunteers to work in the shop, but lots of 'em needs us just as much. Works both ways, give and take, like.' And she went back to sorting donations.

I was surprised and touched by her empathy and perspicacity. There was obviously more to our Kylie than met the eye. After a moment I joined her at the pile of bags. We sorted stock for a while, me showing willing to be one of the team and she chattering as I listened and learned more about her, the shop and her crew of helpers. After a while, she resumed her 'guided' and introduced me properly to the first shop on my new patch.

I didn't meet all the volunteers that day and knew it would take quite a while to catch up with all of them. They came and went at different times on different days and I would be out and about, so we would be a bit like ships that pass in the night. Except it would be during the day for us, of course. Kylie showed me her rota and the roll of 32 volunteers' names, which was astonishing. Some of the shops I'd seen in the previous two weeks struggled to stay open and trading effectively with far too few volunteers. I asked her if the other shops in our group were as endowed with plentiful volunteers as hers.

'Nope,' she said, twinkling her baby blues, 'but you'll find out!'

At just after noon I left Kylie and a shop full of customers and made my way back to the office. I was nervous, thinking over what I'd said to Damian a couple of hours ago and realising I hadn't heard a sound out of him in all that time. 'Think positive, girl!' I told myself as I stopped in front of the closed office door. I gave my jacket front a tug (the suit was definitely ruined now, after all the sorting and clambering over bags and boxes in the stock room) and reached for the door handle… to almost fall flat on my face as it was opened from inside. Damian was standing there looking dishevelled and fraught (a rare event, I was sure), but clutching a sheaf of papers in his hand. He waved them triumphantly. 'Found them!' he almost shouted. 'Every last *one* of them! Sales figures, target sheets, contract, the *lot!*'

'That's wonderful, Damian, thank you so much.' I glanced behind him to see the office apparently turned inside out and with dust floating everywhere. 'How are all the other shop managers today? Did you manage to speak to everyone?' His face set as still as a statue for just a moment. He lowered his arms, his shoulders drooped. 'I completely forgot to call them,' he said in a small voice.

I struggled not to laugh at his woebegone expression and took pity on him, grateful for his efforts and warming to his obvious desire to help. I felt guilty about being over-assertive with him to compensate for my failure with the others. 'Don't worry,' I said, 'I'll tell you what, I'll make us some tea, we can share my lunch and then we'll do it together. What if you make each call, say hello and stuff, then pass them on to me so I can introduce myself and ask them about their sales figures. How does that sound?'

'Well,' he said, not quite recovering his exclamation mark yet, 'that sounds fine except... well, I'm vegetarian you see so, well, do you have any meat stuff in your lunch box? Because it really does terrible things to my digestion. You don't want to be in the same *room* as me when I've eaten meat!' The exclamation mark was back.

'Damian,' I said, 'so am I. A veggie, I mean. Come on, time for lunch.'

-2-
Collision Course

Ten shops and no real technology to speak of. Just a collection of keys and cables that masqueraded as a computer in the office, which certainly wouldn't support anything vaguely related to email or the internet, and a semi-manual accounting system. It made for a lot of paperwork – most of it totally illegible. Managers of charity shops are a rare breed and even rarer is the charity shop manager who believes in the value of an effective administration system. Not quite of the same rarity as hens' teeth, but getting on that way. The generally accepted view among this set of retail oracles was that administration systems were designed by HQ solely to make managers' lives miserable and the only way to deal with them was to ignore them.

It was easy to see why, though. Sales targets were supposed to be 'fair but challenging', as my various mentor colleagues had told me during training, with wry smiles and shrugs of the shoulders. I could almost hear what the reactions would be if I said that to my lot at a team meeting, and much of it was unprintable! The cumulative sum of the targets set for each shop in my area was mine, as the Area Manager, to meet by hook or by crook. Still fair but challenging, of course, and totally, absolutely and certainly out of reach as far as I could tell. My job was to run the shops effectively and maximise surpluses that would contribute towards the charity's spending fund. I'd made the heinous error of calling the surpluses 'profits' during my job interview and had been told by the Deputy Director, who looked as though he had a bad smell under his nose, that profits were OK in commercial shops, but we made surpluses. I couldn't see the difference but, just for a change, decided that I should keep my opinions to myself. Clearly a wise move, because the job was now mine. Anyway, shop managers knew they could earn a bonus if they hit or (heaven help us!) exceeded their targets,

17

so what were they going to do when faced with the conflicting priorities of boosting sales and filling in the paperwork? No contest! The fact that the targets were pie-in-the-sky and never reached was neither here nor there; they made a very convenient excuse for getting out of all sorts of inconvenient tasks, or when there was a pressing need for a quick drag on a fag in the back yard.

The sales sheets I examined that afternoon (written in far more different hands than I expected or found explicable, given that we had only ten shop managers plus the odd paid assistant scattered about) might have been in Cantonese characters or Swahili for all the sense some of them made. After an hour or so of head scratching and asking Damian for interpretation, I eventually found one file that acted on my mind just like a ray of summer sunshine on flowers. Illumination! It was a perfect piece of work. Not one score-out, not one splodge of the all-obscuring correction fluid used so liberally on the others (note to self: buy shares in Snopake and Liquid Paper), and a quick check with a calculator showed the arithmetic was spot on. Halleluiah!

Where was this paragon of book-keeping? Kensington Place, that's where, and the paragon was called Miles. I could see that he'd completed every single line of every single report himself, in a clear and stylish hand.

Did he ever take a day off, I wondered? I knew that Kensington Place was a comparatively high turnover shop (only comparatively, of course, and the only one on my patch, more's the pity) in a busy road not far from a new shopping mall. Jean, my boss, had told me that Miles was a very efficient, calm and professional guy who ran a clean, smart and profitable boutique-style shop with the help of a small but bright team of volunteers. Not the usual, then. He had a flair for numbers too, I could see, and I wondered if there was any way of using this rare skill to help out elsewhere among the obviously numerically dyslexic lot I was now responsible for. It was beginning to look as though I was going to need all the help I could get in the next few months. I made a mental note to visit Kensington Place as soon as possible and see what sort of ally Miles might turn out to be. I just hoped he wouldn't turn out to be the other kind instead – the obstinate obstacle that would make life difficult. Would he resent the imposition of yet another newcomer?

Would he assume, like Ivy, that I'd get fed up and just go away like so many of my predecessors had?

Comparing the sales reports Damian had dug out for me I could see that there was an enormous fluctuation in turnover between the shops. To be expected, I consoled myself bravely, given that they were in such vastly different areas: some on busy high streets, some on run down shopping parades and even one marooned on an island in the middle of a busy new one-way system. A large island, granted, with other shops and even a post office, but still an island. Depressingly, none of them was reaching target, not even Kensington Place. Some of the managers had put little cryptic comments on their weekly report sheets that showed they knew it only too well but retained their sense of humour. Or could it be that they were cocking a snook at authority deliberately? One had written, 'Well, I missed again, oh, oh, oh', which identified an ageing Phil Collins fan, and another had noted, 'It's sales, Jim, but not as we know it' – had we a Trekkie in our midst? Yet another: 'Shall I cut my throat now or will you wait until next week?' – gallows humour that suggested a touch of depression around the place, as well as irreverent humour.

The phone rang and I was grateful for the distraction. Damian picked it up and listened intently for several minutes, his face alternately showing amazement, sympathy, disbelief than disgust. He asked the caller to wait a minute, put his hand over the receiver and turned to me. 'It's Shona,' he breathed, 'she's locked her *flasher* in her stock room!'

'Sorry, Damian, say that again,' I asked, my head still full of a jumble of figures and hoping that I'd misheard what he'd said.

'This guy has been *stalking* Shona for ages,' he said, 'and he's just turned up in the shop, taken off *all* his clothes and sung *love* songs to her! He's *refused* to get dressed until she's agreed to go out with him! She has these panic attacks, you know. He followed her into the stock room and she managed to lock him in there! What shall she *do*?' I was gratified that Damian's italics and exclamation marks were fully restored after the traumas of this morning. I took it that he bore me no ill will –

'What did he sing?' I asked and knew immediately that was the wrong thing to say. Damian looked shocked. And disapproving.

He did disapproving very well, I noticed. Delicately raised eyebrows, elongated neck, chin tucked in and not a wrinkle to be seen anywhere on his graceful neck at all. *Rats!* Somewhere, back in my dim and distant past, a line manager had said, 'Gillian, your flippant attitude will get you into deep trouble, one day', and she'd been right more times than I could remember. Damian was too put out to speak for a while, but eventually he grinned and said, 'Shall I ask?' and I struggled not to giggle.

'I'll take it, Damian, thank you,' I said and picked up my extension.

'Hello, Shona,' I said, 'this is Gillian, your new Area Manager. Is everyone safe?'

'Yes,' she said through a quivery sounding voice, 'this berk's been following me for weeks. The police won't do anything, they don't care, nobody believes me, he's making my life a misery and now he's here! I've shut the shop. He was making so much noise all the customers just ran and he's bloody drunk!'

'You've shut him in the stock room and you've left him there, in a locked shop?'

'Yes. What else could I do? He's huge, roaring drunk and he was singing Lady in Red!', which answered my question. 'I hate that song!' she added, as if it mattered. Since everyone appeared to be safe I didn't know whether to be angry that she'd left him in a locked shop, annoyed that he'd disrupted trading or worried about insurance cover for damage. So I decided to play safe.

'Don't do anything, Shona, I'll be right there. Where are you, by the way?'

'We're all in the pub across the road,' she said. Of course, where else? I thought with resignation and a mental sigh.

'It'll take me about 25 minutes to get to you, which is quite a long time to leave him locked in. He'll be quite angry, I dare say. Have you called the police?'

There was a moment's pregnant pause. 'No,' Shona said, in a small voice, 'they said I wasn't to call again.'

Oh, Lord, I thought, what sort of situation have I inherited, here? But something had to be done. I tried to remember whether I'd had my Wonder Woman costume cleaned, and if it was in the car.

Forty-five minutes later, having only been lost once on the way – pretty good, considering getting lost was something I was really good at – I pulled into the car park of the Rat and Parrot. It was only then that I remembered I didn't have a clue what Shona looked like, since we'd never met, and the pub was a big one with four bars at least. I was tempted to seek solace in a large G&T if she wasn't in the first one I tried but, pushing open the a set of double doors, I realised that I wasn't going to be called on to battle with that kind of temptation today. More's the pity. I was very good with temptation, almost as good as getting lost, and knew an awful lot about it. Not good with battles, though. I always lost.

The first voice I heard as I stepped over the threshold was saying, very loudly, 'Where the hell is she, then? She said she'd be here in 25 minutes and that was over three-quarters of an hour ago!'

Excuses about traffic, and finding my way to unfamiliar places, sprang to mind but prudence suggested this wasn't the kind of comment Shona would find palatable just now. I searched around for something useful and encouraging to say as I tried to pinpoint the owner of the voice. Walking across a carpet sticky with beer spillage and heaven knew what else, I said cheerfully, 'Hello, everyone, I'm Gillian, it's nice to meet you and I'm so glad you're all safe' to the six or so people sitting there, all with large glasses of something in front of them and slightly glazed expressions on their faces. 'If you'll let me have your keys, Shona, I'll go across to the shop and see what's going on. Would any of you care to come with me, just to keep an eye on things from the pavement, you understand?'

I hoped my voice sounded confident, commanding and assured. I hadn't a clue what I was going to do with the naked, singing drunk, not having had much experience with that sort of thing, but I didn't want them to see that. They needed to see me as competent and confident, even if I wasn't. *Especially* since I wasn't! I needed them to look at me with trust and belief so that I could trust and believe in myself. Besides, if it all went pear-shaped they'd be there to help – wouldn't they?

'Bloody hell,' said the little devil on my shoulder, 'you sound just like one of those demented callers in a dress, you know, from a church or somewhere, all goody, goody and it'll all be wonderful.

That's not fair, you know, it's hitting below the belt to talk like that in my hearing, I'm a sensitive soul and me and church stuff don't mix well…'

'Oh *do* shut up,' I flashed back, 'or I'll wear a garlic chain around my neck!'

He was right, of course, there was a hint of C of E baptism service in there, but I knew I couldn't muster an awesome power, even though it would have been exceedingly useful round about now. Still, the Lord helps those who helps themselves, as my Granny used to say – unless it's to the contents of supermarket shelves without visiting the checkout on the way out.

Shona and her volunteers eyed each other, aghast at the suggestion that they should come back to the shop. 'I need to do something quickly,' I said, 'in case he's inclined to run amok in there, and I'm sure you won't want to miss the fun.' I tried to grin, inadvertently appealing to the kind of spirit that makes people slow down to watch the results of a traffic accident as they drive by. It worked a treat and three of them stood up to come with me.

My legs and hands were trembling as I put the key in the shop door lock and turned it. Nothing happened. I tried again. Still nothing. I didn't really want to go in there anyway, so was this the Almighty's way of telling me that I shouldn't? 'Coward!' said the little devil on my shoulder. 'You're really no fun at all.' This time I ignored him as I put my shoulder to the door on a turn of the key and fell inside the shop as the door gave way with the ease of a letter dropping into one of HM's red post boxes. Clearly it was a day for falling through doors into the unknown.

Silence. Not a sound. I glanced behind me and three pairs of eyes, all wide and not entirely focused thanks to whatever had been in their glasses in the pub, stared back at me. Their owners took a step backwards, entirely in unison, like the slow motion action replay of a carefully choreographed dance routine. Slowly I moved forward towards the back of the shop and the stock room door, listening for any sounds that might be heard over the drum beat of my own heart. Gingerly I reached forward, key to the stock room door in hand. To my horror and consternation there erupted, from the other side of the door, a wail of despair. Or was it rage? It was obviously drunken, which made it rather difficult to be sure. Should

I call the police now and wait for them to sort this out? That would be the safe, the sensible, the recommended thing to do.

'This is the police!' I bellowed in my best 'let's-be-having-no-nonsense-from-you' tone as a three-voice chorus behind me cried, 'Ooooooooooo!' 'I'm going to open this door and then step back,' I continued. 'Come out slowly with your hands held out where I can see them.' Do they say that in England, I wondered, or have I been watching too many American police shows on TV?

Carefully I turned the key in the lock, pushed the door open a little way and then retreated hurriedly. Just like lighting a firework, I thought. Light blue touch paper and retire. For several very long seconds there was silence. Just as I was beginning to wonder what had happened to the owner of the wailing voice and was on the verge of returning to the lit firework, so to speak, the noise erupted again with a heart-stopping yell. Something catapulted past me, ran straight into a free-standing dress rail full of lingerie, and collapsed in a heap of tangled clothes-hangers and flimsy fabrics.

Another 'Ooooooooo!' from the pavement grandstand, a bit louder this time and with an edge that suggested the thrill of the back seat at the cinema at a showing of The Postman Only Rings Once. Or is it twice? Whatever.

The owner of the wailing voice groaned once, raised a lingerie-shrouded arm in entreaty, let it fall again and lay still. Was he dead? How would I explain that to the local constabulary or my boss? Slowly, gradually, I moved a little closer and peered into the chaos of lace, polyester and clothes-hangers from which a gentle snore now emerged. The body, naked but shielded by various ladies' garments draped about it, appeared to be fast asleep.

'OK,' I said, thinking fast. 'Would you ladies help me, please? I think we should try to lift him out of this tangle and make sure he's not hurt.'

Three willing pairs of hands, whose owners appeared to quite relish the thought of handling a temporarily helpless naked man, made short work of disentangling our intruder. We half carried and half dragged him through the stock room to the lavatory at the rear of the building. Fortunately this one had been built to provide easy access for a wheelchair user and was quite roomy. We laid him out on the floor, found a pair of trousers and a fleece to dress him in and then tied his ankles and wrists with ties from the menswear display. I could just see the tabloid headlines: 'BONDAGE IN CHARITY SHOPS!' they'd scream, or 'CHARITY MANAGER IN SHOP ORGY!'

Trussed up and sleeping as he was, I now had an opportunity to examine the culprit. He didn't really fit Shona's earlier description. He couldn't have been more than around 5ft 7, was very slightly built and had pale, thinning hair. I'm no good at judging ages but he looked about 60. He was breathing heavily, which was reassuring, and every breath smelt of brandy. Obviously this stalker wasn't short of a bob or two. Getting smashed on brandy doesn't come cheap.

I dispatched the volunteers back to the pub with a message suggesting it was time to get everyone back to the shop. Not that there was much they'd be able to do today, I suspected, given the state some of them seemed to be in, and I certainly couldn't see the shop opening for business again today. Still, tidying up would give them a chance to sober up a bit before going home. While I was waiting for them all to return, I located the phone and dialled Head Office.

'Is Jean there, please?' I asked the operator.

'Jean? No, I'm sorry,' said a lilting, Irish-accented voice. 'She's on holiday for the next four weeks. Can anyone else help you?'

Four weeks! We'd just spoken on Friday, and she'd said nothing about a holiday. First day in a new job, my boss says it'll be a bit tough but she'll be there for me, and where is she? On bloody holiday, that's where!

'Um,' I said, speechless for a moment, then 'Um' again. 'Well…' It came out as a squeak. 'The thing is, I have a bit of a situation here and I need some advice. Who would you suggest?'

'That's it, girl, remember the management training, chuck the question back at the questioner – although it's a pity about the squeak,' said the little devil on my shoulder 'doesn't help your credibility, if you ask me.' I ignored him.

'The only person in the office at present,' the woman on the phone said, 'is Mr Barrington, the Shops Director. Would he do?'

He who hesitates is lost! Does that also apply to 'she'? Probably. I took the plunge,

'Yes. This is an emergency. He'll do!'

A second or two later I'm speaking to God. Or at least the right-hand man with his eyes on the big chair.

'Hello, Gillian, how's your first day going?'

He knows my name! How in heaven's name did that happen? Still, I took that as a good omen and plunged straight in without the niceties.

'I'm sorry to trouble you but I've a situation here that's is a bit unusual. I'm at Lupin Lane.' Did he know where that was? Did he care? Did he think I'd lost my marbles? Lupin Lane sounded like something out of a Postman Pat or Bob the Builder storyline 'The volunteers are all well on the way to being drunk and incapable, the manager is hysterical and there's an intoxicated, unconscious man tied up and lying in the loo.' I deliberately omitted the fact that the man had been naked and that the shop had been closed for almost two hours. 'I can handle the manager and volunteers but thought I should get a steer on our visitor.'

There was a long pause before he finally spoke. 'That's quite a first day score, Gillian. The best I've heard yet.' That couldn't be amusement I heard, surely? Could it? His voice had a definite wobble in it that hinted at suppressed laughter. Or anger. I decided on laughter, it was more comfortable.

'Quite,' I said, confused by his apparently relaxed response. 'But what do you advise? He was very loud, apparently, and caused quite a stir. Some of the volunteers were quite upset. Hence the medicinal use of a glass or three of restorative malt at the local pub before I arrived. Shall I call the police and have him arrested? There's bound to be publicity if I do and I'm not sure whether it's the kind of publicity we should generate in our situation. As a charity, that is. I can just see the headlines in the local paper.'

'Was he violent before he keeled over?'

'Very boisterous, from what I can understand. He took off his coat when he arrived at the shop and he was naked underneath. He danced. And sang Lady in Red.'

There was an explosion from the other end of the connection and the laughter that followed was totally uninhibited and not at all what I'd expected, which was exasperation at best and a hanging at worst. If I hadn't been so stressed I'm sure I'd have thought it sexy.

Perhaps I did anyway. Somewhere in the depth of my mind a tiny, silvery bell trilled against a memory, like the forgotten echo of a nightingale's song or a smell of a scented candle wafting over the warmth of a bubble bath. And was gone. A memory? A dream? I mentally berated myself. This was no time for mind games and meandering. Or perhaps I was closer to a breakdown than I imagined. I was talking to His Nibs, the Head Honcho, the Top Cat, who probably already thought I was a lost cause.

'Call the police, Gillian,' he said eventually, through his mirth. 'You've no idea how long he's going to be unconscious or what frame of mind he'll be in when he wakes up. Waking up in a cell might deter him from troubling us again and besides, you shouldn't take any risks. I'd rather risk publicity than anyone's safety. Let me know how you get on.' And with that he was gone. Put the phone down. No 'goodbye' or 'good luck'. Just like that. No questions about how, who, when, where, what or any of the tedious stuff I hadn't a clue about anyway. Very refreshing.

By the time the shop staff rolled back in a few minutes later, I'd already spoken to the police who said they'd 'send someone round' as soon as possible, but they were dealing with a multi-vehicle pile up on the by-pass and didn't know how long it would be. I resigned myself to a long wait.

It took us over an hour to clear up the shop and the stock room, what with the excitement and the booze, but at least everyone was very jolly – or should that be in good spirits? They'd all tried a few of those in the last couple of hours. Just as the last volunteer disappeared for the day, in a whiff of alcohol fumes and cheery calls about tomorrow, there was a squeal of brakes, a great slamming of doors and two large gentlemen wearing blue uniforms knocked loudly on the locked shop door. They left their brightly painted and shiny patrol car parked on the double yellow lines outside. Well, where else?

'Hello, there,' I smiled, opening the door to them. 'We weren't expecting you quite so soon. Is the pile-up all sorted out, then?'

'Pile-up?' said Plod Number One with a beaming smile. 'Oh, that! No pile-up, ma'am. That's just Control's way of making sure people don't call back every five minutes if we're having tea. What can we do for you? Hear you've had an intruder, like.'

'Through here,' I said, directing them through the stock room and opening the door to the loo.

Plod Number Two took off his cap and scratched his head. 'Hum,' he said. 'Drink or drugs, ma'am?'

'Drink,' said Shona from behind us. 'It's always drink.'

Always? Does she know this man, I asked myself, or is it just that he's been stalking her for so long that she's seen him like this before? Store that one away for questions later.

'Ah, well,' said Plod Number One. 'Give us a hand, Gerry, you take one end and I'll take the other.' He turned to me and said, 'Any harm done, ma'am? No? Well, we'll get him into the car and take him in to sober up or until someone claims him. Can you come into the office and give us a statement tomorrow? Good, just give us a call and let us know when.' By this time they'd hoisted our visitor off the floor and were carrying him, not too carefully, towards the door and out to the car.

Plod Number Two piped up, 'What about the car, Jack? If I 'ave to clean up another load o' puke I'll be well pissed off!' And then they were gone in a puff of blue exhaust fumes. Did nobody say 'cheerio' any more?

When I turned back into the shop, Shona had disappeared. I found her in her little cubby hole of an office, which was tucked under the stairs. She was sitting, weeping quietly into a bundle of sodden tissues and hiccupping. In all the excitement I'd rather forgotten that this man was a stalker and that she must have found it all quite frightening when he'd arrived on the rampage.

'He's gone, Shona, it's over.' I tried to sound reassuring. 'I think you should go home and rest for a while. Is there anyone there? Can I call someone for you?'

'No, I live on my own,' she said through the tissue, 'and what happens when they let him out? You don't know what it's like. He's been following me for weeks, phoning and leaving notes for me everywhere.' Her voice was rising towards hysteria. She gazed up at me with tear-filled eyes.

'Well, he's locked up now and, from the look of him, he's going to be spark-out until morning.' I tried again to sound reassuring since it didn't seem to have worked the first time. 'Do you live far away?'

'I have to change buses,' she said, sounding like a neglected seven-year-old. 'It's awkward.'

'Tell you what.' I said. 'let me take you home and make sure you're OK there. Give me your volunteer register before we go and I'll arrange with them to open the shop without you tomorrow. Don't worry, I'll keep an eye on things.' How difficult can it be for one day, I thought?

'Hah!' said the little devil on my shoulder. 'Can I help?' I ignored him.

'Will you?' she said, looking up at me in surprise, her eyes swollen and nose running. 'That's so good of you. Thank you so much.'

Ten minutes later we'd locked the shop behind us and were in the car. Even in the relative quiet of mid-afternoon, before the rush hour had really got going, the traffic was quite heavy and we stopped at the first junction to wait for a bus, a taxi, a white van and then two more buses to pass. The buses carried only one passenger each and for the umpteenth time, I mulled over how traffic congestion could be reduced at a stroke if all the buses were taken off the roads. Not a popular point of view and definitely not politically correct. The green lobby would probably hang, draw and quarter me if they knew my reactionary views. They'd have to stand in line behind the animal protection people, though, when it came out that I had a secret yearning to wear a fur coat. An expensive fur coat, not your bunny rabbit stuff. 'There's hope for you yet!' said the little devil on my shoulder, sounding positively cheerful.

Carefully I let out the clutch, edging forward to see around a van blocking my view – and was instantly propelled forward like a bullet into the path of a motorcyclist. My neck snapped back against the headrest and the sound of crunching metal rang in my ears. A motorcyclist over-steered in his attempts to avoid hitting me and fell over sideways onto the bonnet of a car, which was waiting to turn right. The car driver was so startled that he let out his clutch, shot forward, dislodging the cyclist sideways into the road, and hit the back of the articulated lorry in front of him, getting wedged under the tail. The lorry driver leapt into the road out of his cab almost directly into the path of a van coming from the other direction, which caused the driver to swerve onto the pavement, where his van demolished a crossing beacon, knocked over several tables at a continental-style street café and brought down the café's overhead awning. In the aftermath of screeching and whistling brakes, six drivers – including me and the one from the car behind me, who'd hit me and started it all – plus assorted passengers and passers-by wandered about, scratching their respective heads in disbelief. The street scene looked like something out of a disaster movie

Fortunately everyone was walking and no-one looked wounded. A few pedestrians were standing around, goggling or stunned according to temperament, and several kids leant out of windows at the school on the corner and chattered excitedly, pointing at the mayhem and laughing. It took me a moment or two to realise that my car had been shunted forward when the car behind had given me a clout in the rear end.

The driver walked towards me looking dazed and puzzled. 'I have no idea why I did that,' he said. 'I'm 77 years old and I've never had an accident in all my life before! Am I going mad, or what? I just saw you ease forward and just… well, just… I was looking at the traffic and I saw the gap after the cyclist and just… sort of… well… I thought you'd go for the gap, you see, and just let out my clutch. Only you didn't. Goodness, are you all right, dear lady?'

'Shaken, not stirred,' I said and bobbed my head, rubbing my sore neck, to see if Shona was OK. She was sitting, rigid, in the front passenger seat, muttering to herself. I heard her say, 'Someone hates me. Why me? This is the last thing I need…' before I returned to give my attention to the mayhem around me.

Everybody milled around making sure that everyone else was OK, and various people collected dozens of names, addresses, telephone numbers and sets of insurance details. I spoke to several, making sure that no-one minded if I left the scene after explaining about Shona's stalker and even including the bit about his being naked, which confused the bemused even more since it was entirely out of context.

We set off again, minus a tail light and a wheel trim, and with the tail gate tied down with string. Fortunately the car handled OK and showed no signs of wanting to deviate from the straight and narrow as we made our way to Shona's place a few minutes' drive away. Shona was almost inconsolable and the journey seemed to last for ever as it dawned on me that I would have to explain to the Health and Safety Director (responsible also for the vehicle fleet and insurance claims) how I came to crunch my car within hours of taking it out on the road for the first time. Would Lucas Barrington still see the funny side of things when he heard about this little incident? I shuddered to think. I'm not sure which of us, Shona or myself, was most relieved to reach her front door without further mishap.

As she collected her crumpled tissues together she gave me a tearful and somewhat reproachful look, as though she thought I was somehow responsible for being in the way of the driver of the car that had hit us from behind. Still, she said, kindly enough, 'Would you like some tea? Maybe you need to steady your nerves before you drive back to the office?'

'Thank you, Shona, I'd love to, but I ought to report this to Head Office before they all go home for the day. It wouldn't look good if I left it till tomorrow.' I didn't add: 'It's already bad enough as it is', which we were both thinking anyway. 'Will you be all right, though? I can stay for a while if you'd really prefer not to be on your own.'

'I'll be fine,' she said. 'I'll call my sister, she'll come round and stay with me tonight.'

'If you're sure,' I said. 'I'll tell your volunteers that you'll be back on Wednesday but if you're still shaky tomorrow, give me a call and we can make other arrangements. Bye.'

I turned the car to head back to the office, but halfway there a flash of memory jolted me and I looked at the dash clock. Three-fifteen! Oh, Lord, I'd said I'd be at the office when Cyril arrived! Thank heavens for the hands-free phone kit! At the next red light I quick-dialled the office on the mobile and waited. And waited. And waited. It rang and rang. Nothing. Green light, too late. Disconnect. Oh, hell's bells!

Using the phone while mobile, even though it's actually called a mobile and was on hands-free anyway, was a hanging offence. One of my mentors had told me a couple of weeks earlier about when the first mobiles had been allocated. Within three days three had been lost, one was stolen and one run over – by the owner's own car! Soon afterwards someone was stopped by a police patrol and charged with driving without due care and attention for charging through a red light whilst distracted by his conversation with his bookie over the mobile. Another employee dropped hers into the garden pond. As far as management was concerned, however, the worst was the saga of the revolving door. A regional manager, already late for a meeting at HO, had decided to park at the hotel next door rather than make herself even later by going to the multi-story half a mile away. As she made the sharp right turn into the hotel drive, her phone warbled at her from the passenger seat. She'd reached over for it, dropped it, reached over even further, lost her grip on the steering wheel, panicked when she saw the car park boundary wall in front of her, over-steered and shot into the revolving door of the hotel entrance. Very embarrassing. Very expensive. Now we were not allowed to use mobiles whilst on the street (to avoid snatch thieves), in the car (excepting only when parked with engine off in order to avoid arrest or demolition), and when connected to the phone with a wrist strap (to avoid dropping it or leaving it somewhere). Oh yes, and write down every call you make so that you can tell the Inland Revenue about business and personal use.

So much for making life easier.

I arrived at the little car park behind the shop a few minutes later to find it full of truck. Must be Cyril's, I thought. Nowhere to park and the streets were all painted with yellow lines. The bank next door? I was a customer of theirs, after all, although not at this branch, admittedly. Still, it would only be for a few minutes. I slid my beat-up little motor, even more beat-up now, into a parking spot. I'm sure it gave a sigh. Or maybe that was me.

As I walked through the wide open back door of the shop, with not a soul in sight, I called 'Hello' and waited for an answering shout to let me know if anyone was in earshot.

'Up here!' called a deep male voice.

I wearily made my way to the stairs, feeling the day catching up with me just a bit. In the kitchen (no sign of Marjorie), Kylie was sitting with her feet up on the little table, her chair tilted precariously backwards and at serious risk of dumping her on the floor. A great bear of a man leaned on the kitchen unit holding a large, chipped mug of tea in his huge hand.

'Cyril,' I said, holding out my hand. 'So sorry I'm late. Bit of an emergency. Hope I haven't held you up at all?' His hand clutched mine and I almost yelped from the power of it. Kylie smirked.

'Nah!' he said. 'This is always my last stop of a Monday and the little lady here always makes a good brew. She told me what happened. Shona OK?'

'I think so,' I answered, noting that the grapevine had been active in my absence. 'I took her home and she'll be fine tomorrow. Would you like to come through to the office and we can chat?' I led the way. 'Hello, Damian. Cyril and I are going to talk rag prices. I hope we won't disturb your work?' He shook his head, unable to talk for the remains of a custard doughnut in his mouth. 'Cyril, pull up a pile of dust and sit down, please,' I added, waving vaguely in the direction of a chair. Damian shot me a baleful look at my criticism of his housekeeping skills, but was still verbally challenged by the doughnut. Cyril perched on a chair that was much too small for him and his bulk gradually overlapped the seat.

'I've looked at the contract,' I said, without preamble and determined not to have another disgrace of indecision or cowardice on the debit side of my account that day. 'You collect from all ten of my shops, is that right?'

He nodded. 'Yup, all ten of them, and around 40 others for your lot in this part of the country. Make a mint out o' me, you do,' he said firmly, settling himself more comfortably in the creaking chair and trying, but failing, to cross his huge arms over his broad expanse of chest.

'Yes, I can see that my shops benefit from the arrangement. It's useful income although hardly a fortune. What can I do for you?' And I put on my best 'if you're going to try and stuff me, don't you dare' look

'It's bin a bad year for rag. Market's difficult. I'm paying out too much and can't sell it on. There's more and more geezers working in my business nowadays. All them relief agencies have stopped buyin' for some reason and there's more and more man-made stuff that ain't suitable fur pulpin'. I tell yah, it's an absolute disaster,' Cyril said. 'I've got to cut my prices in 'alf from tomorrah.'

There was a silence in which you could hear a pin drop. Damian snapped to alert in his chair with eyes wide and spine ramrod straight. Cut by half! That would cut my area income by several hundreds of pounds a week! Thousands, perhaps even tens of thousands, a year! Red and purple lights flashed behind my eyes and panic whipped around my brain. It might not seem a lot to many businesses – it was probably less than the equivalent of about 0.5 seconds' worth of trading to some of the High Street giants – but it was a huge amount to us. I cleared my throat and steadied my nerves, wishing I'd downed that G&T in the Rat and Parrot when I'd had the chance.

'Fifty per cent, Cyril?'

'Watch that squeaky voice,' said the devil on my shoulder.

'Oh, *do* push off!' I targeted barbed thought-darts at him, then said aloud: 'According to my files we have a contract until next April, don't we?'

'We do,' said Cyril, 'but that's never stopped a re-negotiation before. The rag market's very volatile, yer know. Where would yer be if I went belly-up? I got to make a profit, yer know and it's bloody 'ard work, this is.' I suppressed a mounting desire to giggle as a vision of Cyril, looking like Fagan from Oliver and belly-up among a pile of rag sacks, exploded in my mind. Eyes watering from the effort of trying not to laugh, I tried again.

'Well, Cyril, I can only go on what's written in the contract and there's nothing here about *ad hoc* changes or mid-term re-negotiations. Of course, I can't stop you breaking your contract. We'd have to make alternative arrangements, of course, although that would be awkward and cause a lot of hassle in the meantime. Some of my shops would have real problems with storage if we have to find another contractor and wait for them to start. That would be bound to adversely affect our relationship with our neighbours. They'd be sure to get a bit iffy if we built up mountains of sacks full of unsaleable goods in our back yards – or even theirs. I'm thinking out loud, you understand?' Cyril was looking thoughtfully optimistic, sensing a quick victory, and I continued: 'Perhaps you can help me, here, since you know my shops better than I do, at present. Isn't one of them next door to the office of the local weekly newspaper?' He nodded. ' I can't see them being too pleased if our rag store starts to overflow, can you? They've complained before, if what I've been told is correct. Is that right?'

I gave him no time to answer and he began to look a bit concerned at the way the conversation might be heading. 'We'd have to explain why we're in a pickle and, of course, newspapers are always quick to pick up on human interest stories, aren't they, especially when it involves charities? How might they present this kind of situation, do you think? "Wealthy local businessman blackmails charity", perhaps? I wouldn't like to explain that kind of publicity to my boss. You've met Jean, I suppose?' I thought I saw him swallow hard and flinch a bit as he nodded. 'And I'm sure you have better things to do with your time than explain the consequences of your actions to either Jean or persistent reporters. Besides, if you were to lose 40 shops in one fell swoop – and I'm sure my colleagues would want to show solidarity with my predicament – how would you service your regular markets, even when demand is low…?'

'Alright!' Cyril gave in. 'I didn't mean it! It was a joke!' He paused to gather his thoughts and I could almost hear his brain whirring into overdrive. 'I always test out the new ones!' He tried a sheepish grin and a nervous chuckle that didn't quite work. 'Business is business and some o' your lot aren't as switched on as others. Yer can't blame me for trying to cut me costs, can yer? Yer win some, yer lose some. No 'ard feelings?' And he offered me his great paw of a hand to shake.

'No hard feelings, Cyril,' I said, grinning at him and gingerly taking it. 'But please don't ever do that to me again, my heart won't stand it.' He grinned back, while I mentally made a note to find out more about Cyril and the rag trade. I didn't want to feel that vulnerable again.

'Can't promise that,' he said, with a wink, 'but I can buy yer a drink, girl, by way of maki' up and cemetin' the relationship, like. Fancy a quick one down the Swan?' Damian rolled his eyes at me from behind Cyril's large, rounded shoulder, pantomiming frantic motions of throat-cutting and mouthing 'No! No!' in my direction.

'Perhaps another time, Cyril,' I said, 'when I've remembered to bring the flagon of arsenic.'

After a prolonged pause and much thought as to the appropriate reaction, Cyril nearly brought the ceiling down with a laughter that matched the size of the rest of him. The second lot of laughter I'd caused today.

Reaction set in as Cyril left. My knees felt like rubber and a small but persistent throb was bumping at both temples. I really could do without this kind of stress. Any kind of stress, really, although I'd already realised that I was in the wrong job if I wanted an easy life. Damian sat back in his chair and grinned.

'I've never *seen* anyone handle Cyril like that before,' he said, 'it was *awesome*! And you look like a piece of chewed *string*, dear girl!'

'Gee, thanks,' I said, 'you really know how to treat a woman, Damian.'

'Me?' he said, chortling. 'You have me *totally* confused with someone else. I've never known what to do with a girl in all my *life*!' Now it was my turn to laugh. 'I'll make you some tea and find the chocolate Hobnobs,' he added, getting up. 'Marjorie's gone home and *I* won't tell her if you don't.'

'It's a deal!'

Three hours later, having left Marjorie's kitchen as she would wish to find it, I extricated my car from the clutches of an irate bank manager, who was also working unexpected overtime, clearly resented it and threatened to have me clamped next time. I'd swallowed half a pack of paracetamol, tracked down three of Shona's volunteers, repeatedly relayed the story of the stalker and rung the police station to make an appointment to go in the next day. For some reason, probably related to exhaustion, it didn't trigger my memory and I was well on the way home before it occurred to me that I hadn't reported the car shunt. Oh, well, that would get tomorrow off to a flying start!

-3-
Sweet Caroline

Day two dawned, after a night filled with dreams of running through endless, cobwebbed cupboards followed by a demented woman floating half a metre off the ground, brandishing a dish cloth and a kettle, and wailing, 'Look what you've done to my kitchen!' It was a relief to wake up to the dulcet tones of John Humphries on Radio Four.

I prepared for the new day by packing a large holdall with cleaning stuff. Pledge, Mr Muscle, Windolene – you name it, I had it. I just couldn't face the dust and chaos of the office again so I planned to devote today to spring cleaning and some serious thought about the situation I found myself in. Jean probably wouldn't think it was a high priority, but she obviously wasn't about to appear suddenly at my elbow today, since she was sunning herself on a beach somewhere, so I figured I was safe enough. I daren't even think about using Marjorie's kitchen cleaning supplies, she'd have apoplexy at the outrage, and I didn't really want a real-life enactment of my night-time experiences, so I raided my own cupboards for everything I'd need. Damian wasn't around on Tuesdays, it wasn't one of his working days, so it was the perfect opportunity to blitz the place. I thought I could figure out later how to explain to him that dust wasn't my favourite design feature.

This time I had the shop keys in my hand as I reached the door and, humming tunelessly to myself, I made my way through the darkened shop to the stairs. There was a full hour before anyone else was due to arrive and it felt good to have the place to myself before the usual bustle started again. It occurred to me that it was probably the only time of today when I could truly be in control of my own destiny.

'Why don't you have a look in Kylie's office, while she's not around to distract you?' said the little devil on my shoulder. I stopped in the corridor outside Kylie's little cubby hole of an office and slowly put down my holdall.

'That's not very ethical,' I said aloud. 'Besides, why would I?'

''Cos she's a dipstick who couldn't organise playtime in a primary school, let alone run this shop. Who knows what she's up to?'

'That's not the point. I'm supposed to tell a manager before I snoop around their records. It isn't supposed to be an exercise to catch them out, you know, it's a… well, it's an audit. That's right, a systems audit and an opportunity to mutually agree improved standards and procedures. It's not a witch hunt.'

'Sometimes you're boringly straight, you know that?' he sneered. 'But she won't know, will she, and you'll know a bit more about how she runs the shop. Or not, as the case may be. She's a bubble head, if you ask me, could be up to all sorts.'

'Well, I didn't ask you!' I hissed, but somehow I couldn't bring myself to move from the spot. Something inside me knew that that little devil had put his finger on a good point. In spite of the short acquaintance with my new job, I knew that my patch was in trouble and one of my main tasks was to find out whatever I could about what was going wrong and then put it right. If the staff would let me, of course. Jean had made it quite clear that she expected me to pull sales up from rock bottom to something approaching acceptable in as short a timespan as possible. In spite of my conscience, and feeling as guilty as hell but unable to resist, I reached out and twisted the door handle of Kylie's office. It wasn't locked, contrary to standing orders and, in a heartbeat, I was standing in front of her desk.

The dust was just as thick here as in the office upstairs and the notices on the wall, including insurance certificates and the other obligatory bumpf, were all about ten years out of date and showing a fine age patina. Perhaps she's Damian's sister, I thought to myself. They certainly had similar ideas about interior design, even down to the rather tasty male pin-up. Mmm. Pause for thought. Then back to reality. The only thing that appeared to be used regularly, if the absence of dust was any guide, was the accounts ledger in which Kylie recorded the daily till receipts, petty cash spending and banking every day. The Church has the Bible, drivers have the Highway Code (and speed cameras) and we have the Shop Manual. Ministers have the Book of Common Prayer, drivers have the Theory Test and we have the Accounts Ledger. No new-fangled nonsense like computers and spreadsheets here. Everything was entered by hand, daily, in column after column, on pre-printed sheets, which were all then totalled at the end of every week and the whole was balanced across the bottom. Except in this case.

Kylie's handwriting was a clear, round, child-like print. Legible but still as incomprehensible to me as Mandarin. Figures were crossed out, written over and crossed out again. Arrows directed the reader to other columns which were either blank or contained other, different figures and there were little post-it notes that said things like 'Forgot to ask for a receipt, sorry' and 'The float's in the you-know-what in the you-know-where' and 'Think I rang this up twice by mistake – or did I do a refund?' in a dozen different hands. From what I could see, the till receipts and the banking were adrift every day, sometimes as wildly as a Florida hurricane – or was I reading the wrong column entirely? Why, oh why did I have to see all this at the start of the day? It was bad enough to be depressed at five o'clock in the afternoon but to feel my spirits sink before the first cup of tea of the day, especially on the second day in a row, was a bit much. Still, I reasoned, it was my fault for being nosy and served me right for listening to that pesky little devil – again!

Now I knew that Kylie was hopeless at the arithmetic and administration, I couldn't un-know it. It's like nuclear technology: once it's there you can't get rid of it. The question was, what to do with that just-at-this-moment-unwanted knowledge? It was a little early in my career to start pulling the heavy-handed manager bit but, on the other hand, I knew it was one of the priorities of my own job description. In my head I heard the voice of Lawrence Smythe, our Chief Accountant, from part of the introduction training/pep talks: 'We must be able to reconcile our shop turnover with the income and expenditure account,' he'd said pompously, 'or else how can we be sure the shops are contributing to our income targets and expenditure needs?' I wondered what he'd make of Kylie's incomprehensible incomes and expenditures, and began to realise how Pandora must have felt when she opened her box. Once the cat's out of the bag and legging it down the garden, there's no way you're going to get it back in a again in time to make the vet's appointment. Or something like that.

But was this just innocent incompetence or something altogether more sinister? Did I think Kylie was a complete nincompoop with figures, or was she hiding a sophisticated trail of deception?

One of the more depressing aspects of shop life was the alarming regularity with which things simply disappeared. Not just my shop's but everyone's. Nothing was safe. Boxes of till rolls, clothes hangers, stock from the shop floor and the stock room, money from the till, each just vanished from different shops at different times with depressing regularity. It was as baffling as trying to figure out how anyone could get hooked on reality TV. Better brains than mine had been applied to the problem but nothing seemed to stop the haemorrhage of an astonishing variety of goods and supplies.

'It ain't stealin',' I'd heard someone say during my tour of the country, 'not really. People gives this stuff away. They don't want it. How can it be stealin' if nobody owns it?' But they don't give us the hangers, I'd thought, and the money in the till is... well... money in the till. Just like in any other shop. And once the donor has given us stuff to sell, the charity owned it until is was legitimately sold on to a new owner. Of course it was stealing, but how to change blinkered mindsets, especially when, as my granny used to say, 'there's none so blind as them that won't see'.

Anyway, Kylie didn't seem the type to be dishonest, with her friendly openness and hard-working attitude. Okay, she was a dipstick and the volunteers ran rings round her, but that didn't make her a tea-leaf. Still, I had to admit that it had taken me six months, when I was 15, to figure out that my boyfriend was seeing my best friend as well as me, so I clearly wasn't a very good a judge of character! I was good at revenge, though. When she'd asked me to shorten a skirt for her so that she could wear it to a party – me being the noble, innocent little seamstress and she being the outrageous, treacherous flirt – I'd sewn kipper skeletons into the hem, finishing it just minutes before she was due to leave for the party and far too anxious about missing her lift to even look at it before she put it on. She didn't notice until after a dance or two, when the bones warmed up a bit and a vigorous bop wafted the scent all over the club. By that time it was too late and she never did live it down in her set.

But I digress. I consoled myself with the thought that my boss was on holiday for the next four weeks and was unlikely to be particularly interested, for a while at least, in how I was prioritising my workload. I had time to decide what to do and how to do it and was a great believer in the maxim that something will always turn up if only you can wait long enough. Just as well, given the sweatshirt, jeans and bucket of cleaning gear I was carrying as my main priority of the day. I decided that Kylie and the accounts could wait. There'd be time and opportunity to check out whether she was doing everything she ought – and nothing she shouldn't – another time.

Back on track and climbing the stairs, I shot a line at the little devil on my shoulder: 'Stay out of my hair today, you've done enough damage already!'

'Who, me?' he said, all huffy, injured innocence. 'You don't have to follow my advice, you know. Don't those do-gooders in the white collars and nightgowns keep banging on about all that free will stuff? Don't blame me, deary!'

Upstairs I set to with a will, my little radio bleating out mindless wallpaper music and a scarf wrapped around my nose and mouth against the dust. By the time noises downstairs heralded the arrival of staff and the start of another shop day, I was up to my elbows in Marigolds, Mr Muscle (Oooo I wish!) and water that was rapidly turning into mud. The vacuum cleaner, which was almost on its last legs (mental note to self: source a new one ASAP) had taken care of about a third of the dust after I'd emptied the bag twice, and wet cloths had almost done for the rest after several changes of water in a cheerfully bright red bucket. The colour added a valiant sort of note to the challenge, a bit like a matador's cloak to the bull – maddening but very stirring for adrenalin levels.

'Well, 'ere's a sight for sore eyes!'

I recognised Kylie's voice although it wasn't easy to be sure it was actually her standing in the doorway for the haze of dust in the air.

'Wotcha, Gilly,' she said, in her usual cheery way, 'you got stuck in then! Good job Damian ent 'ere to see yer, 'e'd go bonkers!' And she disappeared, laughing in a girlish treble that might have been infectious in other circumstances.

The thread of my enthusiasm, not to mention my energy, was

snapped by the interruption and Kylie's humour, so I downed tools and made a cuppa, trying not to leave traces of my passage through Marjorie's kitchen for fear of reprisals. I'd already decided she would be just as happy with guerrilla tactics as with a frontal assault and I didn't fancy meeting her, unexpectedly, on a dark evening in the car park.

Seated at my almost clean desk with the tea and a couple of choccies in front of me on the moderately clean surface, I pulled the telephone towards me and took a deep breath to steady my nerves before dialling Head Office. All too quickly, and before my courage was properly in place, the switchboard operator had connected me to the number for Malcolm Tweedy, the Facilities, Fleet and Insurance Manager, and I was counting the number of times the phone rang. He was bound to be there, they always are when you've a humiliating confession to make, but they're never around when you need help. Sod's law at work.

'Hello?'

'Hello, is that Malcolm?'

'Yes. Who's this?'

'It's Gillian, I'm the new area manager. I started this week. We met at the HQ induction day, do you remember?' My hand felt clammy as it clung to the plastic phone and I wasn't relishing the next part of this conversation at all.

'Yes, I remember you, Gillian. Blue blouse, black trousers, flowery blazer. What can I do for you?'

Well, he sounded friendly enough although I wondered if it was quite normal to have such a clear memory of what people were wearing two weeks after you'd met them once for about 90 seconds. Was he practising for some international World Cup for super memories? Perhaps he had a clothes fetish. A women's clothes fetish?

'Well... er...' I hesitated. 'I'm... er... afraid I've some bad news.' There was no easy way to say it so I just ploughed on. 'Some stupid idiot of a Sunday driver gave my car a rear end shunt yesterday.' I instantly cringed as the chosen words made me sound incredibly petulant and incompetent in about equal measure.

'Ah,' said Malcolm ominously thoughtfully, then paused for a moment. 'Is there much damage?'

'I'm fine, thanks,' I said, 'and so is Shona. She was with me.'

'I meant to the car,' he said and I could hear the frost crackling down the phone line and overtaking the previous comparative warmth in his voice. Yes, of course he meant the car, idiot, I berated myself silently.

'Urm… well… the bumper and rear light assembly on the driver's side are rather dented, and the tail gate is a bit stiff and there's a dent in the wing…'

'Stop!' he said, with a different kind of warmth this time. The lobby of Lucifer's basement sprang to mind, for some reason. He definitely blew hot and cold, did this one. 'Didn't you just collect the car yesterday?'

'Er… Sunday, actually,' I confessed

'Well, that's just about the quickest on record,' he said. 'I just hope our paperwork has caught up with you and you're properly insured. Take it to any main dealer for estimates and repair and I'll send you the forms you need to complete. Call me if you have any more problems.' He put down the phone with a little *snick* that said everything there was to say about new staff, their cars, their carelessness and the volatile combination of the three put together.

Phew! I thought. Still, it could have been much worse. Or could it? What was it he'd said about insurance? Surely they couldn't have sent me out on the road without insurance! Could they? I decided that was his problem.

I'd spent years trying to cultivate a Scarlett O'Hara attitude – the 'I'll think about it tomorrow because tomorrow is another day!' thing – and it had a lot to recommend it. I'd discovered that problems sometimes went away if you left them alone for long enough, a bit like the scabs that just fall off by themselves when your knees heal. Unless you fell on them again, of course. Or wanted an interesting scar that you could boast about, in which case you picked the scabs and made them bleed afresh everyday for a fortnight.

Some, however, just got worse. Problems, that is. Then you had to explain to someone, generally in authority like a bank manager or builder or someone equally humourless, why you hadn't done something sooner. Then there were problems that weren't really problems at all, just the workings of an over-active imagination. They were the best kind. You could congratulate yourself on dealing with them positively, successfully, bravely even, with no risk at all, just as long as you hadn't already allowed yourself to be driven to Prozac!

Feeling that, on the whole, I'd got off lightly with Malcolm, I set to with a will to tackle the rest of the cleaning, starting with the ancient computer. Someone had given me a magic little vacuum gismo for Christmas together with three boxes of anti-stat, chemical-impregnated wipes whose scent made me sneeze. The vacuum cleaner thingy wasn't very powerful, but it seemed to shift most of the biscuit crumbs from between the keys so that was OK. The wipes seemed to be rather wetter than I thought was good for the keyboard but the box said they were 'especially formulated' and that excess liquid would evaporate quickly. After about 20 minutes of scrubbing and two boxes of wipes, the computer looked almost smart and was hugely improved over its former state. I reached over the desk, pushed the plug back into the socket, switched on … and all the lights went out.

'Oiy!' yelled a voice from downstairs. 'Wot's goin' on, then?'

I raced down the stairs to be met by Kylie racing up. We met in the middle, literally, because it was almost pitch black without the lights. My downwards momentum took us to the bottom of the stairs without, thankfully, any broken bones. She picked herself up from the heap we'd landed in and I could see, in the weak light from the cloudy window in the back door, that she was very confused and more than just a little bit cross. She was also rather grubby from the tumble. As was I, of course, but at least I'd brought it on myself from all the cleaning.

'Wotcha bin doin?' she glared at me, accusingly, testing her limbs for breaks.

'Nothing!' I assured her, though hesitantly. 'I'm sure I did nothing. I was cleaning the computer and everything just went dark. What's happened, then?'

'All the bleedin' lights 'ave gone,' she said, 'and every other bloody thing as well. Me till's stuck and the steamer's gone off. Mind you, with the lights out we can't see nuffink in the bleedin' stock room anyway! Did you plug summat else into a socket?'

'Well, yes,' I said, 'should I not?'

'No!' she exclaimed. 'Yer can't do that 'ere! The wiring's all to

43

rats and it'll only take a few bits at a time.' By this time we were back in the office and she explained to me as though I was an infant, ticking things off on her fingers. 'There's the lights and the till – it's electric, yer know, 'cos o' the credit cards. Then there's the steamer, the kettle and the fan, the answerphone downstairs and the one up 'ere and the fridge and the microwave in the kitchen, your compu'er and prin'er and the copyin' thingy and if you put 'em all on at once the 'ole lot blows! The fuses, yer know, they all pops at once. Damian knows and so does we so, when 'e's 'ere in the office we don't put so much load on downstairs. You just messed up our routine!' she accused.

I did a bit of mental mapping of the building and realised that the till and the fridge were always switched on and, when Damian or I were in the office, the computer, with its printer, and perhaps the copier would be as well. When we were out our answerphone was switched on although the other office equipment should be off. If we'd remembered to switch it off, of course. The steamer, a kind of giant kettle with a nozzle that directed a jet of steam through all things fabric (and fingers and hairstyles as well, when they got in the way), straightening out creases, was switched on for almost half the shop's opening hours. When that was being used the fan was almost obligatory, even in winter, because of the poor ventilation in the stock room. So a cup of tea, a bowl of soup in the microwave or the use of the fan in the office (on a warm day) was definitely out of the question without a lot of pre-organisation.

'I'd better check the fuses, then,' I said, with due humility, since it seemed to be all my fault. 'Where is the fuse box?'

'That's the thing, yer see,' Kylie said, looking at me with a grin now, and a speculative gleam in her eye. 'It's up there...'

My eyes followed the line of her arm and finger through the open door, up the wall at the end of the stairwell and... Oh, Lord! The fuse box was about six metres up on the tallest wall in the building, just under the ceiling over the foot of the stairs. Two floors high of empty space. And I hated heights.

'We 'ave a ladder,' she said, still grinning, 'a big un!'

I swallowed hard. Half an hour later, the computer again unplugged and with the fuses checked and all pushed back into place, I was sitting at my desk still trembling and damp with the aftermath of abject terror. I really didn't need reminding of why I loathed heights. Kylie made me a cup of tea and must have felt sorry for me because she brought me another chocolate biscuit as well, still grinning cheekily at my mishap.

'You won't do that again in an 'urry, will you!' she crowed and disappeared back to the shop and her customers to spread the word about the new boss's latest cock up.

It took an hour to locate an electrician who was willing to come in before Christmas (which was OK since Christmas was only about four months away) to see what could be done about the fuse box and, by that time, I'd calmed down and cooled off a bit. Something had to be done. Blown fuses were just a symptom and, although the building was old and pretty grotty, the last thing I needed was to explain to Malcolm why it had burned down. I hadn't a clue yet whether I had any money to spend on things like maintenance and I had a feeling that, even if I had, it wouldn't stretch to new wiring. Still, maybe I could frighten HQ with dire tales of H&S and fire risks threatening to close the shop!

After checking with Kylie that it was OK, I plugged in the computer again, switched on and waited for the screen to warm up. And waited. 'Bloody thing!' I muttered under my breath, and then presto! Lights, action and a strange greenish glow began to appear. Slowly it gathered strength until the whole screen was the colour of a stagnant pond. The licensing logo appeared and I goggled at the date. This machine was almost as old as steam but it seemed to be humming away with a contended little whirring sound nevertheless.

The license screen defaulted to what looked like an accounting package which wasn't anything I recognised and seemed to pre-date even my long computer experience completely. Figures blocked in most of the tightly spaced columns. At the top of the page was the last action date. It was just last week. Hope soared. Maybe Damian was really very efficient and it was just a personal quirk, this thing about dust and piling papers everywhere except in a filing system! After all, he had provided me with up to date sales figures just yesterday. That's if they were up to date, of course, and not just wishful thinking.

I felt a bit euphoric after this little success, after all it had been

'It's Brigid, from Broad Barrow.'

The alliteration, with its Irish brogue, made me smile in the teeth of all expectations of another problem. Broad Barrow was the roughest shop on my patch, a street where the drunks populated the street most of the day, and drug pushers and their customers took over when the drinkers stumbled into doorways in alcoholic stupors for the night. Volunteers for the shop were hard to come by and most of those who did offer to help would work only until twilight or four o'clock, whichever came first, which made staffing the shop in winter rather difficult. Amazingly, the shop did pretty well in spite of the challenges. That is, in terms of results for my patch, which was actually pretty dismal in a global sense, though I tried not to think about that. The customers loved its old-fashioned charity shop image, all higgledy piggledy and an H&S nightmare, but with a weekly turnover that actually challenged belief, in the circumstances, although I doubted that Jean thought of it that way.

'The water's pouring in!' Brigid howled. 'The ceiling has come down all over my shoe display and there's water tumbling down the stairs like a waterfall! What on earth shall I dooooooo?' said the wail, rising higher by the second.

'Where is it coming from, Brigid?' Think, I need time to think!

'From the flat above us. The tenants are always letting the bath overflow or the washing machine pipe get disconnected or some daft thing.'

'Hold on, Brigid, this has happened before?'

'Oh, yes! About four times now, since the new people moved in.'

'What did you do last time?'

'Rang the landlord. He lives just down the road and he had to break down the door, they never answer the bell.'

'Ring him now, Brigid, and I'll ring the Fire Brigade.'

'The Fire Brigade!' she yelped. 'Isn't that a bit extreme?'

'Probably,' I said and put the phone down.

Five minutes later I was in my car and a mile down the road before I remembered that I was still in jeans and sweatshirt with a pair of Marigolds tucked into my waistband and, in all likelihood, smudges of dirt on my face. What a way to meet a shop manager for the first time! Still, it couldn't be helped. Needs must when the devil drives. 'Is that my cue, then?' said the voice of the little devil on my shoulder 'Shut up!' I growled, using the rear view mirror to check my face and scrub at a large smudge across one cheek.

Twenty minutes later I saw the flashing lights whilst still half a mile from the shop. Broad Barrow was around two miles long, straight as a die and it lent itself to the long view which was wasted, really, since it was a bloody awful sight at the best of times! The street was always overcrowded with people and traffic, it was noisy, dirty and permanently blocked by vehicles left double parked with engines running by drivers who'd never heard of emission tests, let alone passed one. There was nowhere for me to park – well, why would there be? – and it was another ten minutes before I dumped the car and walked the half mile back to the shop. Arriving at the front door I found several large, rather dishy-looking hunks in yellow and black uniforms standing around holding cups of tea. Why, oh why, couldn't this happen when I was dressed to impress rather than looking like someone from Molly Maid on a bad hair day?

'Hello, Brigid,' I said to the most harassed looking female I could see in the shop.

'Are you Gillian?' she said. 'Well, I'm glad you're here but this is all *very* embarrassing.'

'Probably,' I replied, opening the conversation where we'd left off, 'but they've stopped the water, I see.'

'Well, yes. But Yusuf could have done that. He was here within two minutes of my call and into the flat with his spare keys.'

'Ah,' I said, nonplussed. 'Yusuf is the landlord?' She nodded at me 'But didn't you say…? Oh, it doesn't matter, I suppose, the main thing is that the water's stopped.'

Brigid was looking me up and down by now, clearly puzzled by the way I was dressed.

'Sorry,' I said, looking down at my old sweatshirt and seen-better-days jeans. 'I was cleaning my office when you rang and didn't even stop to change my clothes.' Her eyebrows rose even higher. Not a boss-like image, cleaning your own office, obviously. 'But how about if I stay to help you clean up? I'm dressed for it, after all,' I said, trying to sound jovial and we're-all-in-it-together. It occurred to me that this wasn't quite the impression I should make on my first meeting with a member of my shop's team – it lacked a certain management credibility, somehow. Still, it was too late by then so I thought I'd try to make the best of it and create a feeling of team spirit. After all, there was a certain pattern of unusual first meetings developing here, and I was sure that Brigid would hear about Shona and her stalker pretty soon, even if she hadn't already.

A few minutes later we were thanking the firemen, who seemed to be taking the whole thing in their stride. 'That's alright, love, we get called out to all sorts of things and this one's better than rescuing cats from up trees,' said one.

'Or jumpers from the tops of multi-stories,' said another, worryingly.

'That's alright, love, anytime,' winked and leered a third.

'I'll have to arrange a few traffic accidents or derail a train for them,' said the little devil on my shoulder, 'they obviously need something more interesting to do.' I ignored him.

When we'd seen the guys and their large, shiny fire engine on their way, Brigid introduced me to Yusuf who was hovering hopefully in the background. He was small, dark and very thin and wore a dazzling smile with one gold tooth, just left of bottom centre.

'Hello, new lady!' he enthused. 'I am very pleased to meet you but would have wished for better circumstances.' He shook my hand and held it just a little too long. His was ever so slightly clammy. I retrieved mine gently and smiled back at him.

'I'm pleased to meet you too, Yusuf. I understand you're our landlord and that you own the whole building?'

'Yes, for my sins that is so. There are actually many other parts also. A small lock-up shop next door and a pied-a-terre over it. Here.' And one arm shot straight up to indicate the ceiling and something beyond. 'Large apartments on the first and second floors.' He paused, seeming to expect a congratulatory response. I obliged with a small smile and he beamed at me again. 'A significant responsibility,' he said, 'when one's tenants are careless.'

'Yes, Brigid tells me this has happened before,' I said, 'more than once, in fact.'

'Ah, yes. They are my countrymen,' he said, tilting his head slightly to one side and shrugging his shoulders gently. 'They have been in this wonderful country for only a short time, they speak little English and do not fully understand British plumbing either. They came to escape persecution but still fear every knock at the door. They will not open unless they hear our native tongue speaking words of reassurance.'

We moved around the shop together, the three of us examining the consequences of people who didn't understand English plumbing. Contrary to expectations the damage didn't look too bad now that water had stopped dripping, although Brigid kept on shaking her head and wore an increasingly worried look on her face. Several ceiling tiles had caved in, scattering polystyrene all over the shoe display, book shelves, record racks and the counter. The torrent had swept through the door and had turned right where it met the counter, carrying small items of stock with it as it tumbled down the stairs, pooling in a debris-strewn puddle in the stock room below.

A closer examination showed that the tiles that had cascaded down from the suspended ceiling were easily replaceable, and Yusuf agreed that he could arrange it quickly. I asked him gently and with my best winning smile about his responsibilities for other utilities and for certain fire risk precautions. He squirmed a bit but agreed he would also check the electricity cables in the space between the suspended ceiling and the floor of the flat above. I'd no idea whether it was actually his responsibility or not but I was damned if I was going to spend money out of my budget – especially since I didn't have one. The counter would dry, the insurance company would probably pay for the lost stock if it amounted to more than pocket money and, since the stairs were bare boards, I thought they'd probably dry out in a day or two.

The stock room floor seemed to be the only real problem. Being a basement, with no ventilation that I could see, drying out down there was going to take some time and would probably be a pretty smelly experience as well. The carpet, if that's what it had once been, looked as though it had been there since the Great Flood, not to mention all the other, local, ones that Brigid had mentioned. Whatever colour it once was had long since disappeared under years of abuse. I could see, however, that there were two boarded-up windows in the side wall of the stairwell and worked out that they were probably just above street level, since the back of the shop seemed to be lower than the street to the front. I chose not to mention them just yet but an idea was beginning to form in my mind.

'What can be done about the damp down here, Yusuf?' I asked gesturing at the damp patches on the walls whilst paddling in the puddle. I just prayed that there weren't any dodgy electrical cables down here. 'There doesn't seem to be any ventilation in here and that can't be good for the staff, even in ideal conditions. The light seems pretty poor too. What can you recommend to improve things?' Delegate, my mentors had taught me years before, especially when you don't have a clue and you want someone else to suggest a solution!

Yusuf put on a show of thinking deeply, putting his fingers under his chin, titling his head to one side and then the other. He'd do well on the stage in an Oscar Wilde comedy, I thought.

'Is very difficult,' he said, 'this is old, old building and, you see, this basement is for storage not for work like these lovely, wonderful ladies of yours! Your people decided to use for working after I said to them, many times, it is not a good place. I did my best, you know.' Now he looked positively hurt at the cavalier way in which his advice had been cast aside. 'But they would not listen. Am I to be penalised? Am I to be forced to find a vast fortune of money from somewhere, I know not where, to do works because they did not listen to me? Now,' and his voice changed to honeyed tones, sensing an opportunity here, 'if your people say it must be done and would care to find monies maybe I would know someone who might do these things for cheaper cost, knowing it is for charity? Some heating, perhaps, you think...?' And he left his little door open, waiting for me to stick my neck through.

Ten out of ten for effort, Yusuf, I thought, not a bad try. 'I could ask, Yusuf,' I said with a show of interest and enthusiasm. After all, two can play at that game. 'I will look through my H&S manuals to see if there's anything that might help us.'

'Dear lady!' he breathed, apparently overwhelmed by my magnanimity. 'How splendid! I will do whatever I can to help you in these endeavours!'

'But these lovely, wonderful ladies you speak of, and whom you seem to admire so much,' I said, 'must get back to work quickly and you and I both know, don't we, that large organisations never see

51

the need for the same urgency as we, who must work so hard, do?'

'Oh, so true'! He wrung his hands and nodded vigorously.

'We can try to help ourselves in the meantime, however.' I smiled at him to strengthen the conspiracy of the 'we' and he gave me a look that was half leer and half sly cautiousness. 'Our lovely ladies would be grateful to you for helping to make this problem better as quickly as possible.' And I took his elbow, gently and firmly, and led him to the boarded windows. 'If you would arrange to open up these windows,' I said, 'we would have ventilation and you would have my unending gratitude, not to mention the goodwill of all the ladies you admire so much.'

He looked as though he'd been stung, which he had in a way, I suppose. Hoist by his own petard. 'But... I...' he stammered.

'Brigid, you and your volunteers would make sure that Mr Yusuf would be well looked after while he was working here, wouldn't you? And I'm sure it wouldn't take him very long to remove some boarding and put in new windows.'

'We... er...' Brigid was dithering as well, which didn't surprise me; I had rather chucked her in the deep end on this one.

'After all, Yusuf,' and I turned my beaming smile on him, full blast, 'the windows are quite small and I'm sure that you, with all your many contacts and business associates, could arrange it quickly and cheaply. Couldn't you?' He was starting to turn a funny colour under his tan and his mouth was working without any sound coming out. 'That's fixed, then!' I enthused, before he had a chance to say anything. 'Thank you so much, Yusuf, you're a gentleman and a saviour! Now, since we need to be back in business, Brigid and I will clear up as best we can and time is marching on, you know.' I took his elbow again and walked purposefully up the stairs to the street door. 'I shall really look forward to seeing you again soon.' I smiled at Yusuf as warmly as I could. 'Shall we say, on Friday? That isn't too soon, is it, for you make your arrangements, so that we can divert the attentions of the Health and Safety people?'

'I...er...'

'Good, that's excellent. So kind.' And I gently closed the door, leaving him on the pavement looking puzzled.

Brigid was looking almost as bemused. 'Do you think he'll be back on Friday?' she asked

'Haven't a clue,' I said, 'I'll sort out something if he doesn't. Now, let's have a look at this lot, shall we? Neither of us wants to be here till midnight, I'm sure, and there's a fair bit of work to do yet.' We examined the scene, me with some relief that I wouldn't have to work here while it all dried out and Brigid with a growing sense of desperation knowing that she and her volunteers would. I just hoped she could persuade/bribe/weedle them into turning up to work here while it was all damp and dank.

'What's this, then?' said a husky voice from the stairs behind us. I turned around to be greeted by one of the most bizarre sights I'd ever seen. A tall, pencil thin figure of well over six feet in height was standing halfway down the stairs, stooping slightly to avoid brushing the ceiling, with a wild bush of hair dyed in at least four different colours. Over henna red there were streaks of primrose yellow, sky blue and magenta. The apparition's eyes would have won appreciation from Cleopatra and the mouth was a glorious *rouge noir*. Long finger nails were painted leaf green with tiny, glittering stars glued to their centres and there were at least three rings on each finger. A long coat reminded me of pictures of Gandalf, the wizard from The Lord of the Rings. It was long and flowing, made of velvet and satin in deep blue and royal purple, and reached almost to the floor. And the face of this figure out of fantasy sported at least two days' worth of five o'clock shadow and a pugilist's nose.

'Hello, Caroline,' said Brigid. Caroline? What? I realised my jaw had dropped to somewhere around my chin and hurriedly closed my mouth whilst trying to compose my features into something more acceptable than the stunned disbelief I knew was showing. Boy, oh boy, was it showing!

'Gillian, this is Caroline. He's my most loyal volunteer and I don't know what I'd do without him.' I was having a bit of difficulty getting my head around this. She had said 'him', hadn't she? And 'Caroline'? I mentally kicked myself into action and stuck out my hand.

'Hello, Caroline,' I said and was quite proud that my voice sounded steady. 'Pleasure to meet you.'

'Likewise,' said Caroline, in a voice that was quite well suited to Hagrid in the Harry Potter books, as he gave my hand a good shake, making my spine and teeth rattle and sending my eyeballs into orbit.

Caroline waved his hand vaguely, indicating his appearance. 'Don't mind me, I'm just back from a lunch date with my friend Daphne, I don't normally dress this way for work. I only stopped off to see what was going on 'cos I saw the fire brigade leaving.'

'Oh, really?' I said, feeling the pressure of his deep, powerful voice on my ears in this confined space. At least the voice matched the size and shape, even if nothing else did.

'Bit of a mess, isn't it?' he said, looking around. 'Looks like there'll be plenty to do when I come in tomorrow. You alright, Bridge, dear?' he asked gently, bending slightly towards her in a motherly sort of gesture. Something wafted under my nose and I could have sworn it was Chanel something or other. Caroline had good taste in perfume even though her – his? – dress sense was just a tad dramatic. The gestures were more than just a bit OTT as well. Everything about Caroline was overwhelming, overpowering and all sorts of other 'overs'. Still, s/he seemed very caring of Brigid's welfare so s/he couldn't be all attention-grabbing drama queen.

'Oh, yes,' Brigid said, gloomily, 'Gillian says she'll help me clear up. I'd really need your help tomorrow, though, it's Nelly's day and you know how depressing she can be when she's upset, and this will really upset her.' Brigit's voice suggested she knew all about upset and depressing. 'See you tomorrow, though, we can sort something out then,' she added, as a kind of afterthought, 'Are you seeing George tonight? You two seem so well suited, I'm so pleased you found someone special.' and she gave him a watery smile. Rather appropriate in the circumstances, I thought.

Caroline sniffed and pulled a face. 'Don't think so,' she replied, 'she's decided she wants a baby, silly bitch. She's gone back to her husband.'

an early start to the day, I hadn't had any breakfast and an overdose of dust throughout the morning so far hadn't done much to improve my mood. Neither had scaling a ladder the height of Everest. The feel-good feeling was seductive so I looked around for the mouse. Nothing. No mouse. Never mind, old systems were controlled by the key board, I remembered. Mice (or should it be mouses?) hadn't been invented when this computer was born, I reasoned and, since I'd learned my keyboard skills in those far-off halcyon days I thought I'd have a go. I raised my hands over the key board, took a deep breath and touched a short succession of keys. Nothing. Zilch. Not even on the most common combinations of F keys (very aptly named, I thought) or any other combination I could think of. Pausing for thought, it occurred to me that maybe it had something to do with cleaning the thing. After all, I had thought that there was rather a lot of cleaning fluid in the wipes. Could it be...? Oh, Lord, what would Damian say if I'd ruined his toy? What would HQ say when I told them I couldn't produce the weekly accounts!

I picked up the keyboard and turned it upside down. Why, I don't know – it just seemed like a good idea to have a look underneath. Five keys fell out to be followed by a thin, dirty, trickle of obviously un-evaporated cleaning fluids. I put down the key board carefully, replaced the keys and the lights went out again.

'Oiy!' yelled Kylie. 'Yer done it again!'

'Tell her something she doesn't know!' said the little devil on my shoulder and I went to find the ladder again.

Two trips up the ladder was two more than my nerves would take. It took four cups of very strong tea and a currant bun to make me feel even halfway steady again. A G&T or three would have been better but there was the car, and the drive home later, and Malcolm was already a little cross with me. I couldn't afford to face a charge of drinking and driving as well and, knowing my luck, a policeman would be standing on the corner watching me before I'd even unlocked the car door. Ah, well, later at home, perhaps.

My hands had stopped shaking – just – when the phone rang. I picked it up and was immediately aurally assaulted by a second semi-hysterical voice in two days. It was getting to be a habit!

'Is that Gillian?' the voice said before I could even say hello.

'Yes, that's me.'

-4-
Party Time

I woke the next morning to the realisation that it was only Wednesday, and only my first week in my new job, but I already felt as though I'd been working non-stop since Christmas. After spending the best part of yesterday up to my Marigold elbows in dust and muck, I'd looked like some kind of bag lady by the time I arrived home. I hadn't dared go to Lupin Lane to cash up but each time I'd phoned to say hello, one or other of the volunteers had said not to worry, everything was under control in Shona's absence. I crossed my fingers and hoped for the best.

On my way home I'd stopped at the police station to give them the statement they'd asked for. I was grubby and wet after a day of being a Mrs Mop and the desk sergeant gave me a look that said I wasn't the only one who thought I looked like a bag lady. I wasn't able to tell him much about our intruder, of course, so it didn't take long to complete a statement. He told me that Shona wasn't going to press charges and I told him that neither would the charity. He seemed a bit surprised but in a worldly 'nothing surprises me any more and anyway, it saves me a lot of paperwork' kind of way. I explained that the chap hadn't really done anything except bend a dress stand and make a nuisance of himself. The desk sergeant said our visitor had had a monumental hangover when he woke up and had gone straight into the Boots store across the road when he's been released. Presumably for pain killers to clear his brandy-induced state of severe delicacy.

I'd spent ages under a hot shower when I got home, sluicing away the remains of the day. My hair had been stiff with dust, my skin as grey as though I'd been shut away from the sun for weeks. My clothes almost stood up by themselves and, even with the protection of gloves, my hands and nails definitely looked the worse for wear. Eventually, with pink skin, shiny face and wet hair, I'd wrapped myself in a bathrobe and gone downstairs to Greg, my other half, and the supper he'd cooked for us. It wasn't the first time I'd been grateful for a husband who was handy in the kitchen. Sometime before we'd met he'd been on a skills re-training programme and passed a catering course with flying colours, much to everyone's surprise. There were those unkind souls who seemed to think he wasn't much cop at anything really, except avoiding hard work, but I'd always had faith that he just needed to find his niche in life. He seemed to enjoy being in charge in the kitchen and created mouth-watering meals out of what appeared to be no more than a lettuce leaf, a bit of cheese and half a carton of milk. I'd suggested once, during one of his spells of unemployment, that it might be an idea to take up catering professionally. He'd been a bit huffy, saying it was poorly paid and a lot of unsocial hours. He'd been even more huffy when I'd said that unemployment was even more poorly paid and if he worked evenings in a restaurant he'd still have his lie-ins in the mornings, as per usual.

Still, every cloud has a silver lining and this cloud produced some truly scrumptious meals, when the chef was in the right mood. OK, that wasn't too often, but it was worth waiting for. While we ate I described my day. Not all of it, there was a lot to tell and I could see he was only half listening anyway. He seemed a bit concerned, though, about what might have happened if our singing flasher had been aggressive instead of unconscious, which I thought was quite sweet since he wasn't normally the most sensitive type, and said I looked shattered. I wasn't surprised he'd noticed the effects of the day, 'cos I felt dead on my feet, although he could have been a bit more diplomatic about his phraseology. He suggested I get an early night and then, almost as an afterthought, that he'd promised to meet a friend down at the pub for a quick one.

I don't even remember climbing the stairs but I guess I must have, and wriggled under the bed covers, because the next thing I knew John Humphries was berating some hapless social worker about yet another supposed failure of social services somewhere. Sunshine slanting through the curtains told me I was late.

While I got myself dressed and ready to face another day of strange events and even stranger people, I reviewed the past couple of days. It had all been a bit trying, to say the least. I'd met a human

56

rottweiler programmed to defend kitchens, a gay icon to elderly ladies, a miniature Albanian version of a spiv, a mountainous transvestite and a drunken romantic with a penchant for brandy. I'd lost half a day's trading each at two different shops, pranged the car, called out the fire brigade and faced my own pathological fear of heights. Twice! Not bad for just two days. What was it Greg had said two months ago, when I was cock-a-hoop at having landed the job?

'That's really great,' he'd said with real enthusiasm. 'Congratulations! I can't see why you're so keen to work for a charity again, mind you, it's bloody hard work and not much in the bank to show for it but what the hell, it's better than being on the dole, isn't it?'

True, how true! Although how he knew that was beyond me. As far as I could recall he'd been out of work more often than not for the past five years. He seemed to think messing about under the bonnet of his car and watching TV in the afternoon was the highest of ambitions. But then, the only thing that seemed to give him any real satisfaction, apart from keeping his rickety old car on the road, was seeing a healthy bank balance, just as long as he wasn't expected to make too much of a contribution towards it.

'Is there a car with it?' he'd asked

'Yes.'

'Even better! You won't need yours then, will you?'

'No,' I agreed, thinking that the proceeds from a sale would be just enough to clear the debts we'd accumulated while he'd been out of work this time.

'I can use it, then. This couldn't have worked out better! I didn't tell you at the time because you were so wound up about being away on all that training stuff but I'd forgotten to pay the insurance premiums on the Volvo. Now we won't have to borrow to buy me another car. Isn't that great?'

Forgotten? *We?* The Volvo was his car, an old, clapped-out thing that he spent hours tinkering with but which was always suffering from some problem or another. He'd driven it into a ditch when he'd skidded off a country road at a crossroads a few weeks ago. All the fault of the farm tractor coming the other way, he'd said, and had avoided all my questions about when it would be repaired.

Deep down I'd known somehow that the car wasn't coming back but hadn't quite made the leap to what would happen next. I was just glad that no-one had been hurt in the accident, especially Greg. He wasn't exactly the most reliable person in the world, but he had a way of making me feel special that lightened my life. He could be tender and thoughtful, gentle and kind. He had a wicked sense of humour and a knack of taking the mickey out of pompous people and bureaucratic nonsense that made dealing with the gas board or the water company seem almost entertaining. It was like living with a wayward child at times – sometimes difficult, never dull and often positively exciting!

Last year the local council had been quite stroppy about an unpaid parking fine. His, that is. Greg had torn up their letters and, when others kept arriving, he'd charge around the house, waving his arms about and getting very red in the face while he lectured an imaginary official about the inequities of the parking regulations. Eventually, however, under threat of being arrested, he'd been forced to give in. But he didn't do it gracefully, not my Greg. He'd withdrawn £40 from the bank, all in two-pence pieces, and dumped it, in bags, on the council cashier's desk. Then he'd demanded a receipt so that the poor girl had to count it while he waited. I was appalled at the way he'd treated her. It wasn't her fault, after all, but I couldn't help thinking that it was an imaginative way of cocking a snook at authority. Not big on authority, my Greg.

I'd given way within a day or so, of course, so now he was driving around in my car. At least I knew the insurance was paid up for the next eight months. He'd read me pretty well on that one, knowing better than I did that I couldn't hold out on him. He'd read my new job right too. It was turning out to be more of a challenge than even I'd anticipated.

Still, here I was on day three, wondering how Damian would react to the new-look office. I'd made sure I arrived early so that he didn't walk in and see all the gleaming surfaces (as much as office furniture of indeterminate age and suffering from umpteen years of neglect was capable of gleaming, anyway) without some prior warning!

As always at this early hour everything was quiet when I arrived. Passing Kylie's office I had a twinge of apprehension, remembering what I'd learned yesterday, uneasy about the underhanded way I'd come by the knowledge. Still, opening up my office soon put all thoughts of Kylie's administrative shortcomings out of my head. The windows sparkled, the telephones gleamed in the sunlight and even the ancient computer didn't look quite so beaten and cowed. I hummed a little tune to myself as I made my first cup of tea of the day and made sure that Marjorie's kitchen was left spotless. I even thought of emptying the kettle and filling it again with cold water in the hope that she might not realise I'd been in there at all but rejected the idea as the mark of a coward. I might very well be one but there was no need to demonstrate it, especially to myself.

I hadn't even sat down behind my clean and completely clear desk when the phone rang. My good mood evaporated as I remembered the other calls I'd taken in the past couple of days and I half expected to hear another hysterical voice as I picked up the handset.

'Area Manager's office,' I said with cheery bravado. 'Good morning, can I help you?'

'Hello, there,' said a voice of bubbling brown sugar, 'is that Gillian?'

'It is,' I answered and waited.

'This is Marc, I'm the Area Manager on the patch next door to yours. We haven't met because I was on holiday when the Boss brought you round on your tour. Thought we'd better touch base. How're you getting on?'

'How long do you have, Marc?' I asked.

'Um,' he said, still sounding joyful. 'That bad, huh? Tell me, who's been giving you a hard time then?' There was laughter in his voice, but it was kind and sympathetic. I'd been told that Marc was one of the more experienced area managers and that he was a good one to have as a friend and mentor.

'Well, I've met Shona and Brigid, Kylie and Damian and Cyril as well as a few of the volunteers. Oh, and Caroline.'

'Good grief, no wonder you sound a bit stressed! All in two days, eh? Did Cyril try to tell you he was dropping his prices?'

'Yes.'

'How did you handle it, if you don't mind my asking?'

'I told him he'd be in breach of contract and I'd feed a strap line of "Local Merchant Fleeces Charity" to the local newspaper. He said he was only kidding and asked me out for a drink. I said no.'

'Excellent! If he invited you out for a drink he must have taken a shine to you even though you tumbled his game. Well done. Be warned though, he's very persistent and he'll try again! Did you meet Shona's stalker?'

'You know about him?' I was taken aback by his obvious knowledge of my patch and sat down so as to be comfortable for a bit of a gossip.

'Oh, yes. Shona tells everybody who'll listen – and quite a few people who don't! What she won't tell you, and you should know, is that the stalker is her ex-husband. Well, actually, if we're being strictly accurate, he's her ex-husband twice.'

'Pardon?'

'They were married first about 15 years ago, Shona and Derek, and she left him on their wedding night. There are almost as many stories as to the whys and wherefores of that as there are empty bottles of gin in the boot of her car.' He paused and chuckled. 'I'll tell you about that another time. Anyway, they got back together a few months later, and then he left her for her best friend. She divorced him then took him back after he mounted a pretty impressive campaign to win her over again. That was when he used a stalking campaign for the first time. Shona's got a bit of a thing for weddings – anybody's really, but her own are best – so they got married again. It didn't last, though, and she left him for an Australian tourist she met at the Notting Hill Carnival. Derek divorced her that time. Anyway, the Aussie went home taking her bank balance, such as it was, with him and she threw herself on Derek's mercy.

'Silly sod took her back and they got married again. Lord knows why the local Registrar keeps doing it but he does. Anyway, Derek's mum turned up at their place about eight months ago. Shona said she was impossible to live with and it was either Mum or her. Derek chose Mum and Shona left. The grapevine says that Derek and Mum have fallen out and now he wants Shona back again. Hence the revival of the stalking thing. He's just trying to persuade her to go back to him and she's trying to make him pay for choosing his Mum over her. Good enough for a book, don't you think?'

Marc was an excellent raconteur. As I listened to the tale of Shona and her husband/stalker, his voice injected a jaunty wit that brought a smile to my face at the chaotic absurdity of the whole thing. I was amazed by how he managed to keep such a convoluted tale clear in his mind.

'If you know about all this,' I said, 'how come Damian's in the dark? I get the impression he knows the patch quite well but he was knocked out yesterday when Shona rang. He didn't know anything about it.'

'I only know because Derek confided in me one day. I've been caretaker of your patch a few times, when your lot got too much for your predecessors, and I met him once or twice just after his mum moved in and Shona moved out. I've no idea why he told me, maybe I've got the kind of face that invites confidences. What else?' he asked, pausing to re-order his memory. 'Oh, yes, Caroline. Wonderfully camp, isn't he? Or perhaps we should say "she" now. What happened there, then?'

'The ceiling fell in at the shop and I called the fire brigade,' I said and his shout of laughter nearly deafened me. I joined in and a second later we were both lost in gales of mirth that brought tears to my eyes.

When we'd both recovered a bit he spluttered, 'You've really had a good start, haven't you, but rest assured there's more to come.' I groaned, he chuckled again and I asked him about Caroline.

'Caroline was in the Army,' he said, 'three tours in Northern Ireland then some secret stuff. You know the sort of thing, Colonel Calamity sends his troops in as cannon fodder, General Disaster sends in special forces to save the day, scatter gun threats from the MoD under the official secrets act to keep the story out of the papers and so on. Anyway, he had a breakdown, lost his family, career, the lot. Rescued off the streets ages later by a working girl who needed someone big and strong to watch her back against aggressive clients. For some reason he took to wearing her clothes until she introduced him to charity shops as a way of getting him out of her wardrobe and into something more his size and shape. Not easy, I'd imagine. Finding stuff his size, I mean. Anyway, that's how he met Brigid and signed on as a volunteer. He's like a mother hen to her chick, only sometimes the roles get reversed because he still has patches of spectacular depression.'

'Good grief,' I said, 'volunteers come with all sorts of baggage, don't they? Whatever happened to the blue-rinse brigade everyone expects to find as the stalwarts of charities?'

'Long gone,' he said, 'if they ever existed, that is. My lot are all absolute marvels but they keep me on the hop. More Hell's Angel than blue-rinse. It was a year before I thought I could handle my patch but they still manage to surprise me about twice a week and I've been at it six years come Easter. Don't let it get to you, Gillian. It's in the nature of the job and we're all in the same boat, working too hard and trying to do the next-to-impossible. You've got my mobile number?' I told him I had. 'Don't hesitate to use it,' he said. 'Martin, Sally and I will help you all we can so please feel free to call any one of us whenever you like. Which was why I rang, really. We normally have a monthly team meeting but the Boss cancelled this one because of her holiday. We three have decided we should meet anyway, more of a social thing really, so can you make it to the regional office next Friday? Start at 3pm for a bit of business and then we'll repair to a local hostelry for a jar or three.'

'I'll be there,' I said, looking forward to meeting Martin and Sally and to putting a face to Marc's duvet-warm voice. 'And thanks, Marc, you've been a great help. Bye for now.' And we both hung up.

By this time there were voices downstairs and I heard the Damian morning chorus as he made his way through the shop to the stairs.

'Yo, ladies!'

'Yo, Damian!' a chorus of trilling female voices sounded up the stairs.

I went back to the kitchen to make him a cup of tea, resigned to any loss of face at the boss making the tea – again – and waited. He stopped in the office doorway as suddenly as if he'd walked into an invisible barrier, his face showing stunned disbelief. His mouth opened, then closed again, as his eyes swept around the office.

'Bloody hell, you've been busy!' he said and I couldn't hear anything other than shock in his voice, which wasn't very helpful when I wanted to know if he was resentful or pleased at the transformed environment. After all, I'd ignored all the management-of-change issues ever discussed on training courses, hadn't I? Where was the invitation to staff for their in-put, the negotiations on priorities and timescales, the joint decision-making, the team work? Nowhere, that's where, and that was why I was waiting, nerves jangling and all confidence in my so-called management status shot to hell.

'I'll never find anything!' he said, still in neutral and standing stock still, eyes locked on the cup of tea I'd placed on his desk. 'How *could* you!' He shot a look of bewilderment at me. 'Why *would* you?'

Wow, I thought, italics, capital letters and exclamation marks! Have I hit the jackpot or what? I took a deep breath

'It was filthy, Damian. You're obviously a really snappy dresser and I can't understand how you'd want to risk your expensive wardrobe on a place that looked like the drawing room of Miss Faversham's mansion.'

'Miss who?' he asked, puzzled and momentarily diverted.

'You know, the mad old bird in Dickens' *Great Expectations*, the one who didn't clean house for 20 years after her lover jilted her on her wedding day.' He looked at me as though I'd grown two heads then blinked, slowly, and a half smile appeared.

'Oh, yeah, I remember. Not as good as thingy, though, you know, that guy with the picture in the attic, Dorian Grey.' I nodded, although I couldn't see, for the life of me, what *A Picture of Dorian Grey*, which was a horror story after all, had to do with our office. Still, I kept quiet on that score since Damian seemed to be recovering a bit.

'What have you done with all my files?' he asked in a rather accusing fashion.

'They're all over on that table,' I pointed to a large, refectory style table in the far corner, tucked behind several filing cabinets, 'in the same trays and boxes they were always in. I haven't touched them at all. Honestly. Still, we'll have to do something with them, you know. How am I to find anything in all those unlabelled piles…?' He looked miffed and I rushed on '…even though I'm sure you can put your hand on any paper I ask you for within moments. But you're not here all the time, you see…' My voice wobbled to a stop. Still, he looked less aggrieved and a bit smug although I was sure I detected a smidgen of self-doubt as well, although it was swiftly suppressed. I seriously doubted that he could find anything but thought discretion and flattery would get me further than blunt honesty. 'You mean cowardice,' said the little devil on my shoulder but I ignored him.

'Perhaps we could spend some time going through them all and decide together what we need to keep and what we can throw away?' I suggested gently. He opened his mouth again but before he could say what he'd intended, I added: 'In your own time, of course' and he closed it again.

The phone rang and my heart did flic-flacs. What now?

'Hello,' I said. 'Area Office, Gillian speaking, how can I help you?'

'Hello, Gillian,' said a well moderated, very gentile voice, 'this is Miles. I'm the manager at the Kensington Place branch. Welcome to the team.'

'Well, thank you, Miles. I'm heard a great deal about you and all of it complimentary.'

'Oh!. Thank you. That's... er... really nice.' He was obviously pleased albeit a little flustered at the praise but I wasn't going to apologise for embarrassing him. The whole region knew about Miles and his spotless, successful shop. The consensus was that he could sell fridges to Eskimos and would be one of the most successful managers in the country if only he could lay his hands on the right stock. His area was quite well-to-do but, for some reason, the donations the van driver collected on his rounds of the neighbourhood never seemed to reflect the obvious wealth of the local population.

I knew that Miles was in his mid 60s and that he'd retired early from the teaching profession some years before to care for an ailing mother. After Mum's death a few months later, and a bout of loneliness (he'd never married or had a family) he'd come to us to work as a volunteer partly, at least, as a kind of therapy. He'd been persuaded to apply for the manager's job when it became vacant and had proved to be worth far more than his weight in gold ever since.

'I called to ask you if you were free for an hour or so,' Miles continued. 'I know it's short notice but I though it was an excellent opportunity for you to see the positive side of what we all do.'

Cutely put, I thought. I'd seen some of the downside in the last couple of days. In one short and very subtle sentence, Miles' invitation seemed to say he knew that already.

'Go on, Miles, I'm all ears.'

'We have a young volunteer here who came to us from a local training-cum-residential centre. Her name is Bianca and she has Downs. She couldn't speak when she came to us six months ago and needed constant supervision. We found her some simple things to do and then a few more and she's come along beautifully. In fact, she's so much confidence now that she can hold quite a long conversation, she can shop if we give her a list and send her to a place she knows, and she's learned how to use the till. She's done so well that her carers want to make a video of her, here in the shop, to show other youngsters and their parents. A "this is what can happen and don't give up" sort of promotional thing. They'll be here in just over an hour and I thought you might like to join us.'

'That's the best piece of news I've had all week, Miles, bless you,' I said. 'I'd love to come. I'll be there in about 45 minutes if that's OK?'

'Good, we'll make some tea and we've apple doughnuts today. You can meet my team, they're all really lovely people.'

I told Damian what Miles had said and he looked relieved. Whether that was because it wasn't another problem to deal with or because he thought getting me out of the office for a couple of hours was a good idea, I wasn't sure. Anyway, I picked up my keys and my bag and left him to it, sipping his tea and standing in the middle of the floor looking as lost as Little Orphan Annie.

Just over 40 minutes later I pulled into the service lane behind the Kensington Place shop. I'd got lost only twice on the way, which wasn't bad going for me – I've been lost in all the best locations and seen loads of places I'd have missed otherwise. Once I'd ended up in Brighton instead of Croydon, which turned out to be a happy mistake because... well, that's an entirely different story!

Anyway, my usual luck was running true to form because there was nowhere to park. There were several vehicles in the lane at the back of the shop, most of them tucked against fences or in loading bays. I'd seen a sign for a multi-storey car park on my way down the High Street but, not knowing the area, I had no idea how long it would take me to find it, park and walk to the shop. Given my complete lack of a sense of direction and total inability to walk past more than three shops at a time without being kicked inside one by my credit card, probably about three days at a guess. My plastic isn't safe on a High Street and all sense of time just vanishes if I find myself next to a John Lewis or House of Fraser.

Then I noticed a small gap at the top of the lane and went for it. It turned out to have just about room for a child's trike in front of a set of double garage doors. The silt, weeds and general debris in front of them made it obvious that no-one had opened them in months, maybe longer, and there were no visible tyre tracks to indicate that access was frequent or even needed at all. In for penny... I thought and carefully manoeuvred the car, backwards and forwards, until I was as close as possible. That'll do, I thought, admiring my handiwork at getting into such a tight spot, and locked the car behind me.

Miles was waiting for me and it looked as though his entire team had turned out for the occasion. I was introduced to two Mabels, Jo, Laura, Gladys, Pauline, Sheila, three Margarets, Ivy, Susan and John, the lone and token male among the volunteer force. Men were almost as rare as hen's teeth and it was often only where there was a male manager that male volunteers came forward. Bianca was due to arrive at any minute, so they told me, and a couple of absentees sent their apologies, citing care of grandchildren, hospital appointments and other reasons why they were unable to join in.

Jo made tea for everyone and handed around huge doughnuts, some with apple fillings and some with custard inside and with chocolate coating. Blow the diet, I thought, I'll start again tomorrow. There was much chatter, lots of affectionate teasing and laughter and the atmosphere was like that of a birthday party. After a while I took Miles to one side and said, 'Everyone's having a really good time, Miles. Is it always like this here? Bianca's a lucky girl to have you all care for her so much, no wonder she's flourished.'

'We're a happy crew here,' he said. 'I know it isn't the same in all the shops on the patch but my volunteers are really wonderful and I let them know it. You only have to look around to see how hard they work and how much they care. Our customers forget that this is a charity shop, you know, and seem to think it's some kind of unique boutique. If you visit us often you'll see what I mean.'

I could see what he meant already as I looked around. The whole place was spotless, including the stock room, which was normally the most chaotic place imaginable in any charity shop. The shop floor merchandising was imaginative and the presentation just shouted 'Look at me!' and 'I'm a bargain, buy me!'

The womenswear was arranged in groups of colour families, just like a regular fashion shop: blues over there, black and white over here, red by the window. Some of the menswear was hung in complete outfits – a suit, shirt and tie on the same hanger with pens in the top pockets and shoes on the floor underneath. One had a briefcase hanging from the end of a sleeve, tied to a piece of string threaded through the sleeve. Clever! But it was the children's corner that caught my eye. Two outfits, one for a boy and one for a girl, had been stuffed to make them look just like little children. The boy figure was arranged to look like a child hiding its face in its arms, leaning against a wall, for all the world as though he was counting 100 for a game of hide and seek. The girl figure was sitting astride a rocking horse, legs stretched out in front, pigtails flying, painted eyes closed in a vision of ecstasy. It was enchanting.

At that moment Bianca and the film crew arrived and for the next hour everyone was arranged, re-arranged, disarranged and lectured about lighting, camera angles and not looking directly into the lens. I watched from the side-lines or held things for the crew, excusing myself from being in front of camera on the grounds that I hadn't been part of Bianca's renaissance and didn't want to claim any credit. The fact that I look like a cross between Dracula's mother and Lassie when on film had nothing to do with it!

After a while, as filming seemed to slow down a bit, I managed to catch Miles on his own, between takes, and drew him to one side again.

'Thank you for inviting me, Miles,' I said, 'it's been an education and a pleasure to be here and meet you all. I'll leave you to recover and perhaps we can have a proper tour of your shop soon?'

'I'm glad you were free to come over,' he said, 'I can imagine what your life's like just now.' He looked at me sympathetically, as though he really could. 'We're a bit different here. This is a good place to work, we're a happy team and you're always welcome.' We smiled at each other and I took my leave feeling more optimistic than I had since before I'd arrived at the office on Monday morning. They say pride comes before a fall but maybe that goes for a feeling of wellbeing too.

I was standing next to the car, keys in hand, when I noticed the waspishly yellow boot fastened to the front wheel. Plastered to the windscreen was a large notice that said 'WARNING! Do not attempt to move this vehicle!' and another that had the name of a clamping company and dire warnings about towing, secure compounds and the selfishness of people who obstruct private property.

I looked around. There were no signs about clamping, or privacy, or anything else as far as I could see. At the second floor window of a building across the lane a guy in a dazzling white shirt and large, loud Snoopy tie called to me.

'Got you, did he? Gets two or three a day sometimes, he does. He comes out to sweep around and make it look as though nobody's so much as stepped in front of those doors since Christmas before last! Parking's so tight these days loads of people take a chance, like you did, and he catches 'em every time. Didn't you see the sign?'

'What sign?' I shouted, too loudly and with aggressive venom.

'Bottom left on the right hand door,' he said, 'behind the nettles!' Using my bag to brush aside the vicious looking plant, I saw a small sign, about the size of a post-it note, pinned to the door. It was rusting and discoloured but it said 'Private. Clamping' and that was it! I kicked the door. The man was still hanging out of the window, obviously enjoying my predicament and grinning hugely.

Angry with myself for being stupid, angry at the garage owner for being malicious and livid with the guy in the Snoopy tie; feeling frustrated and impotent, what was there to do but throw a tantrum? I kicked the garage door, then the yellow boot, then the rear tyre wall. I growled loudly, stamped my feet, waved my arms about like an out-of-control windmill and swore, using words that would have made a sailor blush.

Almost out of steam from the physicality of it, I saw, from the corner of my eye, a flutter of something red. Into instant full-stop, I turned slightly on my heel to see, just a few metres away, a woman holding the handle of a child's stroller so tightly I could see that her knuckles were white. Her other hand was holding tight to a small boy's jacket collar. He was around three years old and was gazing at me, wide-eyed, with his fist in his mouth. The little red plastic windmill in his other hand turned slowly in the breeze, the only thing in the tableau we three made that moved for several seconds.

I grimaced an attempted grin and tried a chuckle. It sounded like a hollow, squeaky, sort of hiccup.

'Sorry,' I said, 'didn't mean to frighten you... er... car... got clamped... so frustrating' and I could feel the hot colour flood to my face. The poor woman just turned and fled, the small boy screwing his head around on his neck, unwilling to lose sight of the demented creature who'd completely distracted his mum from scolding him.

After a few minutes of deep breathing and muttering 'calm, calm' like a mantra, a technique some long-distant, totally crackpot boyfriend had taught me years ago and which I'd used occasionally ever since, with dubious results, I used my mobile to call the number on the windscreen notice. For the next 15 minutes I tried to scrape off the tacky stuff that stuck it, like super glue, to the glass. It smeared everywhere but wouldn't let go. The tow truck eventually arrived an hour later. It disgorged two scruffy guys, both the size of Jack's beanstalk giant and both wearing identical Led Zeppelin T-shirts, Doc Martin's and scowls. I wasn't feeling diplomatic or cautious. And the mantra clearly hadn't worked on this occasion.

Ten minutes after that I drove away, £65 lighter in the bank balance and with my ears ringing from a mixture of my own incautious comments (on greedy private landlords and their equally greedy, unscrupulous, clamping cowboy co-conspirators) together with their equally choice responses. I'd learned a couple more words for my own obscenities repertoire, though. We learn something new every day, don't we, even in difficult circumstances?

There was time to calm down a bit on the way back to the office, or at least time to repair my injured pride a little and put on a good face. No point in prolonging the agony, after all, when you've just been well and truly stuffed. I found Damian surrounded by black plastic sacks, many of which were bulging, in a most satisfactory manner, with paper and ancient file covers. He looked a little dishevelled, which must have been a novelty as far as I could tell from our short acquaintance, and his beautifully designed hair showed a slight tendency to stand on end.

'I thought I'd make a start,' he said, sounding tired, triumphant and irritable all at the same time, 'while *you* were off *enjoying* yourself!'

I opened my mouth, but remembered where my tongue had put me less than an hour ago, and closed it again. Instead I took a deep breath, conjured a smile and said, 'You look as though you're doing very well without me, Damian, how's it going?'

'Well,' he said, 'I started to go through *all* those files and folders, looking for the stuff we should keep. You know, H&S reports, personnel records, van maintenance, that sort of stuff. But there was *just* so much of it. Judy, the one that did this job before me, just kept everything. Can you believe that? Absolutely *everything*.' I let that one pass although it almost tugged a smile from my mouth. Almost. 'That's why all my work was on table tops – the filing cabinets were full and there wasn't any room. But I realised it was going to take a *month* of Sundays the way I started so I changed tactics.' He paused and looked a little unsure about how to continue.

'And?' I prompted him.

'So I've chucked out *everything* except the last financial year,' he said in a rush.

I was nonplussed. Gone were all the useful things as well as all the rubbish. Everything. Sales records, target calculations and results, annual staff reports – all consigned to the local dump. Still, maybe it wasn't that bad. Personnel had copies of all the people stuff, Accounts had copies of the figures stuff and Fleet Management had copies of all the vehicle stuff. Should we need to refer to any of it again, which I seriously doubted anyway, there were copies elsewhere and I was almost glad of charity bureaucracy for that reassurance. And we had an almost empty office! Except, of course, chucking all that paper around had stirred up a whole lot more dormant dust. Never mind, you can't make an omelette without breaking eggs.

I grinned at Damian. 'Well done, that's going to make life a whole lot easier. From now on we can plead ignorance to all sorts of things. Isn't that liberating!'

He relaxed and grinned back. At that moment there was a loud bang from downstairs and Kylie's voice could be heard above the rest as several people all started shouting at once.

'Yer daft prat!' she yelled and I cringed, hoping against hope that there were no customers in the shop. 'Are yer blind or what? Yer've run right over that pram and the wendy 'ouse! We could 'ave got mega bucks fer that, yer dozy pillock!'

Damian grinned at the consternation showing clearly on my face. 'One for you, boss,' he said, 'that'll be Ginger.'

'Ginger?'

'One of the drivers. I think you're needed downstairs.' With that, he sat down, put up his feet on a spare chair and picked up his mug of tea and a chocolate biscuit.

Downstairs there was absolute chaos. There were surely far more people in the stock room than there should have been and the place seemed to be full of exhaust fumes. Kylie was assaulting a bemused, cowering man with both her fists and a well-aimed, boot-shod foot.

'Just what is going on!' I bellowed over the hubbub. For a second there was silence and everyone froze. It looked like a children's party when everyone is playing 'statues' and the music stops. It was the second time today I'd reduced everything to stillness. Then everyone started talking at once and I could hear '…all his fault…' and '…bloody fool…' and '…could 'ave killed someone…'

I tried again. 'Can we have a little quiet, please', and I waited till the noise subsided again. I picked out one of the more sensible volunteers 'Brenda, will you go back to the shop, please, and apologise to any customers brave enough to still be there after the noise and, er, the language they've heard. Kylie, tell me, please, what this is all about.'

'This bleedin'…'

'Quietly, please, and without the expletives.'

'Eh?'

'Without the language.'

'Oh. Right. OK. This… idiot driver backed into the car park wivout lookin'. 'E ran over some kiddies' fings we'd bin cleaning. They was really good and worth lots o' dosh. 'e's ruined 'em. 'E's alus doin' stuff like that, 'e never looks where 'e's going, 'e's a …' she almost choked trying not to swear '…menace!' she ended triumphantly.

71

'You're Ginger, I take it?' I turned to the man in question. 'I'm Gillian, the new Area Manager. I'm pleased to meet you, although I could have wished for a calmer introduction.'

''Morning, Gill,' he said, straightening his sweater and recovering rapidly now the fists had stopped pummelling his chest. 'Nice to meet you, too. This daft cow's always getting on 'er 'igh 'orse.'

'Would you follow me, Ginger, please?' I asked mildly. 'These ladies are far too busy to want us standing around here, chatting and getting in their way.'

And I turned for the stairs. Muttering sounds followed us as the disappointed sensation-seekers went back to work. In the office Damian was eyes down to his desk. He looked up as we arrived and Ginger grinned at him.

''Ow do, Damian?'

Damian all but sniffed as he replied, somewhat haughtily, I thought: 'Very well, Ginger, thank you.' then, to me 'We need fax rolls, Gillian, I'll run down to the stationers on the corner.' Then he was gone, closing the door gently but firmly behind him.

'Take a pew, Ginger,' I invited and sat on the corner of my desk. Maintain a higher eye level than the person you're talking to, management advisors said, when you want to intimidate. 'That was all a little unfortunate, wasn't it?'

'You can say that again,' he agreed, 'silly cow's always getting on 'er 'igh 'orse.'

'Yes, so you said. But did you run over those things?'

'Well, yeh, I suppose. Shouldn't have left 'em there, should she?'

'Maybe not. Has it happened before?'

'Well…' he fidgeted '…only two or three times.' I waited 'There was the two chairs they used to sit on outside when they was on their breaks when the weather's warm, and then Marjorie's bike and… oh, yeah, the box o' glasses and china that somebody left round the back when the shop was closed.'

'Why, Ginger?'

'Why what?'

'Why do you run over things?'

'Easy. I can't see where I'm going when I'm reversin'. There's no mirrors on the van!'

'No mirrors?'

'No. They was ripped off when it was parked on the street outside my place one night and there's bin nobody 'ere to authorise to get 'em fixed. I can't see a damn thing when I'm in reverse.'

I resisted the temptation of asking why, in that case, he reversed at all but realised that was a pretty stupid question to ask this particular white-van-man. I picked up the phone and called HQ.

Malcolm wasn't in the office and the girl on the switchboard asked if I'd like to speak to Hilary, his secretary. Hilary was very sweet and completely at sea. She didn't seen to have a clue about vehicle repairs, budget authorisations or what papers should be completed, if any, so I asked her to pass on a message to Malcolm that I was sending a van driver to the local main dealer that afternoon. He wasn't going to be pleased to hear from me again so soon and the proverb about sheep and lambs came to mind.

'Blimey,' said Ginger, 'you're a fast worker!'

'Ginger,' I said, 'you're responsible for the van. For keeping it clean and in good condition and for making sure that any damage is reported immediately. I know there has been no area manager here for ages but there are alternatives ways of getting these things seen to. It was all covered on your training and it's in the info pack in the glove box of the van. Supposing that pram had been a real one, with a baby in it? And who compensated Marjorie for her bike?'

Ginger looked first astonished and then truculent. ''Ere,' he said, 'are you tellin' me 'ow to do my job?'

'No, but I am telling you that you haven't fulfilled part of your responsibility properly.'

'You can't talk to me that way! I've worked bloody 'ard for this charity for years, I 'ave, and got paid peanuts for it! You ask anybody 'ow 'ard I work!'

'Ginger, I'm sure you do,' I said, torn between a cowardly wish to pour oil on troubled waters and anger at his cavalier attitude to other people's safety, even if he cared nothing for his own. 'That isn't the issue. You put yourself at risk if your van isn't up to scratch, as well as other people, surely you can see that?'

'I'm not stayin' 'ere to be insulted like this!' And before I could think of anything else to say or do, he'd leapt out of his chair and clattered off down the stairs in a stream of verbal protest and bluster.

When Damian came back a few minutes later, he found me with my head down on the desk top, cushioned on my arms.

'Oops! I gather he's gone, then?'

I lifted my head and ran my hands through my hair. Now we both looked like overworked lavatory brushes.

'Gone but far from forgotten. Do we have any brandy around, Damian, or a valium or three?'

'Oh, tut, tut,' he said, wagging his finger at me, 'resorting to an alcohol lift already, are we?' He paused for effect then smiled, slowly and wickedly. 'But now that you *mention* it…' And he pulled open a drawer in his desk. With a flourish and a '*Voila!*' he was holding a bottle of Scotch aloft.

'Damian!' my surprise was real enough, my comments had been in jest. 'No alcohol on any of our premises' was one of the charity's golden rules (which made staff Christmas parties a bit difficult) as was 'anyone found drinking on our premises shall be deemed guilty of gross misconduct', a sacking offence. I'd seen it written down in the 'Bible' (Shops Manual, to the uninitiated) during my training and had refrained from asking, since it wasn't specific, if the rule included customers as well. Perhaps I could have invoked that at Lupin Lane yesterday?

Damian grabbed my hand and hauled me to my feet. 'Come with me,' he ordered and made for the door, me in tow. Through the kitchen and out of the door on the other side that opened on to a fire escape. We clattered along the cast iron gantry, with its rust and peeling paint, and emerged on to a little platform that bridged the alleyway between the shop and the bank next door. There was an old wooden bench up there and a faded canvas director's chair.

'Sit,' Damian ordered and he put the bottle to his lips for a pull at what I could see from the label was an excellent malt. Grinning, he handed the bottle to me and I followed his example. The liquid hit my insides like rocket fuel in an afterburner.

'Haaaaaaahhhhhhhh!' I squeaked and sat down heavily. After a few seconds I looked up at Damian, still standing, and tilted my head slightly to one side in an attempt to see him clearly against the glare of the sky. 'Why are we up here. Damian?'

'Because it's not *on the premises*,' he explained, 'they can't touch you for it up here. 'This bit isn't on *any* of the plans. I checked.

According to the land registry deeds it isn't attached to *either* property. We're in *no man's land*. Not like me, deary,' he chuckled, 'I'm *any* man's after a Scotch or two!' He said it with such a twinkle in his eye, and with the sweetest smile, that I couldn't help but laugh.

'No, that's not what I meant. I've only been here a couple of days and you're sharing a single malt with me after I ordered you about on Monday and blitzed the office yesterday without telling you. Ginger just yelled at me for less!'

'*Somebody* has to comfort you when the rest of them give you a hard time. Who better than *me*? I'm *always* looking out for waifs and strays, I am, and at least they're not going to accuse *us* of having an office affair, are they?' He passed me the bottle again and I took another pull, a much shallower one this time, and grinned at him, feeling the effects of the silky smooth liquid already.

'That's true,' I said and then, apropos of nothing, really: 'You and Kylie seem to be the only up-front ones around here.'

Damian looked at me in comical astonishment for a second or two then said, with the drama of a truly hammy Hamlet, 'Oh, Lord, she's cast me in the same mould as *Kylie*! Has my life come to that, then? What a *sad* person I am!' And we startled the pedestrians on the pavement below with our Scotch-tinted laughter.

It didn't take long to finish the bottle (even though vodka was normally my tipple), and we gossiped quite a bit in between gulps of firewater. Damian told me about his latest flame, Randolph, whom he described as 'small, sweet and the dearest thing' and I told him about Greg. I might have been a little indiscreet because I vaguely remembered, much later, using words like 'lazy' and 'thoughtless'. I might even have said 'feckless' or something close but it all became a bit of a blur around then so maybe that wasn't quite right.

I do remember, however, that after a while I suggested we go somewhere to eat. I think Damian said it was a bit early for dinner and I said it was after five o'clock so we weren't in working hours any more anyway and we might as well find some food to soak up the whisky. We found an all-day pub and ate steak and ale pie with mashed potatoes. It didn't seem to do much to soak up the whisky, but things might have been complicated by the very good ale, which complemented the pie beautifully and kept appearing next to my elbow magically, and with pleasing regularity.

The rest of the evening was just a series of grainy snapshots in my memory. Later, much later, I remembered walking along the top of someone's garden wall holding an umbrella and pretending to be a high wire act in a circus. Damian perched on the roof of a VW Beetle, cross-legged and with his chin on his fist, like a pixie, telling me something about wanting to be in the Brownies instead of the Cubs when he was seven. A very nice policeman asked us, in a serious tone, to be a little quieter or he'd find us a bed for the night. For some reason I found that hysterically funny and couldn't stop laughing, even when the tears streamed down my face and I had a painful attack of hiccups. Which didn't help much when I rang Greg to explain that I wasn't coming home that night. I could recall telling him, between hiccups, that I was unfit to drive and I think I managed to do that in reasonable fashion, but then spoiled it by telling him that I'd no idea where I was, couldn't remember where I'd parked the car anyway and that he wasn't to worry because Damian was looking after me and would take me home.

Then it was morning. I knew it was morning, even though I didn't open my eyes, because a radio was on somewhere and the lugubrious John Humphries was trying to sound like Mr Niceguy while he pulled some poor politician smuck to pieces with his sarcasm. Then I remembered bits about the night before, and groaned. It must have been me because there was no-one else in the bed. I was stretched out across it diagonally. Naked.

'Morning!' said Damian's voice somewhere close by.

Oh Lord!

-5-
Headache and Headroom

Oh, Lord! What a way to start a day, let alone a working one. I lay, inert, for a moment while jumbled memories from last night started hammering at my brain along with the hang-over. I opened one eye, very carefully, then closed it again, immensely grateful that curtains hid much of the daylight from outside, although it still seemed inordinately bright. My eyeballs cringed, even though my eyelids were closed. Carefully I arranged my body, trying to keep all of it under cover, which wasn't easy because I felt curiously numb and my skin couldn't feel the duvet. As I experimented by opening one eye again a little bedside clock came slowly into something approaching focus. I saw but didn't understand what the clock was telling me, so gave up.

'Glad to see you're awake,' said Damian, 'I've made some coffee.' I heard a mug click, much too loudly, on a surface somewhere close at hand. 'Shower's through there, help yourself. Your clothes are *all over* the floor so you'll look a bit *crumpled* today, but who's going to remark on that in a *charity* shop?' And he chortled merrily at his little joke. Jolly laughter would have been bad enough this early on any day, but after the sort of night we'd had, it was unthinkable! Did I say 'we'? An awful thought entered my head and I tried, as determinedly as I could in my weakened state, to push it away.

'Did you sleep well?' he asked pulling back the drapes and letting in all that blindingly cruel sunlight. I must have yelped because I heard a kind of strangled sound that came from quite close to my own ears. Gingerly I lifted my head from the pillow and, as Damian disappeared out of the door back in the direction of, presumably, the kitchen, I sipped the scalding hot coffee and wondered if I could let last night slip from my memory through an act of will. Amnesia was a wonderful defence against embarrassment.

Carefully I left the bed and wobbled on jelly legs to the bathroom. I found some painkillers in the wall cabinet and, after the coffee, the tabs and a shower I felt a bit less shaky, although not much. In the bathroom mirror an apparition like Frankinstein's monster's mother looked back at me.

The smell of toast and fresh coffee tempted me down the corridor towards its source. I passed an open door on the way and spotted a rumpled bed draped with the clothes that Damian had been wearing yesterday. What a relief! I took it as a very good sign that I hadn't done anything monumentally stupid last night, like sleep with Damian. I wasn't at all sure if even the most committed of gays wouldn't take an opportunity, if propositioned determinedly, when the propositioner was blathered. I wasn't very knowledgeable in that regard and had no previous experience on which to base an opinion. Even had I been able to think clearly. Which I wasn't. Besides, for all I knew Damian might even swing both ways. Nevertheless I was relieved that I hadn't, apparently, put it to the test.

'Dry toast?' Damian offered. 'Looks as though that's all you're ready for!' And he chortled again.

'You've no sympathy,' I said.

'You've no *shame*!' he retorted with amusement.

'Why? What did I do?' The alarm resurfaced again.

'Can't you remember *anything*?'

'Erm… not much.' I admitted, then one very vague memory gradually surfaced. 'Was there a policeman?'

'There *was*!' he said, gleefully, as though I was a schoolgirl answering a hard exam question correctly. 'And I'm meeting him for a drink on *Saturday*!'

My eyelids lifted into my hairline, much to the discomfort of my aching head. 'How on earth did you manage that?' I asked, stunned and admiring.

'The same way I don't get hangovers like *yours* any more,' he said. 'Lots of practice!'

'But what about Randolph, the love of your life?' I asked, confused.

He pouted. 'He didn't come home last night! Left a *message* on the machine! Said he was going down to *Brighton* for a few days! We all know what *that* means, don't we?'

Did we? Perhaps I'd work that out when I could think properly again. It occurred to me that there was something not quite right with the logic, here, something about meeting the policeman before we'd got back to the flat and before he'd heard the message on the answer machine but I couldn't quite pin it down in my fragile mental condition.

'Come on then,' he said, 'it's time *you* were at *work* and *I'm* late for the gym. Have to keep the body *beautiful*, you know, it's a *very* valuable asset.'

Gym? After last night? I'd be lucky to just sit in a chair all day, I thought. How does he do it? And I resolved to ask him, one day, when he wasn't shouting so loudly and I could understand his answer.

Coffee and toast helped a bit. The sandpaper of the toast took most of the fur from my tongue, although the vibration clanging around my head from chewing, and the decibels from crunching the crispness, were pretty painful.

The car was still parked behind the shop when I arrived after a careful and very gentle stroll over the half mile from Damian's flat. I'd had visions of controlled explosions after vigilant neighbours reported it abandoned by terrorists, or vandalism at least, but it was quite safe, and I thanked heaven for that. I also promised not ever to drink again. I was late, of course, and Kylie plus several volunteers were already hard at work. I'd arrived before them on each morning that week so far but I could tell from the quizzical looks that the parked car minus me had aroused a little curiosity. No doubt they'd tested the bonnet to see if the engine was warm.

I put on a jaunty air and said, 'Morning everyone. Just fancied a little breakfast this morning!' implying that I'd arrived early then popped out again, but without actually telling a porky. I could tell from their expressions that they thought it was a bit lame, especially since I was wearing the same clothes as yesterday and looked decidedly crumpled. I made straight for the stairs before anyone got around to asking any innocently awkward questions, or even deliberately awkward ones, such as 'Where did you go, then? Fred's caff do a really good breakfast...'

The office now looked a lot cleaner and tidier than it had earlier in the week and Damian had left me a list of jobs that needed doing. It occurred to me that he'd turned the tables quite neatly from Monday, when it had been me telling him what to do but what the hell, I couldn't have cared less just then. I settled down to what I hoped would be a quiet day of physical and mental recovery over some steady paperwork. As usual, my little devil had other ideas. The phone rang.

'Good morning,' I tried to sound cheery, 'how can I help you?'

'Gilly,' a voice said and I cringed. I just hated being called Gilly, that was for Jilly Cooper types and I hoped I had a bit more… you know, sort of… well, credibility than that. The little devil on my shoulder said, 'Who are you trying to kid? What about last night, then?'

I hissed, 'Don't go there, just don't go there!' to shut him up.

'Gilly, I've got a problem.'

'Who is this, please?'

'Ginger. It's Ginger!' I braced myself for what was coming next. 'I've had a small accident, nothing really serious but you did say everything had to be reported.'

'I did indeed, Ginger. I hope you're alright? Not hurt? Was anyone else involved?'

'I'm OK,' he said, 'and there wasn't anyone else. Except Tesco, I suppose, if that counts.'

'Sorry? You've lost me.'

'It's all Tesco's fault. I alus go to Tesco for breakfast. It's cheap and quick and me girlfriend works in the caff so I get extras, see. Only yesterday they was doin' stuff in the car park. Like, they put up a barrier.'

I felt as though my brain was full of cotton wool. I couldn't see the connection but knew Ginger would enlighten me if I could just concentrate a bit longer.

'Yes, I'm with you so far.' Was I? I said it anyway, just to encourage him to tell me more although I would much rather have been listening to gentle waves lapping on the shore somewhere, with me in a hammock swinging gently in the shade of a large palm tree. Bliss!

'It's plenty high enough for cars.' He paused and I had a sudden and awful image of a car park barrier and a hi-top Transit van. It couldn't be! Could it? 'The barrier was a bit low, see, not designed for vans and it… sort of… got stuck.' There was silence for quite a long moment while I composed myself. First things first.

'Stuck? The van?' I had visions of irate shoppers trying to get into the car park and an even more irate Tesco manager examining his new barrier with a van stuck firmly beneath it. 'Er… it's stuck on the barrier?' No, please, no!

'No.' Sigh of relief. Too soon. 'Not now' Oh gloom!

'Is the van damaged?' I managed through gritted teeth.

'Er… yes.' Misery!

'Much?' This was like pulling teeth.

'Er… well…'

'Is the barrier damaged?'

'It's in one piece!' he said triumphantly. 'And it looks like it was supposed to be that shape. Even, like, yer know, like it was made all curved.' I felt like growling but decided against it on the grounds that the vibration would only bring back the headache that had just started to recede. I sighed instead and put my head down into my free hand.

'Come back into base, Ginger, and we'll have a look. In the meantime I'll ring Tesco and see what we can sort out.'

The General Manager at Tesco was called Ronald and he sounded about 12 years old. A rather irate 12 years old and, clearly, far too young to be in charge of his own corner shop let alone a giant superstore. I asked him to tell me what had happened.

'HGVs have been parking in our shoppers' car park overnight,' he explained, 'using it as a night stop, and fly tippers have been using our waste skips instead of the council tip. Our textile re-cycling bins has been broken into and emptied as well. We thought a barrier to restrict the height of vehicles coming in would help. It was put in yesterday. It had a fringed length of bunting hanging from the top cross pole to attract attention. The bunting was silver and red and fluttered in the wind and the barrier was painted in red and white stripes! We even put a maximum headroom notice up! ' He was getting worked up, I could tell. 'Nobody could miss it!'

'Well,' I said, brightly, 'he didn't, did he? Miss it, I mean.' Ah, I could have bitten off my tongue!

'I'm glad you find it amusing,' Ronald said, rather frostily. 'He was lucky not to hurt someone. As it is, we'll have to replace the barrier at considerable cost.'

'It can't be repaired then?' I asked, already knowing the answer but trying to keep hope alive. 'My driver said it was a little bent out of shape.'

'It is. The top is now the shape of a Transit van roof. And it's lying on the ground because he hit it so hard both uprights snapped off at ground level!'

'Oh, my!' I said, mentally wincing from imagining what the impact had been. 'I'm so sorry. Not what you need at the start of a busy day, is it?' And I rambled on with variously phrased apologies and platitudes for a while until I could sense him calming down a bit. I said that I was sure we could help towards the cost of a replacement or even, perhaps, pay for the whole thing. I made all kinds of promises that I was sure would give Malcolm apoplexy.

Still, it had the desired effect because Ronald said, a bit more calmly, 'Well, that's good of you to offer. Really it is. But you're a charity and it doesn't seem right to take your money. It was an accident, after all, even if it was a damned silly thing to do. It isn't a fortune when you look at our daily turnover. Leave it with me, I'll have a word with my Head Office and we'll see what we can do. I did tell them we should have put up notices to tell customers what we were doing, in advance. As usual they didn't take any notice of a sensible suggestion so they can't complain too much.'

'You're a gentleman, Ronald,' I said, 'and rest assured I'll do what needs to be done here.' Whatever that is, I thought, and we said our polite goodbyes.

Twenty minutes later I heard the sound of a diesel engine and braced myself for a lively discussion with Ginger. He swaggered a bit as he walked into the office and sat down before I had a chance to say anything, for all the world as though yesterday hadn't happened, much less today's incident.

'I'm glad you're not hurt,' I said, which wasn't quite what I'd intended to say and the little devil on my shoulder sneered 'Wimp!' I ignored him. 'Tell me what happened please.'

'Well, it was like this…' Ginger began, before pausing to gain a little thinking time. 'I drove over to Tesco's, like I alus do in the morning, and drove under this new barrier. There's a crunch and a judder and I'm stuck, like.'

'You drove into it? You saw it, then?'

'I saw it, but I didn't see it, if you know what I mean.'

'Not exactly. Indulge me and explain.' The sarcasm almost went over his head. Almost, but not quite. I saw his eyes narrow briefly and I mentally reprimanded myself. Which training course was I ignoring this time? I thought. Personal Effectiveness? Relationships in the Workplace? Or perhaps Inadvisable Words and Phrases when Dealing with White-van-man?

'I saw this ribbon fing flutterin' about and was watching that, see, not really lookin' anywhere else. I thought it were just the ribbon thing tied onto poles – didn't see the bloody top barrier at all. Wind fluttered it, sort o', up like an arch thing, you know, high like, so I just went for it. Then *crunch*. Van stopped and stalled, I started 'er up again, pulled forards and we only moved a few inches so I went into reverse and damned thing came with me! Wrapped itself around me an that was that, weren't it?'

I moved over to one of the filing cabinets and ferreted about in a couple of folders until I found an insurance accident report pack. Further conversation seemed pointless and I wasn't up to it, anyway. I held it out to him and he took hold of it very carefully, as though it might bite him if he jolted it. I almost wished it would.

'You'll need to fill in one of these, Ginger,' I said, 'and be as accurate as you can. I'll have a look at the van while you're busy. Do you have the keys, please?'

He handed over a bunch of keys whose size probably rivalled those of the Governor at the Scrubs. 'You'll 'ave to use the passenger door. Other one got a bit stuck, like, didn't it?' Then he bent over the papers, chewing the end of his pen, forehead furrowed in concentration. I left him to it.

Downstairs the stock room was empty. Everyone was outside, standing around the van in an eerie silence. Both sides had been scraped almost clear of paint, with deeper tram lines where metal had scraped against metal. The handle of the driver's door was squashed, buried into its recess, the sides of which had collapsed around it. On the passenger side, the loading door was buckled and its runners were twisted and torn. From a vantage point a few steps up the building's metal fire escape I could see that the roof was similarly stripped of paint and a piece of red and white bunting waved jauntily from the twisted guttering. There wasn't a lot to be said, in the circumstances. Shout and scream, maybe, or yell and curse but I held it all in check for fear of losing face in front of the massed crowds of volunteers and a few customers. As if that would make any difference after the last few days – who was I kidding! Still, I restrained myself.

After a circuit of two of the injured beast I stopped pacing, folded my arms and sighed deeply.

'Not a pretty sight, is it?' Marjorie said. She nodded towards her fellow volunteers. 'And they wonder why I won't let him use my kitchen and bathroom upstairs! Can you imagine…?' She left the sentence unfinished for added effect, shaking her head in disbelief.

Kylie began to shepherd her flock back to work. 'No need to arsk weffer you went 'ome last night, eh?' she said, looking me up and down, a broad smirk on her face. I grinned at her, not minding her misunderstanding and grateful for her irreverent humour.

Upstairs in the office, Ginger was still chewing the end of his pen and struggling with the report. I made some tea while he was busy and stayed in the kitchen to drink it, knowing I was being petty not to offer him a cup but still angry enough not to care. After about 20 minutes or so I went back to the office and sat down to read through what he'd written while he fidgeted around on the chair at the other side of the desk.

'Mmm,' I said when I'd finished, and let the word hang in the air for a while. He fidgeted even more and looked sheepish. 'Do you really think Tesco is to blame, Ginger?' I asked. 'That's what you've said where the form says "In your opinion, what caused the accident?"'

'Too right,' he said, leaning forward in his chair for emphasis. 'Stands to reason dunnit? If they 'adn't put up the thing I wouldn't 'ave 'it it, would I?'

'That's not quite what the questions means but never mind, we'll just let that pass. Is the van safe to drive, do you think? There's not much paint left on it but, apart from the doors, everything else appears to be untouched.'

'Yeh. It was fine when I drove it over 'ere. I got 'ere safe, didn't I?' His habit of answering a question with a question was beginning to irritate me.

'Good, because there's still a collection to do and the other two guys are out on the road by now on their own rounds. It's too late to ask them to cover your patch as well as their own and we've enough to do without placating irate householders whose donations are sitting on their doorsteps instead of in our stockrooms. Besides, what would we tell them? Our van driver had a disagreement with a car park barrier? I think not. I want you to drive over to the dealership and get them to have a look at the van then leave it with them. I'll call ahead and arrange for them to let you have a temporary replacement. OK?'

'Well, I was 'oping to have the rest of the day off.' He hitched up one shoulder and pulled a face 'I think my shoulder got strained.'

'Fine,' I said, picking up the phone and holding it out to him. 'Are you going to tell Gordon, or shall I?'

Ginger looked at the phone as though it were a hand grenade with the pin out. Gordon was the manager at Chilton Street and he had a reputation that struck dread into the hearts of all his fellow shop managers, volunteers and van drivers alike. I'd met him just the once, on my first tour of the area, and immediately understood how he had come to earn his fiercesome notoriety. A martinet of the first order, ruling his little empire with a rod of iron, he suffered fools badly and both Ginger and I knew that Gordon would think him a fool. And today's collection of donations was the stock for weekend trading. He'd go ballistic if the delivery didn't arrive on schedule.

'Er...' said Ginger, staring at the phone, '...maybe I'll give it a try, then. P'raps it's just a twinge, eh?' and he beat a hasty retreat.

Resigned to another difficult conversation with Head Office, I dialled the number and asked to speak to Malcolm. It was worse than I expected. He was not pleased. He was very quiet, very controlled and very, very angry. The only bright spot in the whole affair was that this time I wasn't the culprit. Malcolm was, however, sure I'd had something to do with it – I could tell by the tone of his voice. Or rather, the total lack of any tone at all in his voice. Perhaps he thought I was a jinx or a djin or whatever those things are called. I almost told him about the little devil that lived on my shoulder, thinking I could blame him for the bad luck that afflicted the vehicles in my care, but thought again and decided that, if I did, it might be the final straw that would convince him I was completely off my trolley.

I replaced the phone in its cradle with a shaking hand. Whether that was a result of the conversation, or the dying throes of my hangover, I had no idea but I was glad I didn't have to talk to him any more. Outside the sun was shining. Just the weather to get out and about a bit, I thought. I really needed to blow away the last hour or so.

Jean had said that it was always a good idea to get the measure of the 'opposition' and an expedition onto the High Street was just what I needed to cheer me up. Grabbing a jacket and my bag, I legged it down the stairs before the phone could ring again. In the shop Kylie spotted my intention to escape and started to close the portcullis.

'Goin' somewhere?' she asked, sweetly. 'Ain't it a bit early to go 'ome?'

'To see what the opposition is doing, Kylie.' I raised an eyebrow in her general direction. 'Would you like to come with me?' Always look out for recruits for the escape committee, I say, you can never have too many allies.

'Good idea!' she said enthusiastically, dusting herself down. 'I could do wif some air. Jenny, can you 'old the fort for a bit?' And she handed over her keys to the volunteer.

'Of course, dear,' said Jenny, a little doll-like pensioner with twinkly eyes and a nice line in 1940s' hairdos. 'You go and enjoy yourself.' She stationed herself next to the till clutching a large pile of carrier bags, ready for anything.

'OK, Kylie,' I said when we were outside, 'which of the charity shops on the High Street would you consider to be your closest rival?'

'That one.' She immediately pointed across the road to a branch of one of a large, national chain of shops supporting medical research. 'It alus looks just like one o' them posh boutiques.' We crossed the road and gazed through spotless windows. Inside, the window space was fitted out with a new, laminated wood floor with posts and rails in matching wood that formed a stylish display area. There were two very contemporary display units and lots of shelves fitted down the wall on the right hand side. It made our shop look distinctly tatty and I felt a bit like one of those children you see on a Dickensian Christmas card – the one that stands outside in the snow looking in through a window at perfection. The goods on display were an eclectic mix of the usual donated stuff (although I noted that the labels were from the collections of expensive department stores – no bog standard BHS or Top Shop here), brand new 'new age' giftware and quite a few non-sale props such as a tastefully arranged dried flower arrangement enhanced with ribbons, and a curvy tree branch that had shoes hanging from it. It was striking and very appealing.

'Give me a few minutes, Kylie,' I said and went inside. I assumed that she would be known here and, since I wanted to be anonymous, it would be better to go in without her.

I moved around the shop, flicking a few items along clothing rails, checking out prices and manufacturers' labels, and then hovered close to the counter, glancing over a shelf full of china, glass and wooden ornaments, noting the display techniques. Don't re-invent the wheel, someone had once said to me. If you see an idea that works – pinch it for yourself!

Two volunteers were chatting to each other, as they stood behind the counter ignoring their customers, and soon gave me an opening to join in the conversation.

'I told her I couldn't come in and she said that only left the two of us for Friday afternoon, as if that was my fault!'

'It's getting a bit difficult, you know,' said the other, 'there doesn't seem to be enough people around nowadays, who want to volunteer to do this kind of thing.'

'I know. They're all out at work, aren't they, the younger ones, and they don't have time for anything else. Still, that's not my fault if we're short-staffed, she's the manager, she should sort it out.' She sniffed. 'We had to close on Wednesday afternoon last week, you know, there wasn't anybody here. We lost a lot in sales.'

Cue me to join in.

'Excuse me, ladies, I'm sorry to butt in and I don't mean to be rude.' They both turned to me with quizzical smiles. 'But I couldn't help overhearing what you were saying. I'm new to the area…' I let it hang there for a while. Devious or what? I deliberately let them think I might be a new volunteer. They gave me all their attention. 'It must affect your takings quite badly, not being able to open, I mean. This is a beautiful shop, you must be very proud of it. Does it raise a lot of money?'

'Oh, yes,' said the first, eagerly. 'We take around… well… what would you say, Betty?'

Betty looked thoughtful and named a weekly turnover figure that made Kylie's shop look decidedly sad, even though it did reasonably well, considering. I placed a small purchase on the counter and rummaged around in my pocket for some money. One of the volunteers found a bag and the other took my money while I fulsomely admired the shop and said that I'd call again.

Outside Kylie was hopping from one foot to the other and grinning widely. 'You're devious, you are!' she said happily. 'I'll 'ave to warn everybody about you! What they tell yer, then?'

We walked down the street a little way and I told her what I'd heard. She whistled when she heard about their weekly turnover and nodded at the news about lack of volunteer help. We both found it reassuring, albeit a bit depressing, that we weren't the only ones who had that problem.

Long ago, when women only burned their bras by accident with a hot iron, those with time on their hands did 'good works'. They visited housebound neighbours with soup and gossip, they made jam and sang 'Jerusalem', ran jumble sales and campaigned against graffiti. They helped their sons and daughters raise children, entered the fruits of their gardening labours in the local flower show and harassed the council about refuse and dark streets. Nowadays it's given a name – volunteering – and people hurry away with their heads down, muttering about being too busy as though they were being asked to give up their cars for a month and their two weeks in Val d'Isere.

Many of them are, of course. Busy, that is. If they're not working all the hours God sends, building a career and juggling family life around it, they're going to art appreciation classes, having their nails done or shopping on-line. The blue-rinse 'do-gooder' is no more, defunct like the dodo. Even Granny is off to work every morning, running a corporation or an NHS Trust. The fellas, never much ones for giving time for no-pay anyway, do macho things like play rugby, hide in their garden sheds or disappear under the bonnet of the car. Would teenagers help? No way, unless they can be bribed, coerced or blackmailed.

Working in a charity shop as a volunteer is un-cool. Being a shop assistant is bad enough but to do it for no pay at all… well, just how cracked can you be? It was tough finding volunteers, no argument there. But do it we must.

As Kylie and I were moving on to the next stop, chatting about recruitment strategies, my mobile rang.

'Hello?' I shouted above the traffic noise, a finger in the ear that wasn't plugged into the phone.

'Hello yourself!' said a rich, deep voice. 'This is Brian, one of your drivers.'

'Yes, Brian, we met last week, didn't we? Nice to hear from you again. What can I do for you?'

'Well, I've had a bit of a mishap…' my heart sank '…but don't worry, I've got it sorted, I just thought you should know.'

'What happened? Are you OK?'

'Sure, I'm fine, don't worry on that score. You'll think I need my head examining though. I don't know what I was thinking of. I've just filled up with fuel and put petrol in the tank.'

Just for a minute my mind went blank and I couldn't see the problem. Then it hit me. The vans ran on diesel.

'Brian!' I exclaimed. 'What a daft thing to do! What happened?'

'Well, I didn't even realise what I'd done until I was in the shop, paying for the fuel and my paper. I called out the breakdown service and got a tow down to the dealer – I'm there now – and they've flushed out the tank and filled me up again. They say it'll be alright, no damage or anything because I didn't start the engine, but I feel like such a prat!'

'I can understand that, Brian,' I said, 'that seems right on the button to me.' I paused, smiling, waiting for him to catch up and recognise that I thought he was a prat too. 'Still, no harm done, I suppose. Your mind must have been on Mars, though.'

'Not quite Mars. Down at the hospital. My missus just had our first,' his voice rose with excitement, 'and I'm a bit distracted! We had a boy, nine pounds four ounces. Called him Alexander 'cos he's got loads of red hair.' His voice was filled with pride and I didn't have the heart to castigate him further.

'Congratulations!' I said and then, aside to Kylie, I mouthed: 'Brian. It's a boy.' Kylie's face lit up and she made a clapping motion. 'Have you any leave booked?' I asked him.

'No. Kid arrived early. I was going to take some time when Fliss came out of hospital but that wasn't for another three weeks or so.'

'Take tomorrow, Brian, and spend the weekend with Fliss and your new son. Come into the office early on Monday and we'll sort out how to cover your patch so you can take leave. I assume they'll be home by then? Just drop the van off here before you go home this afternoon, so we can use it tomorrow.'

'All being well they'll be home later today,' he said, 'and… well, thanks, Boss. I owe you one.' And he hung up.

'I think that's cause for a celebration, Kylie, don't you?' I asked and, without waiting for an answer, made a sharp right into the invitingly open door of the Morning Star. I needed a hair of the dog and Brian had just given me the perfect excuse. A modest glass of wine was just right!

Bearing in mind the family matter that had given rise to our ten-minute break, I asked Kylie about herself and her boy, Charlie. She told me that she'd met his Dad on a coach day-trip to Clacton when she was 15. Her brother had introduced them over a can of 4X. Considering this was at seven in the morning, and the rest of the day was fuelled by alcohol and other excesses, the results were pretty much a forgone conclusion. Two months later Mum was in tears, Dad went ballistic, brother said it must have been all her fault because his mate wasn't like that and the culprit had taken a job on a dam project in Malaysia. Charlie arrived seven months later into a reconciled but still noisily reproachful family. He was Kylie's pride and joy, her bane and nemesis. He was utterly delightful, absolutely charming, totally uncontrollable and love for him shone out of her every pore.

Back at the office later, having left Kylie spreading Brian's news around the other shops on the patch and to her volunteers, I pondered how to find another driver to take out Brian's van tomorrow. There were around 100 donation sacks out on streets somewhere, which had quite some potential for irate phone calls from householders who had left them out on their doorsteps to be collected, and from the local Council who didn't like what we did anyway. Far too messy. Much more so than refuse collections. Absolutely.

I rang Damian at home. There were two intertwined, trilling

voices on the answerphone. 'This is Damian and Randolph. We're busy and no, we're *not* going to stop and answer the phone.' Much giggling. 'Just leave your message and, if you sound sweet, we'll call you back.'

'This is Gillian,' I said. 'Sorry if I'm interrupting, Damian. Just need your advice, if you can spare five minutes. Call me in the office, please? Oh, by the way, Brian's Fliss had a boy and I'm sorry if I was grumpy this morning. Just a slight case of alcohol poisoning. Thanks for the toast and coffee!'

The phone rang. For a second or two I thought it was Damian with a quick response but it was Miles.

'Hello, Gillian. I'm afraid I have a problem for you. It's rather delicate and I'd rather not discuss it over the phone. Would you be able to come over?'

'How urgent is it, Miles?' I asked. 'Things are just a bit hectic here at the moment.'

'I think it's quite important that we should deal with it as soon as possible. I have a customer with me who you might want to talk to and she'll stay for about half an hour but then has to pick up her grandchildren from school.'

'OK, if it's that urgent I'll be over there as quickly as possible. See you soon.' I put down the phone, heart sinking to my shoes. I could do without this. When was I going to find the time to do all that strategic planning stuff that managers were supposed to do?

After another quick message left on Damian's machine to explain that I'd gone out, I sprinted down the stairs and did a racing start in my little car, leaving small patches of rubber on the road with a delightfully sinful squeal. Eat your heart out, Schumacher!

The traffic was light for once, and I made good time. The seductively empty space in front of the garage behind the shop didn't attract me this time, although I had to take a deep breath and repeat 'calm, calm, calm' like a mantra when I remembered the whole sorry episode of last time. I was lucky enough to slip into a parking bay vacated by a delivery van that was leaving the shop next door just as I arrived.

Miles was waiting for me, sitting in a quiet corner of the shop next to a lady whom I took to be the customer she had mentioned. The customer had a cup of tea in her hand and a plate of biscuits on a shelf next to her elbow. Miles really did know how to look after people! He introduced me to Mrs Woodley and then asked her if she would repeat to me what she had already told him earlier.

'Well,' Mrs Woodley began, 'I came into the shop this morning because I put a coat in a donation bag yesterday by mistake. I saw the van drive off. The number of this shop was the first one I found in the phone book so I phoned here. The lady said that the van that collected from my street yesterday would have brought everything here. I came over to see if I could get my coat back.' She was a bit flustered with all the attention and kept pressing her hand to her flushed cheek. 'I should have put it in a bag for dry cleaning, you see, but I stupidly put it in the wrong one. It's a very expensive coat and I only bought it four months ago. My daughter, you know,' she added, as though we did. 'She'll take it very badly. She'll say I'm a silly, forgetful fool.

'Anyway, when I got here these lovely people went through every bag that had arrived yesterday but couldn't find my coat.' Her voice wobbled a bit.

At that point Miles took over the tale. 'We'd only opened three or four bags of yesterday's delivery,' he said, 'and none of them had had any outerwear in them. While we were looking for Mrs Woodley's coat I found an envelope in one of the bags. It was empty, just scrap really, but the address was a street about two miles from where Mrs Woodley lives. I knew that Ginger wouldn't be collecting from streets that far apart on the same day so I checked my records to see where he should have been yesterday, just to be sure.'

Mrs Woodley took up the story again. 'I saw the driver,' she said. 'He was about 5ft 10 and had gingerish hair that was a bit thin on top. He was driving one of your vans. You can't mistake them, can you, with that advertising on the side?' I smiled. Our vans really were a garish collection of street-art from all sorts of sponsors as well as our own name. 'I saw him again when I was on my way here today,' she continued. 'I was a bit puzzled, though, because he was in a different van but it was him alright. He was parked outside a house on the Robespierre estate and was taking bags out of a garage at the house and putting them into the van. Is that usual? I thought it seemed a little odd, really, otherwise I wouldn't have mentioned it.'

Miles and I looked at each other, he with a 'this is a can of worms, isn't it?' expression and me with a 'Oh, Lord, now what?' kind of look. Ginger certainly *did* have a different van today, thanks to the fight that his usual one had with the Tesco barrier.

'Mrs Woodley,' I said, 'I'm very grateful to you for staying to tell me all this. It does sound odd and we'll try to find out what it all means. I'm sure you'll understand, though, if I ask you to be patient with us for a few days while we look into it? Perhaps you'll leave your details with us? I promise I'll call you in a few days and tell you what we've learned, or at least as much as we can. Is that alright with you?'

'I suppose so,' she said, with the merest show of reluctance. 'Would it help if I let you have the receipt for the coat?' Clearly Mrs Woodley didn't really care much about the oddities of the situation, all she wanted was her coat!

'I think it would, Mrs Woodley, thank you. A copy would do, and there's no need to bring it to us. If you send it by post, that will be OK. We'll keep looking for your coat and we'll talk soon. Thank you again. Please finish your tea and biscuits, take your time, Pauline will look after you.'

Miles and I left her munching a shortbread fan and went to the little office at the very back of the building where we shut the door behind us firmly.

'What do you make of all that?' I asked him.

'Well,' he said, 'my records show that Ginger was working in Mrs Woodley's area yesterday, although her description of the van she saw today was different from the one she saw yesterday.'

I explained about Ginger and the barrier. He was horrified. Not much of a sense of humour, our Miles, for all his gentle ways. I'd better remember that, I thought, or my flippant side could seriously upset him one day.

'The bags Ginger brought us today,' he continued, 'are from streets he was in last week. We've had some other puzzles with Ginger's collections before but couldn't quite get to the bottom of it. I asked Marc about it when he was looking out for us while we had no area manager, before you arrived, and he did some detective work but couldn't find anything. At least, he didn't tell me what happened. Perhaps you should talk to him?'

'Yes, I will,' I agreed. 'I'm not sure what to do about Mrs Woodley's coat, though. The party line says that we should return goods in these circumstance, if we can find them, but that we don't have to compensate people if we can't find their stuff. Still, Mrs Woodley might have done us a good turn, in an odd sort of way, and I'm not happy to tell her just to go away, however politely. Leave it with me, though, I'll take some advice and see what's to be done.'

Miles smiled at me – sympathetically, I thought – and said, 'Let me make you some tea, you look as though you need it, and we've a jam sponge today. One of the volunteers brings something different in every day. Lovely idea but it plays havoc with good resolutions about diet!'

White chocolate cherry cake – bliss!

An hour later I was back in the office and on the phone to Marc.

'Hello, Gillian,' he smiled at me down the phone. Why was it, I wondered, that some people's voices seemed to smile and others always sounded like anally-retentive morality guardians? 'Still standing, are you? Not buckled under the stress and the pressure?'

'Not yet!' I tried to match his cheerfulness. 'But I do have a problem. Have you got a minute?'

'Sure,' he said, 'anything to interrupt this. I'm planning a shop re-fit and there are too many doors and not enough walls on this plan to let me do what I want. The stairs are in the wrong place, too. Bloody annoying! Anyway, how can I help?'

I told him about Mrs Woodley, her coat and the van driver and he listened without interrupting until I'd finished.

'That's a toughy,' he agreed, 'and it could be a bit of a bastard to deal with. You'll have to play detective, which is a bit rough on you, considering you've only just come on board. You'll have to follow him, I'm afraid, just like those movies where the guy says "Follow that car!", only you have to do your own driving which rather takes the gloss off it, really!' He chuckled, a rich, satisfying sound. 'Pick a day and find out where he'll be working, then follow him and see if anything untoward happens. To be absolutely sure you need to follow him all day, although you could just do the highest risk hour or two just before he's due back at the shop to drop the load off, if you think that would be enough. All day is tedious to say the least, and you're bound to get a bit sloppy so that he's more likely to spot you eventually. A lot depends on what you think might be happening. Remember to tell someone where you'll be and let them know when you're finished so we don't put out an unnecessary missing person alert.'

'Not the easiest thing in the world, is it, being a detective?' I asked a rhetorical question. 'Still, our transits aren't likely to lead off on a 100-mile-an-hour car chase around here, it's hardly Chicago or San Francisco, is it?'

He chuckled. 'True, but don't underestimate the madness of a long distance white-van-man, to coin a phrase. Driving a van may not be rocket science but you'd be surprised what they can do with those things on a roundabout at the end of a clear piece of dual carriageway!'

I thought about Ginger and the car park barrier. Ginger at speed towards a roundabout didn't bear thinking about!

'How would you suggest I handle it if he spots me?' I asked.

'Lie!' he said, even more cheerfully. 'If you're sure you've been spotted, stop for a chat. Tell him you're on your way to visit a sick volunteer, or check on an overflowing donation bin or something. Tell him you spotted his van and thought you'd just stop to say hello. He'll know you're lying but it might still have the desired effect. If he *is* up to no good, it might scare him into being a good boy, at least for a while.'

'Hadn't thought of that,' I said, cheering up a little under the barrage of Marc's optimism. 'Thanks, Marc, I owe you one. Wish me luck?'

'Luck!' he said, and put down the phone.

-6-
Loose Ends

Today was the day, I decided. No point putting off the horrible jobs, they only hang around spoiling things so it's best to get them done and dusted. Oh Lord, I thought, when did I start thinking like my mother? She used to say that about homework, or making my bed or peeling potatoes, jobs I always hated. Or was she haunting me and speaking to me through my conscience? As if I didn't have enough to cope with when the little devil on my shoulder got going. I couldn't remember a time when he wasn't there, poking his nose in and giving me bad advice. Mind you, I'd have missed a lot of adventures if he hadn't egged me on to do mad stuff, although I'd always tried to avoid the really bad, much to his disappointment. Like the time my friend Pauline and I climbed on to the roof of the village hall on a Saturday night for a lark, with a Jolly Roger and a pair of the knickers for the flag pole… well, perhaps another time.

I'd woken early and lay listening to Greg's gentle snoring for a while before realising that I wasn't going to get back to sleep so I might as well get up and at 'em. With plenty of time, just for a change, I took a leisurely shower and then had tea and toast while I laid out the kitchen table for Greg's breakfast. The past few weeks had been tough on him and I thought a loving gesture might help. OK, it wasn't much but it was 'something better than nothing', as my Gran used to say.

Anyway, after surprising Greg with a home cooked breakfast and with time still to spare I decided to make a detour on the way to the office and call in at Broad Barrow to see how Yusuf's project was getting on. It was too early for Brigid to be there but I had sets of keys for all the shops on the patch so it wasn't a problem. Besides, I liked being in the shops when they were closed; they were different then, kind of secret and full of suspense and promise.

If I thought that finding a parking space would be easy because it was early, I was wrong. It was worse! The locals hadn't left for work yet and the early birds like me were circling, already waiting like hawks in search of a poor misguided creature that might make a tasty breakfast morsel, for a sign of vehicle movement that might mean a parking space and success. After about ten minutes of frustrating circling I spotted a space up ahead, only a few metres from the shop. Joy!

The shop was in darkness but I thought I saw a glimmer of light shining up from the foot of the stairs. I called and moved across the shop floor to the stairs. I could see daylight down there, and dust. A haze of tiny particles floating in air that seemed to be as thick as soup.

A disembodied voice answered my hail and I called again 'Hello, who's there?' in a kind of wobbly falsetto.

'It's me!' boomed the voice, helpfully. 'Come on down and see what we've done.'

Much to my surprise I realised it was Caroline. Motivating volunteers to turn up at all was a bit of a challenge at the best of times at Broad Barrow, but to see one of them here at this hour was amazing.

'This is amazing,' I said as I trotted down the stairs, 'what on earth are you doing here at this hour?'

'I could ask you the same question,' he said – a bit coolly, I thought. 'Actually, I was having breakfast.' 'Want some?' And he indicated the kettle and a loaf of bread next to a toaster.

'Well, thanks, yes please,' I said and watched him pop two thick slices in the slots. He was a bit more conservatively dressed today, wearing a Malay-style batik sarong, a yellow Arran-knit tank top over a wide-sleeved, muslin shirt and thong flip-flops studded with rhinestones. Quite modest, really. He caught me gazing at his footwear.

'Like them?' he asked. 'Brigid gave me these for my birthday.' He wiggled his toes. The nails were painted shell pink and there was a silver ring on both very large, and not especially clean, big toes. 'She's an angel. I'd probably be dead now if it wasn't for her,' he said. 'She taught me to listen to my inner voice, showed me how to be myself, not what I thought other people wanted me to be. I'd do anything for her.' He fixed me with hazel eyes that were filled with something I couldn't interpret and I suddenly knew how a rabbit feels, caught in the glare of headlights.

The toast popped up.

As we munched he said, through crumbs and marmalade, 'Look at this', and pulled aside a heavy curtain from around which the daylight washed. One of the little windows had already been replaced and I could smell old fashioned putty. The window wasn't new, exactly, but it looked solid enough and would look even better with a lick of paint. The little top fan light was open and a slight breeze stirred the dust again. I grinned at Caroline.

'That's an improvement, isn't it? Daylight and fresh air. Well, fresh-ish, anyway, as fresh as it can be below ground level on a city street.'

'We'll do the other one today,' he said, 'and clear out the yard tomorrow.'

I peered out of the putty-smeared glass and saw a tiny light-well in the edge of the pavement outside, a bit more than a metre wide. It was choked with McDonald's cartons, cigarette packets, chocolate wrappers and what looked suspiciously like a few used condoms.

'Yuk,' I said, 'rather you than me! Thanks for helping out, Caroline, I really appreciate it, you're a star. Not many volunteers would do all the extras you do. By the way, I hope you don't mind my asking, but why Caroline?'

I wasn't sure if he was going to laugh or pick me up by the collar and hurl me around the room but he decided he could be nice today and he said, 'I called myself after a lady who was shunned, cast off and ridiculed but lived in style anyway. Her husband was a king, so that made her a queen!' His eyes lit up and he laughed till he hiccupped. My history was pretty sketchy but I vaguely remembered a history lesson about a king that banished his wife to a house in Kew, or Richmond or somewhere like that, and bitched about how horrid she was for years. Looking at this strange man I realised that he'd probably had an ordinary chilhood like millions of others and that he was living a life he couldn't possibly have imagined, as he sat in his lessons learning about Queen Caroline, all those years ago. For a moment I reflected on the threads that run, unchecked and unrecognised, through all our lives, and found the thought sobering.

We exchanged a few more pleasantries, stuff of no consequence and, reassured that repairs were well underway, I left him munching the last of the loaf and drove on to the office.

An hour later I was checking drivers' schedules and saw that Ginger was due to drop his collection load at Chilton Street today, so I dialled the shop number and waited for Gordon, the manager, to answer. Instead there was a female voice, quivery and vague-sounding, which I didn't recognise.

'Hello,' I said, then 'Hello?' again to what sounded like dead air. 'This is Gillian, the new Area Manager. Who's that, please?'

'This is Belinda,' she said, rather breathlessly. 'I'm the assistant.'

I thrashed around my memory until I recalled that Belinda was Gordon's assistant manager and I tried to remember what Jean had told me about her: thirty-something, single, mind in another place most of the time was the description that came to me.

'Hello, Belinda, we haven't met, have we? How are you?'

'Fine,' she said and then added, 'I think' – still in that rather vague, disconcerting way. 'I didn't get much sleep last night so I'm not quite myself today.'

'I'm sorry to hear that,' I sympathised, 'are you feeling unwell? Should you be at work?'

'It's Gordon's day off today,' she explained, 'so I have to run the shop. Besides, it's my own fault, really, I started a course a little while ago and sometimes I get carried away with the studying and don't go to bed till late.'

'That's very dedicated, Belinda, what are you studying?'

'Klingon,' she said and I thought I'd misheard her.

'Pardon?'

'Klingon,' she repeated, 'so I can converse with the Confederation's enemies and foster greater understanding. It's a difficult language, you see, and too few people learn how to speak it properly. Not many of us learn it at all, really. About six in this country, actually, which makes conversation practice rather difficult.'

What can you say? What *can* you say? I find 'Er...' is always a good one when you're uncertain.

'Try "Eh?"' said the little devil on my shoulder. 'That's almost as inspired.' Go away, not now! I shot in his direction.

'Well, yes,' I tried again 'I'm sure it does. Er... are you sure you're OK then, Belinda, not too... er... worn out to work today?'

'No,' she said, 'I'll be as right as rain as soon as I've had my first cup of Vulcan coffee. That's a blend we can buy at the conventions and it's much nicer than regular Nescafe. I went to a convention two weeks ago. I'm a Star Trek fan. So exciting. We get to do all kinds of things. I have a video of myself on the flight deck of the Enterprise. The original one, not the ones from the movies or the other spin-offs. So exciting! I'll show it to you sometime, if you'd like.'

'Quite. Um... can you help me please, Belinda? I don't want to keep you from your coffee but I wonder if you could just let me know where Ginger is working today? Do you have his route schedule to hand?'

'...or is it with Mr Sulu, the helmsman?' said the little devil on my shoulder and I wasn't sure whether to giggle or send for a doctor.

'It's here, on Gordon's desk,' Belinda said and I could hear a rustle of papers. 'Gordon is so efficient. Not like me.' And I thought I heard a sad little note in her voice. 'Ginger is collecting around the Triangle today.' She gave me a list of around eight or nine street names.

'Thanks, Belinda,' I said, 'live long and prosper.' With that I put the phone down, though not before I thought I heard a breathless and grateful 'Oooooooo, thank you soooo much!'

A driver's job is pretty simple really, although very physical and they need to be fit. In the morning, they pop bags through the doors of homes in an area they've previously agreed with the shop manager. In the afternoon they revisit the streets they dropped bags in three or four days before and pick up the full ones that generous householders leave out on their doorsteps. Simple. Except sometimes it's raining. Sometimes it rains hard. Sometimes householders aren't generous and the drivers get depressed because they work so hard for not a lot and sometimes there are dogs, unsympathetic people and mischievous kids. And traffic wardens. And clampers.

Belinda had told me that Ginger was working in an area known locally as the Triangle, a fairly new housing development that we'd only recently started to visit. Whether it would yield a good return we had yet to discover. Sometimes new developments were productive, when people realised that bits and bobs from their previous homes were out of place in the new, ultra modern box they'd moved to, and a timely plea from a charity for donations helps them off-load their old possessions without hassle. They feel good about their generosity, then go out and spend lots of dosh on new stuff which pleases the local retailers. So everybody's happy!

At just after noon I parked the car on Beecham Avenue between a van decorated with the slogans of a double glazing firm and another car of the same colour and make as my own. I'd figured out that Ginger had to drive up this road to reach the street which seemed, from my examination of a map, to be the logical start of his pick-up route. As my car was just about the most common model on the market these days, I stood very little chance of him taking any notice of mine. On the doorstep of a house facing the T junction at the top of the avenue, I could see a brightly coloured bag that told me some, at least, of the people here had responded to the call.

I waited. And waited. After a while I began to fantasise about what it would be like to be a private detective, spending interminable hours waiting for illicit lovers to leave quiet suburban houses in the middle of the afternoon. Did it pay well, that sort of thing? Would I see people such as sanctimonious politicians, the local vicar, famous TV stars perhaps?

Day-dreaming almost ruined the whole project. It took me a few precious moments to realise that the bag on the doorstep on the other side of the junction had gone and I'd seen nothing. Some detective I'd make! Couldn't even hold my concentration to spot the very thing I was looking for! I left the car and jogged to the corner. There was a tree at the edge of the pavement and I thought it might be possible to see the whole length of the street from its shelter. I felt ridiculous and more than a little guilty, being so furtive. It didn't feel right to spy on someone, especially one of my own staff, no matter what the reason. It occurred to me that the local Neighbourhood Watch might take a dim view as well; I could see a few of their shiny new signs on the bus stop and the corner lamp post.

Then I spotted the van, parked some distance along the road, and there was Ginger, rapidly collecting bags from doorsteps and putting them in piles of four or five on the edge of the pavement. He moved along the street at an efficient pace that covered the ground quickly. Reaching the end of the street he turned back to collect his van and, driving slowly and stopping to load each pile of bags before moving on to the next, he finished the street in less then half an hour. Impressive, I thought, very impressive.

He stopped for a break about an hour later and, from my vantage point crouched behind a kiddies' slide in a playground, I could see him pour something from a thermos and unwrap what looked suspiciously like a large bar of chocolate. My stomach grumbled in sympathy and protest.

Easing aching muscles, cramped by crouching slightly so as not to raise my head over the frame of the slide, I looked around the edge of the metal ladder and... caught sight of a child on one of the swings a few metres away, staring at me. Behind the swing, Mum was frozen in the act of reaching out to push, her face a picture of consternation and uncertainty. Both had recognised me before I'd spotted them and, to my horror, I realised they were the same mother and child who'd witnessed my demented temper tantrum of Wednesday. I straightened up in a hurry, making matters worse, natch, and gave them my most winning smile. It felt remarkably like a leer, and I wasn't surprised to see the mother gather up the child in her arms and hurry away. He gazed at me over her shoulder with round eyes, his mouth a perfect 'O'.

'Humiliation time, eh?' said my little devil and I growled at him.

I resumed my vigil, thoroughly cheesed off but determined to see it through and, after a few minutes, was rewarded when Ginger started up the engine of the van and moved off down the street. A gentle drizzle began falling and I remembered my umbrella, virgin and unused, in the car half a mile away. If I went to fetch it I'd lose him so, not being dressed for rain, I just turned up the collar of my jacket and prayed that the shower would pass. No such luck, of course and 15 minutes later I was soaked, shivering and miserable, and firmly resolved not to apply to my friendly neighbourhood detective agency for a job.

At last Ginger was done, fully loaded and ready to make his way back to the shop. I'd seen nothing unusual and, in fact, had to admire the way he stuck to the rules. Always close gates behind you, don't walk across a garden and don't step over a fence to reach the house next door, always lock your van even if it's just for a moment's absence. He was good, certainly, so why did it feel so wrong? Was it that he was just too good? Too perfect?

'Now you're paranoid,' said the little devil on my shoulder, 'you need to relax more. You're cold and wet and look, there's a pub over there. Why don't you go have a stiff drink? You've done your bit for today and no-one will thank you if you catch pneumonia.' Get lost, I fired back at him, stiffening my resolve. I wasn't giving up now or all this would be wasted.

'Oh, alright then,' he said and I wondered how an imaginary voice – and my own imaginary voice at that! – could sound so like a sullen 'you never take any notice of me any more, you're no fun at all!'

I sprinted back to the car as Ginger pulled into the parking area of the neighbourhood shopping parade and had the engine started when he came out of the newsagent's shop carrying a copy of Sporting Life. Carefully, and from a safe distance, I followed as he turned left, down the duel carriageway in the direction of Gordon's shop, a couple of miles away.

At the roundabout, however, he made another right turn when I'd been expecting him to carry straight on. We drove for about ten minutes and then he made a left, a right and, after about ten minutes, pulled up in front of a neat little semi in a street that looked just the same as thousands of streets anywhere in England. A woman came out of the house and he gave her a cheery wave as he reversed the van into the drive and she opened the up-and-over door to a double garage. I felt my jaw drop when I saw that the garage was half full of the charity's doorstep bags.

There was a narrow pathway through the pile and a smaller stack of bags slightly to one side at the front. Ginger and the woman began to unload the van, carrying bags towards the back of the garage, until the van was empty. Then they loaded it again from the pile at the front. When they'd finished, Ginger put his arm around the woman's waist, gave her a loving kiss, and they both went indoors.

For several minutes I sat, physically still but with mind buzzing, then found my mobile phone and dialled Marc. His phone rang several times and I began to think I'd have to leave a message on his answer service, when he answered, somewhat breathlessly,

'Hi, Gillian, how you doing?'

'Marc, you'll never guess – it's mind-blowing!'

'Try me,' he said, 'this must be safer than the other mind-blowing stuff I was offered last night!' He laughed a dirty chuckle. I'll think about that one later, I thought, momentarily distracted.

'Sounds interesting,' said the little devil on my shoulder, 'I think I could work with this guy.'

'I've been tailing Ginger today,' I blurted out. 'He's outside a house – I think it's his home – and he's just unloaded his collection into a garage and loaded it again with bags that were already there.'

'Bingo!' yelled Marc down the phone. 'Got him! I knew he had some kind of scam! Well done, Gill, you've cracked it!'

'Have I? What have I cracked, then?'

'Sure you have,' he said, 'that's his house, that's where he lives. He's skimming!'

'What's that?'

'He's sorting through the bags to take out anything that's worth more than, say, a fiver, then re-packing them to take on to the shops. It might take a couple of days but the re-packed bags will turn up at one of the shops he services, just not the one you'd expect. I've seen it before. Clever, isn't it?'

'How can you say that! It's despicable!'

'I know. Still quite clever, though not subtle. Not subtle at all. Most of the stuff will find its way to car boot sales but some will go to second hand dealers and even auction houses. That's not really relevant just now, though. You need to ring HQ first and turn it over to the personnel people and the legal eagles. Don't go wading in there until you've spoken to them. Promise me you won't confront him?'

'Her?' said the little devil on my shoulder, who knew what a coward I was. 'She's as likely to have a go as my granny is to fly to the moon.'

'You're imaginary,' I said, 'you don't have a granny.'

'Exactly!' said the little devil.

''Scuse me?' said Marc.

'Not you, Marc,' I assured him. 'Take no notice, I'm just going crazy here. I'll call you back when I've spoken to HQ' Oh Lord, here we go again.

Personnel was closed. Closed? How could they be closed?

'A staff meeting,' said the girl on the switchboard, 'would you like to talk with the Shops Director?'

Oh, yes, please, I thought, that will be just yummy.

'Hello again,' Lucas Barrington said and I swear I heard an echo of the laughter from our previous conversation. I decided that it was sexy, after all, and that I could become addicted to his voice quite easily.

'Well, yes,' I said, 'and I'm sorry but I think this is quite serious and urgent and Personnel is closed. I'm in my car, outside the home of one of my drivers, looking at a pile of several days' worth of donation collections in his garage. There was an indication that something was wrong at one of the shops a couple of days ago and Marc Haslam has been guiding me. It looks as though the van driver is skimming the stock.'

'Oh, boy, Gillian, you are having a week of it aren't you? First things first. Are you absolutely sure that what you think you've seen is what you're actually looking at?'

'I can take some pictures, if you think it would help, Lucas,' I said. 'I have a little disposable camera in the glove box.'

'That would be useful. However, on no account are you to expose yourself to any risk. Do you understand me?'

'Yes. Do you want me to call the police?'

'I should say yes. But I'm not going to, I'm afraid. We never do. This isn't the time to explain properly but I will, another time. For now, I'd like you to start your car, point your camera, take a couple of pictures and leave immediately. Is that clear?'

'Perfectly.'

'Good. The next thing isn't so easy. When you get back to your office you should call someone to help you. Do you have anyone there who can back you up on a tough job?'

'Not really. But I can scout around.'

'When you've someone there, call Ginger and ask him to meet you at your office. When he arrives you'll have to tell him he's suspended from duty. Don't forget to take his van keys and ID card. You should ask him if you can recover any charity property from his home. As a driver he'll probably have boxes of donation sacks there, which is OK, so it's within your authority to ask. You have no automatic right to go there but you can ask his permission and do it if he agrees. Once there you should ask if there are any other goods he wishes to return. On no account should you tell him what you've already seen but, if he tells you about the stuff in his garage, so much the better. If he doesn't, don't push it. Whatever you do, don't go alone. Ask one of your area manager colleagues to go with you. I know I shouldn't ask you this but Jean's away, I can't get to you in time and the people in personnel are out on their annual away-day, as you know. This should be done today. Can you handle it?'

I paused. Away-day? What kind of corporate gobble-de-gook is that when I'm staring this catastrophe in the face? I'd handled difficult situations before but nothing as potentially tough as this.

'I have no idea. It sounds like a mission for the CIA! Still, we're about to find out, aren't we?'

'Does a bit, doesn't it?' he agreed, 'and I know it isn't really fair to throw it all at you. I wouldn't ask if it were something that could wait a while, something trivial, but this is serious.'

After he'd given me a few more words of encouragement we ended the call, I found my camera and took the shots. My hands were shaking and I'd no idea if the shots would be worth anything; only time would tell. Fortunately the garage door was still ajar enough for me to take a couple of useful angles.

A few minutes later I beat a hasty retreat. Half way down the road I remembered Marc's offer of help and, in the next street, I pulled the car over to call him.

'Marc, I need your help again,' I said, and repeated what Lucas had said about back-up.

'I'm about an hour's drive from you,' he said, 'buy me a pizza after we're done and I'm your man. See you at the office.' He rang off.

Just over an hour later, back in my office, I heard a commotion in the shop and Marc's voice making itself heard above the rest.

'Ladies, ladies!' he said. 'How lovely to see you all again! Put me down, please, I'm here on business, not for your pleasure or mine!'

I had to smile, in spite of everything. His irrepressible good humour was a relief from the tension of the day and an excellent pick-me-up. A moment later we were saying hello. He was about my height with white-blonde hair cut very short, violet-coloured eyes and a round face. I couldn't help noticing that his chunky figure was completely at odds with his delicate hands and neat, tiny feet, which were encased in training shoes, in complete contrast to the grey business suit. He saw my eyes stray to the footwear and followed my gaze.

'Comfortable!' was all he said by way of explanation, then gave me a bear hug and said 'sod political correctness, you can't beat a hug for a greeting!'

'The circumstances could be better though,' I said when he'd put me down, flushed but pleased. 'Anyway, I'm really grateful to you for coming all this way to help me out of this mess.'

'Don't mention it,' he said, arranging himself as comfortably as possible in an uncomfortable chair. 'I enjoy a good scrap. When's the miscreant due?'

'In about ten minutes. I thought I'd allow a little time in case you were delayed. He was very reluctant to come back to the office today, said it would take him over his hours. He sounded a bit suspicious but that might have been me being paranoid.'

'All ready then?' he said. 'Know what you're going to do?'

'Yep. What I don't know is what *he's* going to do.'

At that minute we heard a diesel van pull up outside the stock room entrance.

Ginger was clearly somewhat puzzled by the summons to the office and his expression was guarded. I invited him to sit, but he refused, eyeing up Marc's presence across the room. I took a deep breath and began. I explained that I was suspending him from duty and told him there'd be an investigation into his conduct and, perhaps, disciplinary proceedings. While my mouth dried up and I struggled through it, he was impassive, watching me through half-closed eyes. Then I'd finished and mercifully, Marc stepped in and asked him for his keys and ID. He handed them over without a word. I felt the hairs on the back of my neck stand up, waiting for the sky to fall. This was too quiet, too easy.

I said that we needed to recover anything belonging to the charity that he might have at home. For a minute I thought he wasn't going to respond to that either, but then the colour came up to his face and he started to shout. I lost track of what he was saying fairly quickly but caught a few bits about 'over my dead body' and 'touch my house and I'll have your hands off' and lots of other stuff, much of which would have made a Royal Marine blush.

When he'd finished – or simply run out of steam, I'm not quite sure which – there was a brief moment of quiet and Marc said, 'We'll take that as a "no" then, shall we?'

The next moment Ginger was down the stairs and gone, still ranting as he went. We sat down, quickly and heavily, in the nearest chairs.

'Phew!' said Marc. 'I thought we'd got away with it for a minute. I should have known better. Quite a dictionary of obscenity, isn't he? There were a couple in there I haven't heard before! Do you think he made them up just for us?' And we both started to giggle, somewhat hysterically.

'But now what am I going to do?' I wailed through the giggles. 'Brian's gone off to be a new dad and I've just lost Ginger as well! How on earth am I going to do next week's collections?'

'Ever driven a transit?' Marc asked and we both cracked up again. It must be a reaction to trauma, I thought, 'cos it's certainly not funny.

'Well, yes, I have. But I thought my days of humping stuff were long gone.' Marc was beside himself by now and it took me a minute to realise that he was laughing at me this time. The double meaning of what I'd just said sank in and I pitched a well-aimed notebook at his head. He ducked, but not before it caught him across one ear and he let out a satisfying yelp.

It began to look as though tomorrow would be a working Saturday trying to sort out next week's van schedules. How on earth was I going to explain to Greg? He'd planned for us to visit his mum and she was expecting us for lunch. Perhaps we could go on Sunday instead, I thought. After all, Sunday lunch with the in-laws was more traditional anyway. In the meantime, however, I'd promised this man a pizza.

'Come on,' I said to Marc, 'stop humouring yourself at my expense or I'll put something nasty in your salad!'

Over a pizza and a beer, I told him more about my day following Ginger, about Shona's gang in the pub and Trekki Belinda. He told me about his patch, some of his staff and snippets of satisfying gossip about Jean and the other two area managers who were our colleagues. He swore me to secrecy on pain of awful things. He was a mine of information and the time flew by until I realised, with a shock, that it was after eight o'clock and, apart from leaving a quicky message on the answer phone at home earlier, before Ginger had arrived at the office, I hadn't spoken to Greg.

I made an excuse and left Marc hugging a beer while I found a quiet spot in the ladies to use my mobile. Greg answered the phone right away and yelled. What else?

'Where the fuck have you been? I've been worried sick! I've left five messages on your phone already! What's the use of the damned thing if you never switch it on, you stupid cow!'

'I'm sorry, Greg, I really am. I put it onto message service because we had a difficult interview to do and I didn't want it ringing in the middle of that. I must have forgotten to switch it back on again.'

'That's it,' said the little devil on my shoulder, 'grovel again. What about all those times he's stayed out late, come home pissed and told you not to be such a clinging vine?' I ignored him, I was far too busy grovelling.

'I'm really sorry you were worried…'

'And what do you mean "we"?' he said. 'Who the hell is "we"?' Oh, Lord!

'One of the other area managers on my team came to help, it was difficult…'

'I bet it was! Is that why you're not home now, then? Out with the boys are we? Or should I say out with just one boy?'

'It isn't like that, Greg, really it isn't. He came to help and I offered to buy him a pizza, to say thank you. It seemed like the least I could do.'

'Yeah, the least maybe, but what else do you have in mind then? Tell me that! I want you home right now, do you hear me?'

I'm surprised the whole county can't hear you, the woman in the next door loo certainly can, I thought, but kept it to myself 'cos I was in enough trouble already. At least he wasn't likely to want to visit his mum tomorrow after this, she'd sense all in the garden wasn't rosy and would want to know what was going on. Shrewd sort, Greg's mum, not a bad old stick really, just a mite too fond of her son for his own good.

'I'll be there as soon as I can, Greg.' And I rang off.

Back at the table I smiled at Marc and said I had to go, thanking him again for his help and time. We parted with another hug, which was just what I needed to cheer me up, though it gave me a twinge of guilt at the same time. 'Wimp!' said the little devil on my shoulder. 'If you ask me he's a better bet than that specimen you've got at home, even if he is a fruit!' I ignored him.

Half an hour later I let myself in at home and found my dearly beloved crashed out on the sofa, TV blaring and the floor littered with empty beer cans. It was all my fault, of course. Wearily I ran myself a bath and then went to bed, too tired and cowardly to want to wake him now.

Over breakfast coffee the next morning I told a bleary-eyed Greg that I had to work today. It went down like a lead balloon but I sensed a certain relief there as well. He had a fierce hangover that mummy dearest would 'tut tut' at and generally make her disapproval felt, something Greg hated and tried to avoid at almost any cost. He was mollified by my offer to phone her and take the blame for the cancellation.

The shop was busy when I arrived, being Saturday and the busiest trading day of the week.

'What yer doing 'ere today?' Kylie greeted me. 'Yer not supposed to work Saturdays, not like us. Summat up, then? Abart Ginger, innit?' she said, leering at me.

'I do have work to do, Kylie, the electrician is coming this morning to have a look at our manic fuse box and I'm looking for drivers for next week. Know anyone?' She looked a little startled at being asked to participate again for the second time in a week, in things normally beyond her remit as a shop manager.

'Well yeah, I might,' she said, 'my bruv is between jobs just now. Can yer pay cash?'

I smiled. The underground economy was alive and well and living in one of my shops.

'Sorry, Kylie, no can do. But we could pay at the temp rate, if that's any good?'

'Might do,' she said. 'Give me half hour and I'll see wot I can do fer yer. Wuz yer thinkin' o' puttin' the kettle on, then?' She gave me one of her cheeky grins as she turned back into the shop singing 'Who's fer tea, then?'

While the kettle boiled I rang Greg's mum and explained that I had an emergency at work. She was remarkably understanding, saying that of course she realised how important charity work was, and of course I had to make it a priority, especially since it was a new job. I got the strong impression that she was actually quite relieved and wondered what was going on. She'd normally have given me a hard time, reminding me that I should look after her precious son better than I actually did. But there'd be time to think about that later. I still had a driver to find.

The phone rang. After hesitating whether to let the answer phone get it, I decided that it might be Greg and not answering it could cause even more ructions. It was Mrs Ginger.

'I'm sending back your stuff,' she said coldly, after the briefest of non-introductions. 'Ludwic is out at present.' Ludwic? Good grief, no wonder he prefers Ginger, I thought. 'He's not due back until around four this afternoon. He told me what happened. If I let you have it all, can you make your people keep it out of police hands?'

I was stunned. I hadn't expected anything like this and didn't know what to say. My first thought was that it was impossible, that at such short notice we had nowhere big enough to take all the stock I'd seen in Ginger's garage. Then I realised I couldn't say no and that, in any case, there'd be a few Brownie points in it for me if I could recover all that stock. It wasn't as if we were planning to prosecute; the crime scene wasn't needed for detailed forensic examination.

'I'll need a little while to sort out where it's to go,' I said, 'and I can't make any promises about police involvement...'

'Liar!' said the little devil on my shoulder triumphantly 'You're leading here up the garden path! Well done! My training bears fruit at last!'

'...but I'll do what I can and I think I can persuade HQ to listen. Can I call you back in around an hour?' She said that would be OK and we rang off.

But first, a call to HQ to leave a message on the weekend service for Lucas, to let him know what had happened. Monday morning would be frantic, with shops reporting their sales figures and two new drivers to brief and I wanted him to know that Ginger was properly suspended so that Lucas could do whatever he had to do next. To my amazement, the head honcho himself answered the phone and, for a moment or two, I was too surprised to speak.

'Oh, hi,' I eventually managed. 'Um… I wasn't expecting anyone to be there. I thought I'd be talking to an answer phone.'

'I'm real enough,' he said, 'just overworked like we all are. But what are you doing in the office today? I thought you'd be recovering from yesterday.'

'I wanted you to know what happened,' I said, 'and Monday mornings are so frantic I thought a message on the machine would hold things until I could talk with you properly later. Besides, I need to find a new driver today, for Monday morning.'

'Ah, yes. How did it go? Who did you have with you?'

'Marc came over. Ginger is officially suspended, I have his van, his keys and his ID but he threatened to cut off my hands if I went to his house. What happens next?'

'Did he really? I guess he was a bit annoyed to be found out by someone as new as yourself.' Annoyed? Oh, you betcha! 'You need to write a statement of everything that happened. How you came to be involved, what you did, who you spoke to – everything. Get that to me as soon as you can. There'll be a hearing and you'll be expected to attend. I'll let you know when and where but in the meantime, relax, you've done your stuff for now. Sounds like you handled it very well. Congratulations.' Listening to his voice, something stirred again in my memory. For the space of a heartbeat I smelled the ozone of sea air and thought I was going mad.

'Thanks. Do you know where I can store several vanloads of stock? I need to get something arranged within the next hour so that Mrs Ginger can deliver it.'

'Pardon? But I thought you said… My God, how have you pulled that one off?' The tone of his voice said he was stunned by the turn of events and I milked it for all it was worth.

'Oh, just call me magic,' I crowed, 'and maybe I'll tell you one day.' He laughed and my toes curled at the sound of it.

'OK, Magic, send the stock to Sally's new shop. She has a team there today getting ready for Wednesday's opening and she's desperately short of stock to fill the rails. Let's hope Ginger left something worth having! I'm sure you can arrange between you to return the favour another time. Remind me to ask you again some other time how you did it. I'm intrigued. We'll talk again next week and good luck with your hunt for new drivers.'

Mrs Ginger was cool when I spoke to her again but said she'd direct her truck to the address I gave her (I thought better of asking how come she suddenly had a truck at her disposal) and I rewarded myself for a productive and satisfactory morning's work with a cup of tea and a chocolate éclair. Well, two actually, but I felt I'd earned them.

Just for once I managed to hang on to the sense of accomplishment for all of half an hour, which must have been a record. Then Kylie clattered up the stairs with a chap in tow and a broad smile on her face. She was positively glowing although I couldn't help noticing that he didn't look quite so enthusiastic.

'Electrician,' she announced, 'and 'e's OK, 'e's the best yer can get!' With that she positively bounced out of the office and clattered back down the stairs singing 'Girls just wanna have fun' at the top of her voice.

'Well!' I said, astonished. 'Do you always have that effect on women?'

He looked uncomfortable. 'No,' he said, 'we just knew each other once. I 'aven't seen 'er for a while. She's a bit daft, that one.'

I smiled. That was one way of putting it, I suppose.

I showed him where the fuse box was and his reaction was to grunt. 'Bloody 'ell! Never seen anyfing like that before.' I left him to do whatever electricians do in these circumstances, having made sure he knew where to find the shop ladder, the one that could have passed muster at the Eiffel Tower, and went to sort out the driver problem.

Half an hour later, with a replacement and a stand-by reserve sorted out, just in case, I just had to ask Kylie what on earth had turned her into a raving lunatic this morning.

'It's Bingo!' she said and I thought she meant she'd won the jackpot at the local bingo hall last night. Wrong again. 'The electrician!' she explained at my bemused face, "Is name's Charlie but we all calls 'im Bingo, 'ave done since school. 'E's my little Charlie's Dad! I 'aven't seen 'im since I left school, just after the coach trip! Don't say nuffink, please, Gilly. 'E don't know abart Charlie, see, I didn't know I wus expecting till later. After he'd gone. I never told 'im.' And her face went sort of sad and small.

What can you say? I must have muttered something appropriate before I escaped back to my office because she seemed satisfied. Whatever next? I soon found out. Bingo was waiting. He told me all the electrical horror stories he'd gathered in his years as a skilled electrician and then told me that putting right the wiring in the building was going to cost the equivalent of Argentina's national debt. Weakly I thanked him, asked him if he could put it all in writing and said goodbye.

Time to give up and go home. Maybe there'd be a little peace there. I felt pretty whacked after my week and needed just to chill for a while.

The house was deserted. No sign of Greg and no note to tell me where he'd gone or when he'd be back. Never mind, I thought, I can have a little space to do my own thing. I decided on a little retail therapy and, after a cuppa and half a pack of chocolate digestives, I went into town to visit my favourite department store. I couldn't ever afford to buy anything there but I liked to look at shoes and floaty dresses and lots of lovely leather luggage that smelled glorious. I stopped off to collect groceries from Sainsbury's and had a long, leisurely bath as soon as the shopping was safely stowed away. It was a good excuse to use the new smellies I'd bought to celebrate the new job. Greg still wasn't home but I dressed carefully, trying for a little glamour without being too over the top, and waited. I wanted to make up for wrecking his Saturday.

I was still waiting at two o'clock in the morning.

-7-
Monday Mayhem

Monday came as a relief. Greg had arrived home just after three on Sunday morning, in a mini cab that sounded like bonfire night at the rugby club – a mixture of loud roars and large men after several hours in the bar, singing at the top of their out-of-tune voices. He was totally incoherent and as truculent as Scrooge. He was really angry with me for staying out all night on Wednesday and still hadn't forgiven me which, if I stopped to think about it, was pretty understandable, I suppose. I'd explained what had happened till I was hoarse with talking but he wasn't going to let me off lightly. The fact that Damian was gay seemed to make it worse. After all, what woman in her right mind would rather spend a celibate night with a pansy than come home to the delights of an all-man he-man like my Greg? My paraphrase, not his words; but his question, not mine. Somehow I found it a tough one to answer. My hesitation in coming up with a satisfactory answer just made matters worse.

Anyway, we eventually got to bed in the wee small hours of Sunday morning and slept late. I'd tip-toed around his hangover for most of the day longing to tell him how close to hysteria I'd been when he didn't come home and what a thoughtless, selfish sod he was not to call me. Under the circumstances, however, that didn't seem like a very good idea. He was only paying me back, wasn't he? Pretty childish really, and I had actually called him on Wednesday, hadn't I? But who's to say we don't all behave like four-year-olds at times? Cowardice, or discretion (I'm not sure which) finally won the day and I kept my thoughts to myself although I nearly bust a gut holding it all in. OK, OK I'd been blathered when I phoned, but it hadn't been that late. Not late enough for him to be seriously worried. Maybe being late on Friday as well hadn't been the cleverest thing to do, though. Even I had to concede that it certainly hadn't helped.

Still, I couldn't remember him playing tit-for-tat like this before.

He'd normally found a more subtle way of making me feel guilty, like saying he hadn't had anything to eat while I was out because he wasn't sure if I was saving the ham for something special and he didn't want to upset my plans. All in that little-boy-lost voice. I'd not seen him jealous before, either, even when a straight guy paid me attention, so I didn't have a clue what was going on. Was I not paying him enough attention? Was my new job distracting me too much? Maybe he was sickening for something? 'Maybe he's just sickening,' said the little devil on my shoulder and I ruthlessly buried the thought in the deepest depths of my soul.

Still, we managed to get to his mum's for lunch, in spite of the atmosphere between us. I think we both thought a change of scene and a third party around might distract us. There wasn't much party in the third party, though. Greg's mum seemed as distracted as we were and nervous as a cat. I was too confused and tired to bother much and sat in the garden, in the early spring sunshine, while they did whatever mothers and sons do on a Sunday afternoon when they don't see each other much.

I dozed for a while. Greg's mum's garden was quiet and full of the scents of early spring flowers and new-mown grass. I could feel myself drifting even though my mind was still sifting through some of the week's events. Caroline and his bizarre collection of clothes and his fierce devotion to Brigid. Belinda the Trekkie and her passion for a two-dimensional representation of a non-existent culture in an imaginary universe. Damian with his heart of gold and tangled love life. Lucas and... That must have been my last conscious thought because I woke to Greg's hand shaking my shoulder.

'Time to go,' he said, 'although you've not really been here, have you, you've been sleeping most of the time. Good job Mum didn't mind. Come on, shake a leg, we'll miss the start of the match on telly.'

My dream vanished in the mist, in that unfortunate way that dreams have. As it vanished, however, I thought I caught the faintest scent of salty air and the impression of a hand held gently at the small of my back. Fantasy stuff.

Monday morning, decidedly not fantasy stuff, came around soon enough and I decided that this week I'd start on getting to know the shop managers properly and see how they ran their little empires. What is it they say about good intentions and the road to hell?

Damian was already slaving over a hot computer when I arrived at the office, punching ruthlessly at the keys. He was setting up a new page on our very grandly titled, Management Expenditure, Sales and Statistics Update Programme, or MESSUP for short. His concentration level was fierce and he didn't even look up when I put a cup of tea next to his elbow. He just said, 'Figures ready by ten' without taking his eyes from the screen or his flying fingers from the keys. I left him to his telephone and computer and wandered downstairs to see if I could find any signs of life. Much to my surprise, Kylie was already perched on a high stool in her little office, chewing a pen and bending over her shop accounts. I'd already reached the conclusion that this really wasn't her thing, messing with accounts and sales statistics, and that she'd rather scour the lavatory with a toothbrush, given the choice.

'Morning, Kylie!' I breezed. 'You're here early this morning.' I was amazed and alarmed at the look of despair on her face as she lifted her eyes from the ledger. Her forehead was furrowed, there were shadows under her eyes and I could have sworn I saw too much moisture in her eyes.

'What on earth's the matter?' I asked. 'You poor thing, you look as though you haven't slept all weekend.'

'I ent,' she said, much subdued from her usual self, then blurted out 'I can't find it!' and burst into tears. I was completely foxed and, for several heartbeats, just stood there like a dummy with my mouth hanging open. It took several bundles of tissues and much persuasion but she eventually told me that she couldn't reconcile the week's sales figures with the till rolls. Given what I'd seen the previous week, during my illicit visit to her office, I couldn't feign surprise but she didn't seem to notice. What did surprise me, though, was her obvious distress. Her figures were a riot of nonsense every week, so why should it upset her so much now?

'How much is it out?' I enquired. She lowered her head again and whispered something. I thought I must be mistaken and tried to stop my heart sinking to my shoes.

'*How* much?' I asked, trying unsuccessfully to keep the disbelief from my voice.

'Three hundred and twenty-five pounds,' she said again and I sat down on the stool next to her as she added 'down' in a small voice.

'Kylie! How on earth has that happened?'

She shrugged, helpless in the face of figures that wouldn't do what she wanted them to.

'Could you look for me please?' she asked, sounding like a six-year-old with a splinter in her finger.

'Er… well, I'll have a go. Why don't I take all the bits and pieces upstairs while you make yourself some tea? I'm sure you'll feel better with a drink inside you. It's too early for a G&T so plain T will have to do!'

She smiled valiantly but damply at my weak humour, gathering up a startlingly large bundle of till rolls, petty cash receipts and odd scraps of paper covered in scribbles.

Upstairs I spread everything out on my desk and tried to make some sort of order out of the chaos. Till rolls over here, in date order – receipts over there, also in date order, and the shop ledger directly in front of me. The ledger was a bit of a mess, with Tippex and pencil rubbings everywhere. It seemed sensible to start from scratch. Two hours later, hunched over my desk like Bob Cratchett in Scrooge's office, I slowly unwound myself and stretched. There it was, a labour of love and all finished. Well, not love exactly, but done anyway.

'Are you *finished* with that now?' asked Damian. 'Only I have last week's figures from all the others and *this* shop is the only one missing from the accounts.'

'Yep,' I crowed, 'all done and I found out where it all went wrong so that I can explain to Kylie.'

'Humpf,' he said, or something that sounded like it anyway. 'They'll *all* be expecting you to solve their problems now, you know. Word'll get round like a *bush* fire spreading. You won't *know* what's hit you this time next week. Or, to be more accurate, *I* won't know what's hit *me* when I ring around and they'll all say the figures aren't ready and can *you*, meaning *me*, help them out.'

'So what do they do now, when they can't make it all balance?' I asked

'Fudge,' he said. 'Creative accounting, being *economical* with the truth, however you care to label it.'

My heart went cold. Was it really that bad?

'Yup!' said Damian, reading my expression and my mind. 'Do you want one of my Valium? It's a *bit* early for the Scotch!'

'I'll manage. You could distract me, if you like, and tell me what happened on your date with the policeman.'

'Well,' he said, grinning, leaning forward and putting both immaculately clothed elbows on the desk with his smoothly shaved chin in his beautifully manicured hands. 'We met at the Blue Bell, do you know it? No, you wouldn't, *of course*, not your sort of place. I *could* introduce you, if you liked? I know someone who'd be *just* right for you. Lois. Very butch but *refined* with it, right up your street. No? Oh well, never mind. Anyway, his name's Justin, he's 23 – oh God! only 23, what am I *thinking* of? We danced, and talked and went to a quiet little place I know and then went *home*.' He sat back and folded his arms over his chest, a glowing smile on his face with a classic 'don't ask me any more' signal, if I remembered my courses on 'Human body language – how to get your wires crossed without speech'.

'You can't stop there!' I protested. 'What happened? Are you seeing him again?'

'If you think I'm telling *you* any more, you've got another think coming!' he said gleefully. 'You might have slept in my bed but that *doesn't* mean I'm going to tell you my most *intimate* secrets, nosy cow!'

'OK, OK, sorry.' I felt my face break into a grin. Damian had the happy knack of raising my spirits every time. 'But are you seeing him again?'

He grinned from ear to ear. 'Course,' he said, 'he's moving in next week!'

Half an hour later the weekly figures were ready for inspection and I could see at a glance that we were in the doldrums. We were hundreds of pounds off target and, even though I'd been there only a week, I could see that this was going to be a hard nut to crack. How on earth was I going to cut through the apathy, suspicion and the 'you don't know anything you've never worked in my shop' syndrome of long-serving staff faced with a new manager? How was I to raise morale, standards and sales? Gloom and depression hovered over my head like my own private rain cloud. There were a couple of bright spots, though, and I picked up the phone to call Miles at Kensington Place and then Kenny Choudhury at Canon Hill to congratulate them on an excellent week. Not good enough for HQ, I knew, but still bloody brilliant compared with the rest of my lot. And also if they knew how they'd done it so I could crib any good ideas for the others! Miles was encouraging but reluctant to share too much of his expertise over the phone – or, if I read him right, with someone as new as me who might not be around too long. I couldn't blame him. Kenny waffled a lot but didn't really give me much that was useful.

Then I had to pass on the bad news to HQ that we'd missed target again, by a fair old margin, whilst trying to make it sound less of a disaster than it was. In spite of my efforts to keep the call as short as possible, so that I didn't have to be more depressed than I already was, they asked me to hold on. Two verses of 'Raindrops keep falling on your head' later, I heard Lucas's voice, sexy as silk on bare shoulders, and experienced an immediate lift of the spirits as well as other, decidedly more carnal, stirrings.

'Morning, Gillian. Tell me, does anyone ever call you Gill?'

'Not if they want to stay on my good side,' I said, 'and my not-good-side is a bit like Mr Hyde on a bad hair day.'

'Ah,' he said thoughtfully, with a gentle chuckle. 'I'll just stick with the Gillian then, shall I? OK? Good. Well, thanks for your report about Ginger. I've just signed a letter to him confirming his suspension from duty pending an investigation and I want to arrange a hearing as soon as possible. It should be a formality really, on your part, just to confirm your written report and, perhaps, add a few details if we need you to. How do you feel about that?'

'OK. I can't see a problem with that. I'd rather it hadn't happened, of course, especially on my first watch, so to speak. What happens next?'

'Personnel will ask for written statements from everyone concerned and then there'll be a hearing. Ginger will have every opportunity to present his version of events. If a hearing panel decides to dismiss him, you'll have to give him the bad news. One of your jobs as his line manager, I'm afraid, and there's a stunning amount of paperwork that goes with it. There always is for this sort of thing. Ever done this before?'

'Once, quite a long time ago,' I said, 'and the rules have changed since then. It's a lot more complicated now.'

'I'll arrange for a briefing for you as soon as possible, to get you up to date on procedure. It's unfortunate that this should happen so soon after you've joined us. The training on discipline matters comes a bit further down the line so this has caught us all on the hop. Still, it can't be helped. I'll call again when we're a bit clearer on dates. Call if you think of any questions, OK? Try not to worry, it's a bit of an ordeal for everyone but you shouldn't lose sleep over it. If Ginger has really been caught with his hands in the cookie jar he's brought all this on himself, you know. Even if there's a decent explanation, which seems very unlikely, he's still the author of his own troubles. See you soon.' And we both hung up.

See you soon, he'd said. Oh, yes, please!

Damian had been hanging on to my every word, and smirked a bit at the expression he must have read on my face. I filled him in on the conversation and told him to be discreet. I knew him well enough to realise that he could easily fill a vacuum with speculation, better known as gossip, if I didn't tell him what was happening, and things were difficult enough without any added complications. He nodded sagely, crossed his heart with his ring laden, well manicured hand and promised solemnly to keep it to himself.

I found Kylie working her way through a rail of garments all awaiting the magical touch of transforming steam that would turn them from crumpled cast-offs to desirable bargains. She seemed very subdued and clearly had her mind somewhere else. Not her usual self at all.

'Kylie.' I interrupted her reverie and she turned sorrowful eyes on me. Even after such a short acquaintance I knew this wasn't the Kylie all her volunteers and customers knew and loved. 'I've sorted out your ledger. Would you like me to show you how? It might help you in future.' She shrugged but turned off the steamer and followed me in to her office where I spread out the now neatly stapled bundles of papers.

'Are you sure you want to do this now?' I asked. Her attitude was making me uneasy and I wondered if I'd be wasting my time if she wasn't paying attention.

To my consternation she burst into tears again. I'm generally pretty useless in those kinds of situations., and today was no exception. I catch the bug and have an overwhelming desire to bawl my eyes out alongside the one who's sobbing – not very helpful in any circumstances. I'd always wanted to help people ever since I was a little girl and I'd seen an ancient movie about a lady missionary saving children from marauding Chinese armies. I'd had a vision of myself as a ministering angel in a crisp uniform, a nun perhaps or a nurse in Florence Nightingale style, drifting through wards of grateful patients. Just a tad extreme, as I found out when my cat was run over and I had bury the poor little thing, all crushed and bloodied. I'd been hopeless and helpless in the face of that small carnage. Still, it was one of the reasons I'd come to this kind of work – apart from the need to earn a crust, of course. Realising quite early on that my brand of empathy was a little less than helpful, I'd decided instead to help raise the money that paid for the missionaries and the nurses.

Now, in the face of Kylie's distress, I felt my eyes get all scratchy, like they do when tears threaten.

'Oh, yuk!' said the little devil on my shoulder. 'You really are a wuss, aren't you? What did I do to deserve such a soppy heart-bleeder? My mate, Cockroach, got Jake thingy, you know, the one in last week's paper, to look after. He got drunk, flattened a set of bollards with his Norton, tipped two supermarket trolleys in a canal drain and flooded the town centre! That's what I call a devilish success story!'

'Shut up, can't you see I'm busy?' I hissed at him. But he served a purpose; the threatened tears went into reverse.

'Can you tell me what the trouble is, Kylie?' I said as firmly as I could, given my slightly wobbly voice. 'It isn't just about ledgers and stuff, is it?'

She snuffled into a damp hankie. 'No,' she said, 'it's Charlie.' I waited and, after a brief pause, she carried on: ''E ran away on Saturday. We 'ad the cops out and everyfink. They found 'im in an old bus, back o' the garage, fast asleep at four o'clock Sunday morning. Then they came to arrest my Rupe.' Rupe? Her fella, perhaps?

She paused, leaving a long gap, and I let the time pass quietly until she was ready to start again. 'Charlie told the police Rupe 'ad... you know... done fings to 'im.'

For a heart beat the world was a very still place. I even held my breath.

'Oh, Kylie,' I murmured at last, 'I'm so, so sorry. How is Charlie?' My heart went out to a six-year-old child who felt he had no option but to run away from the place where he should have been safe.

"E's at me mum's,' she whispered, her voice wobbling. 'The social worker lady said maybe 'e was best somewhere different for a bit, you know, not where it 'appened. Me mum's really good wiv 'im and he luvs her to bits.'

'Do you want to be with him?' I asked. 'Maybe you'd both feel better if you were together?'

Her voice sank even smaller. "E's angry wiv me,' she said, her voice breaking again. "E says I let it 'appen.' The words hung in the air between us and I had absolutely no idea what to say.

Just then Iris stuck her head around the door and said, in an voice that was appallingly cheerful in the sad air, 'Kylie, can you come and do a refund for the witch please?'

I was guiltily grateful for the interruption and said 'The witch?' in a voice that was, I knew, much too sharp.

Iris blanched and stuttered, 'Er... Mrs Witcherly. We call 'er the witch 'cos she's got a long pointy nose and she wears a poncho thingy instead of a coat – it looks like a cloak like witches in pantomime wear.'

'Right. Fine. Does she know?'

'Lord, I 'ope not!' said Iris chuckling with an odd, grating sort of sound, as though that part of her vocal cords didn't get much use 'We don't mean any 'arm, you know, it's just a bit of fun. She's one of our best customers, she is. In 'ere every other day or so and always spends something. For 'erself, 'er grandchildren or 'er old man.'

'I'll see to Mrs Witcherly's refund,' I said, trying to shield Kylie from prying eyes, and closed the door gently behind me as I steered Iris back towards the shop.

'Good morning, Mrs Witcherly,' I said, greeting an elderly lady who did indeed look like the witch in 'Babes in the Wood'.'I understand you'd like a refund? Can you tell me what the problem is?'

'Hello, dear,' she said, smiling gently and gazing at me with cornflower blue eyes. 'I bought this little dress for my granddaughter last week but it's too small. I've had a good look around and there's nothing here I'd like instead so can I have my money back please?'

Oh, sugar, I thought, why can't it be easy for once? Shops' policy said no refunds unless goods are faulty – exchange instead. No such thing as credit notes either, too complicated for accounts, elderly volunteers and so on and so forth, and too difficult to keep track of. The volunteers knew all this as well as I did and I felt four pairs of curious eyes turn on me, waiting to see what I'd do now. They knew that I knew they gave refunds but I knew they knew I couldn't break the rules, even though I knew they did it when no-one was looking, or I'd never hear the last of it.

'Mrs Witcherly,' I said brightly and with what I hoped was a winning smile. 'Has anyone ever actually told you that our policy says we can't give refunds unless the item is damaged, dirty or sub-standard for some reason?'

'No, dear,' she said, looking a bit startled and widening her eyes even more, 'they haven't.'

'Well,' I said, still smiling and being as chipper as possible, 'they should have', and I felt, rather than heard, the sharp intake of breath from four mouths. 'I'm afraid I can't give you a refund but are you sure the dress is really absolutely, positively alright? Not damaged at all? You've checked it carefully, I assume?'

'Yes, I…' She paused and frowned a little before smiling at me knowingly. She caught on quick, this innocent little lady. 'Now you mention it,' she said, 'the stitching around these little loop button holes is coming away and one of the buttons is missing. Such a shame, dear, it's a lovely little dress – a designer label you know, very expensive. It's damaged, then, isn't it?' I took the dress from her and reached for the refund book. While I took down her details for the record, I launched into my speech.

'Our refund policy has been around a very long time, Mrs Witcherly, and our Head Office is quite strict about it. It's there for a reason, although I'm sure you're not interested in our stuffy internal rules so I won't bore you with the details. Your statutory rights are unaffected, of course.' I smiled at her again. 'Still, I'm pleased to have had the opportunity to tell you about it without causing you any inconvenience on this occasion. It's part of my job to make sure our staff uphold the rules and it would make it very difficult for me if I had to keep nagging them, especially when it inconveniences our best customers, such as yourself.'

Mrs Witcherly listened closely and smiled at me again. She almost applauded. She knew full well that my speech was for the volunteers – bright lady, Mrs Witcherley – and she went along with my little charade like a seasoned campaigner.

'I quite understand, dear,' she said cheerfully. 'I had no idea, of course, and wouldn't dream of embarrassing you by asking again. Unless the item is damaged, of course.' Her voice was all honeyed innocence and we smiled at each other. All those smiles wouldn't have looked out of place on a training video called 'How to be civilized while telling a customer to go away and stop bothering you'. Still, I'd made my point and so had she. I felt sure that every item she tried to claim a refund on in future would be 'damaged', but we'd cope with that little problem another time – and there would be another time.

I escorted Mrs Witcherly to the door and we parted with a few more mutually understanding smiles from the opposite sides of our respective positions. When I turned around, four pairs of eyes belonging to the volunteers were still fixed on me and so were three more – customers who'd witnesses our thespian interlude. There was spontaneous applause and I took a little bow. Jenny said, 'Luv a duck, I never thought you'd get around that! Never seen anything like it. We'll 'ave to watch it now, girls, this's a live one and no mistake!' And they all laughed.

''Ere,' said one of the customers, holding up a rather smart cream silk shirt. 'Have you got this in a blue size 16?'

I fled, leaving the volunteers to get out of that one.

Back in Kylie's office, I found that she'd dried her eyes while I'd been away and I explained what had happened with Mrs Witcherly. She listened and I suggested she could do the same sort of thing, if she practised a bit. After all, every pound she paid out in refunds reduced the sales total for that day and she had targets to meet. I could see that her heart wasn't in it, though.

'Would you like to talk with someone, Kylie?' I asked gently. 'Someone who'll listen and not make judgements, someone who isn't involved?' She looked at me from huge pools of pain.

'Can't see 'ow that'd 'elp,' she said.

'It can, I promise. Let me find someone? Leave it to me.'

She nodded half-heartedly. I suggested that she took an early lunch break and get some fresh air. She struck a figure of solitary pathos as she wandered away from the back door, avoiding contact with her volunteers in the shop, and disappeared around the corner.

Back in the office Damian was waiting for me, almost hopping around in his excitement.

'You'll *never* guess!' he said. 'Go on, then, try!'

I pantomimed a moment of deep thought, finger under my chin, eyes to the ceiling.

'Haven't a clue,' I said, 'you'll have to tell me.'

'Hell's bells,' he spluttered 'you're no fun!'

'Tell me about it,' said the little devil on my shoulder in meaningful sarcasm.

'Lucas Barrington rang!' He paused for effect. My puzzlement must have shown. '*We* ring *him*,' he explained, '*he* doesn't ring *us*! And this is the *second* call today! He thinks he's centre stage at the top table usually, he doesn't normally bother with us mere *mortals*!' I couldn't help smiling at Damian's mixed metaphors and he tutted at me. 'You *know* what I mean. Right hand of *God* and all that. He says you're to phone him *back*.'

'OK,' I said, moving over to my desk and picking up the phone. I swear Damian's ears tilted forwards as his eyes stayed glued to my face.

Lucas answered after the third ring and my fingertips tingled at the sound of his voice.

'Hello, it's Gillian,' I said, as composed as possible in the circumstances.

'Thanks for calling back so promptly,' he said, his voice like warm honey. 'It's about the investigation. We've fixed Monday morning next week for most of the interviews and I thought I'd check that you were free, before we send out confirmation letters. I'd like you here at eleven.' No 'if you can' enquiry, I noticed. Very much the head honcho.

'Yes, that shouldn't be a problem.' Still, I was puzzled that he should call me to ask. This was a three-line whip, after all, and I'd expected to drop everything else, short of plague and famine, to be where I was supposed to be at the time I was supposed to be there.

'It's quite a long trip,' he said, 'to HQ, I mean. We'll lay on coffee and sandwiches but…' he hesitated for the space of a heart beat '…I wondered if you'd mind having a working lunch so that I could run through the rest of the disciplinary procedure with you, before the hearing? Since Jean is away and this is urgent, we need to be sure you're properly briefed. We can't afford any technical hitches, after all.'

'That sounds like a good idea,' I said, trying to keep that annoying squeak, the one that appears when I get anxious or excited, out of my voice. I couldn't help wondering why he wanted to do the briefing; I felt sure that someone in Personnel would have done it just as well. 'I'll be there.'

'Good,' he said, 'I'll look forward to it.' And he put the phone down abruptly.

'What did he *say*?' Damian was almost beside himself. It struck me that, for such an outwardly suave and sophisticated social animal, Damian was really just a big kid when it came down to it.

'Training, Damian,' I said. 'While Jean is away, Mr Barrington is my mentor. He can't afford to have another disaster on this patch and too many area managers have come unstuck here already. Another would be just too much. What with this Ginger business, he's determined to make sure that nothing goes wrong. He wants to make sure I don't up and leave like the others so he's lending a bit of extra support and training this time. That's all.'

Damian looked doubtful but the story had a ring of truth to it – it might have been true, for all I knew – and the bubble of his curiosity gradually deflated.

'Oh well,' he said, 'one can always hope for a little *excitement*.' He bent his head over the file in front of him again. I'll go along with that, I thought.

We had a quiet but depressing hour while I studied the sales figures that Damian had collected that morning. We were way off target and I hoped, but didn't really expect, to be inspired into some new and magical strategy that would increase our sales by 100 per cent by the end of the month and deliver two dozen new volunteers as well. Fat chance! Still, hope springs eternal, as they say, and I gave myself a headache trying to find some inspiration in the columns of figures.

After a while a little germ of an idea began to tickle at the back of my mind. I picked up the phone and dialled Kensington Place. 'Hello Miles, I'm going to be a bit cheeky here and ask for your help.'

'Go ahead,' he said, albeit with a cautious tone.

'Well, our sales are disastrous, we don't have enough volunteers and Mr Barrington is going to be on my case if I don't do something soon. Most of the other shops don't have enough volunteers or sales skills, they don't know what to do about it, they aren't listening, or they don't care. I'm new and haven't proved myself yet. They're waiting for me to fall flat on my face and it's going to take a bit longer than a week to win any confidence at all. But you've been here for a while and they all know you.' It came out in a rush, then I paused. There was silence for a moment.

'Yes,' he said, guardedly, 'that's all true.'

'Will you work with me on a strategy for recruitment and training? I can provide all the materials we need and do the design work but I'd like you to front it. You know, the PR, presentations and general up-front part at a staff meeting. We need a proper on-going programme, working in the shops to do the whole thing very hands-on in the real world, not some remote classroom that has no resemblance to life at all. I don't need an answer now, but I'd like you to say you'll think about it.'

There was another long pause and I could almost hear his brain sorting it through.

'Well, I don't want my shop to suffer. If I'm doing that I can't do all the things that need doing here.' Reasonable, but depressing. I'd hoped for just a bit more... well, co-operation.

'It's exactly because of all the things you do, and the way you do them, that I want you for this project. Your shop is the best-looking on the patch and, size for size, it delivers more sales per square metre than any of the others. Whatever it is you're doing, the others need to do too.'

'Well... can I think about it for a while?'

'Of course, like I said. I'll find you some help in your shop so your volunteers and sales don't suffer. You'll stay in charge but a good deputy should give you the time we need on this project as well.'

'Right. OK. If you can do that then I'll give it some serious thought. Will we see you soon?'

'I was planning to do a whistlestop tour tomorrow. I haven't been to all the shops on the patch yet and I can call in on you on the way. Shall I call in at around mid-morning?'

'That would be fine. We have Margaret's fruit cake tomorrow!'

Next it was time to see how Kylie was doing but before I went to find her I checked my address book and made a couple of calls. Downstairs the shop was busy and Marjorie was tidying rails of clothes that somehow still managed to look like a badly organised boot sale no matter how much she tweaked and twisted. It's an art, I thought, presentation and shop dressing, definitely an art. And there weren't enough artists in my shops to go around.

Kylie was at the steamer again, her expression no less woebegone than before. I slipped a piece of paper into her hand. She looked at the name and telephone number of the person I thought would be able to help her and her family, then at me. I nodded and she slipped the note into her pocket. There wasn't much to be said so I offered her a Minstrel and she took a handful. Chocolate is a great soother, I find, and although not as good as sex, it comes a pretty close second in my opinion. Her appetite was OK anyway, which was encouraging, and I left her munching as I went through to the shop floor.

By this time the volunteers were all gathered around the till gossiping, while three or four customers rooted through the displays. Voices were low but I could hear that they were talking about Kylie's predicament. I joined them and they fell silent. As quietly as I could I said, 'Even low voices carry, ladies. The shop floor isn't the place for chatter about someone's personal life. Please be more careful.'

The atmosphere chilled. One of the perks of being a volunteer was the increase in gossip potential over normal life and they didn't like my intervention. But at that moment, I didn't really care. Kylie was hurting, I knew what that felt like, and I didn't want a difficult situation made worse. The ladies shuffled off in different directions and shot me looks with daggers in them.

'Are you the manager, ducks?' a customer asked.

'One of them,' I said. 'How can I help you?'

'This sweater. Have you got it in blue?' I could hear the phone ringing upstairs in the office. I summoned a smile for the customer and resisted the temptation to give a totally inappropriate answer that would have sent her scurrying for cover with her ears aflame. I explained as carefully, clearly and politely as I could that our stock was good quality and nearly new, but that it was donated to us by people who didn't want it any more. That we had no idea what would be inside any of the sacks we opened and had no influence over what people gave us.

He listened with rapt attention. I explained that our goods didn't come from a wholesaler and we couldn't pick up the phone to ask for whatever we needed. As I finished he said, 'So you don't have it in blue, then?'

'No, sir, I'm afraid we don't.' And smiled. What else can you do?

'Gillian! Gillian! Where are you?' There was a note of panic, almost hysteria in Damian's voice and I heard his footfalls loud on the stairs. I bolted.

'What's wrong?' I said, as we almost collided in the corridor outside Kylie's office.

'It's Gordon,' he panted, 'the shop's been demolished by a runaway *lorry*! It came down the hill to the lights and didn't *stop*. It came straight over the *junction* and through the plate glass window!' He stopped for breath. For a moment I couldn't believe what he'd said. Surely it was just a bad joke. It wasn't April Fool's Day, was it? No, it wasn't. Nor was it a bad joke.

'Is anyone hurt? Is everyone safe?' I asked.

Damian took a deep breath to steady himself and went on. 'Amazingly, no and yes. There were no *customers* in the front part of the shop and the volunteer at the till saw the thing *coming* and got out of the way in time. Thank *God* Joan wasn't at the till, she's *blind* as a bat and *wouldn't* have seen it and even if she *had*, her arthritis wouldn't have let her jump out the way! The truck stopped *halfway* into the shop so the *back* part is OK and so is the stock room. Gordon says there's a *hole* in the floor and the truck looks likely to fall into the *basement*!'

I said a little prayer of thanks that no-one was hurt as Damian and I raced up the stairs where I quickly gathered my stuff and

130

barked instructions. 'Damian, be an angel, will you, and call Malcolm at HQ. He's really going to freak but he'll need to arrange… whatever it is he has to arrange. Tell him I'll call him when I've seen for myself what's going on. Ring the other shops, they should know that no-one's been hurt as soon as they hear there's been an accident otherwise they'll all go bonkers. I'll call you before you finish for the day, to give you an update. Byeeeeeee…' And I was gone.

Chilton Street looked like a demolition site. Which it was, I suppose. I had to park the car some distance away because the police had shut off the whole road. Walking down the hill I could see the mayhem long before I was close. There were two fire appliances, three police cars and an ambulance, the sight of which made my heart sink. Had someone been hurt after all?

Gordon and Belinda were standing across the road, looking like human sheepdogs as they circled around their small band of volunteers. They were all dusty and clearly very shaken but apparently unhurt. I just hoped they hadn't left one of their number in the rubble.

'Hello, Gordon,' I said, 'I'm Gillian and this isn't quite the way I'd hoped to meet you. Is everyone accounted for and are you all alright?'

'No, we're not bloody well alright!' he yelled at me, his neck stretched out like a tortoise and his face thrust close to mine. 'We could have been maimed, killed, annihilated, flattened! We're lucky to be alive! Of course we're not alright! What a damned stupid thing to say!'

I stepped back a pace at the onslaught, startled by the strength of his reaction. Still, under the circumstances, it was understandable, I suppose. Jean had told me that Gordon was a bit crusty and was feared by all on his local Residents' Association, School Board and Neighbourhood Watch. Just what I needed, a sergeant major activist!

'Sorry,' I said, 'I didn't mean to be insensitive. Look, why don't you take everyone to that little place over the road and buy them large mugs of tea.' I reached for my wallet and gave him more than enough cash for several large mugs of tea each – and half a dozen doughnuts as well, if they wanted them. 'I'll have a word with the police.' And I bolted. I'd done a lot of that today.

There was one fireman standing looking on from a distance, catching his breath by the look of him, as he wiped his forehead with a large, dirty handkerchief. I showed him my ID and asked what was happening.

'Not a lot, love, at present. I know you, don't I?' I looked at him a bit more closely and recognised one of the men who'd helped us during the flood at Lupin Lane. 'Course, I know, you're that lady wot called us to the other shop when the water came through the ceiling! Well, this one's a bit more exciting but you didn't need to go to these lengths to see me again, you know... another burst pipe would have done the trick, even a cat up a tree!' He chortled at his own humour. True, he looked quite striking in his uniform and had an open, friendly sort of face, but I couldn't quite imagine anyone going to any great lengths to meet him again. Still, every man thinks he's God's gift so this one's belief in himself wasn't surprising. I smiled. He looked pleased, and continued. 'The lorry's well and truly jammed, one wheel's gone through the floor, at the front. We'll 'ave to use jacks to make sure the 'ole shop front don't come down when we shift it. Going to take a long time to put this right, love!' Then he sauntered off to re-join the crew.

I retreated across the road and rejoined Gordon and his staff in the tea shop, several of whom were obviously in shock even though the ambulance crews had cleared them all in physical terms. Gordon was a bit calmer, for which I was grateful since I wasn't feeling particularly robust myself. We arranged for the volunteers to get home safely, calling friends and relatives who could make sure there was someone to take care of them when they got there. My mobile's battery was almost flat by the time we finished but at least I was using it indoors, sitting down and over a soft landing (my lap). All in accordance with the rules. Malcolm might moan about the size of the phone bill but at least I was conforming with instructions on 'Mobile phones, care and use of'.

Eventually I got back to the car, took my mobile out of my bag for one last call and stared at it for a good ten minutes trying to decide how to tell Malcolm what had happened. And Lucas! What on earth was I to say to Lucas?

-8-
On Tour

This was the day of the grand progress. Not quite in the style of kings and queens of old, but still the day I planned to visit as many shops as possible, and especially those I hadn't been to even once yet. Actually, that meant half the patch. I knew Bell Lane pretty well by now and I'd already visited Kensington Place, Lupin Lane and Broad Barrow, and Chilton Street had been demolished yesterday, but that still left five waiting for the first visit. I intended to spend some time at Broad Barrow to see how Yusfef and his lads were doing, so it looked as though it would shape up to quite a long day.

I wanted to meet the managers on their own territory, so to speak, and invite them to our first team meeting personally. So much better than a phone call, or asking Damian to do it. The last thing I needed was to have them all think I was the arrogant sort, summoning them to my presence like some big cheese. Plus there'd be much less scope for 'Oh, I thought it was next week' or 'Your message didn't get to me' later. The first team meeting was important and everyone should be there – no excuses!

Hopefully I'd also find something for Gordon and Belinda as I was doing the rounds. I couldn't leave them idle, it was too expensive and I had an idea that the dreaded word 'redundant' might rear its ugly head if I couldn't sort something out soon. Heaven only knew how long it was going to take to put Chilton Street back together again – certainly far too long to just sit back and hope everything would be OK. When the emergency services said it was safe I'd have to go in with the insurance assessor but that wasn't likely to be for at least some days yet. I needed some sort of proposal for HQ soon.

Anyway, first stop Lupin Lane and Shona. She was setting up the till for the day when I arrived, and I suggested that a cup of tea would be nice – get the day off to a good start and all that. She looked a bit surprised when I dug around the little kitchen for mugs, tea and milk and produced a pack of chocolate biscuits from the bottom of my 'everything but the kitchen sink' bag. By the time the tea was ready Fred and Margaret had arrived. We chatted for a while and did Shona's version of a 'guided' while she tip-toed around me, nervously pointing out all the plus points in her shop – the clean windows, the shelves free from dust, all the right customer information leaflets in the dispensers – and tried to make sure I was too distracted to take a close look at the prices on the tickets or the way she presented stock on the shop floor.

Charity shop managers are all powerful creatures in their own little empires. They generally decide what goes on sale, what the asking price will be and, within reason, how a sales floor is arranged. A good one can turn a shop into a gold mine, raising a fortune whilst being a PR blessing for the charity they work for. Some of them, however, let the power go to their heads and become proper little despots. Some have the design sense of a squirrel, no real idea of the value of the goods they handle and can lose a sure-fire sale every hour of the day – every minute, sometimes! We all knew a manager who'd sold a pair of Jimmy Choos for £2.50, a lovely piece of crystal for 50p or a customer's coat while she was trying on a dress in the changing room. Some of those stories are apocryphal and even make the national dailies, becoming part of the folklore of retail. Not good for the charity's image, though – or bank balance.

Shona wasn't quite like that, but I soon began to see that there was a lot that could be improved here. The shop was close to an art college and the students there were her biggest customer group: not much money, freed from parental constraint and keen to be seen as more imaginative and outrageous than anyone else, they bought retro and contemporary with equal relish and wore it with panache. Almost every day, within ten minutes of the shop opening, there were a couple of groups of three or four students twitching stuff along the rails, chattering loudly about Friday's party and how they needed stuff to make over for the fashion show at the end of term. Shona didn't seem to notice, she just seemed to stand behind the counter with a vacant expression on her face most of the time. Get out there, I was pleading silently, show 'em the 70s' retro stuff in the corner and, good grief, what's it doing stuck over there in the corner anyway? I took a deep breath. Don't have a heart attack, girl, I mentally shook a finger at myself, this is just a fact-finding tour, don't go off half-cocked until you're sure the gun is pointed in the right direction!

Fred picked up the tour when Shona lost heart and continued to show me around the place. I asked him about himself and he said he'd been in the army. He told me a bit about his time in Suez in the 50s, where he'd done National Service and ended up with a bullet in his back and only half his hearing. He was one of those who proved there was no such thing as an average volunteer, that's for sure.

While we were busy Margaret got stuck in to the bags of donations that people had brought in the day before and within a very short space of time she had a couple of dozen hangers full of 'new' stock ready for steam-pressing and pricing. All of a sudden, she startled us all with a yell that nearly curdled my blood and Fred almost fell off his step ladder.

'Come and look at this!' she squeakled. 'It's… it's… Oh, my goodness!' And she disappeared back into the stock room. We galloped after her and found her standing next to a large blue plastic sack in the middle of the stock room floor. Margaret opened the neck of the bag and we all peered inside. Shona gasped. Fred choked and then started to laugh. Margaret glared at him and I didn't quite know whether to giggle with Fred or go all po-faced like Margaret. Inside the bag was a jumbled collection of leather and I lifted out, in turn, an eight-tailed whip, a pair of extremely shiny, thigh-length boots with heels as thin as my little finger and as long as a new pencil, a stretchy rubber catsuit, two pairs of handcuffs and a black mask with slanting eye holes and cats' ears.

We gazed at the collection.

'Blimey!' said Fred

'Heavens!' cooed Margaret

'Heaven has nothing to do with this,' said Shona caustically. 'Hell's bells, more like.'

'What do we do with it?' Fred asked. 'We can't sell this lot, not in a charity shop.' He paused. 'Can we?'

'Not really, Fred,' I said, losing the battle and laughing out loud.

'Although I'm sure we could ask a good price for this lot. It's almost new and it's good quality too.'

Three pairs of eyes turned on me and I could almost hear three minds thinking, 'How does *she* know?' Fred smirked. Margaret looked startled. Shona sniffed.

'Unfortunately,' I said, 'we can only throw it away. It can't even go in the recycling. I can just imagine what Cyril's lads would say if they found this lot when they were sorting!'

Shona sniffed again. 'Cyril's got enough ideas as it is,' she said, 'he doesn't need any more.' On the basis of my one and only encounter with Cyril, I agreed with her but thought it best not to comment.

'Seems a shame, though,' said Fred.

'Don't you go getting ideas, Fred,' said Margaret, 'not at your age, it ain't seemly. Or healthy.'

'Might be fun to try though,' said Fred, grinning at her.

'I think it might be a good idea if I take this to the local authority tip,' I said, 'and just get them off the premises. Would that be alright with you, Shona?'

'Might be best,' she agreed, 'we sometimes get foxes rooting through our rubbish bin at night. I'd hate to find this lot all over the alley way at the back in the morning.' I couldn't help smiling at the thought of the neighbours having a field day with that little source of gossip.

Shona and I went to the office and she found her 'Take away' book. Shona carefully recorded the items we'd found, noting each item in great detail with a certain intensity, I thought. I signed the book and wrote 'To local tip' next to my signature – there for posterity and all Shona's other volunteers to see and speculate over. Through the open door I could see that Margaret had tied up the neck of the sack and left it for me to pick up on my way out.

I wasn't there long after that, but couldn't help noticing that Shona and her crew put quite a creditable amount through the till, thanks mostly to the students. Puzzling, really, that that morning could be so productive yet the sales figures Shona reported every week were only ever moderate. I could see that the potential was even better if only she took the bait the students offered and put herself out a bit instead of just standing there like a suet pudding.

Still, I'd think it all through later. Now it was time to move on, taking my precious cargo of Miss Whiplash gear with me.

Next stop was Broad Barrow and Brigid. Finding a parking space was a nightmare, as usual, but it was only a half-mile walk in the pouring rain so why complain? The shop was as higgledy-piggledy as usual but somehow managed to be fascinating and compelling for all that. There was a university cap and gown on a model in the window (university? At Broad Barrow?) a huge bed quilt hanging on one wall and a kiddies' plastic paddling pool leaning drunkenly up against the side of the counter. Bit early in the year to sell that, I thought, but still, you can never tell. The counter top was askew, the cable from the till was trailing along the floor and it looked as though several of the shelves were only precariously fastened to the walls. All together an H&S nightmare but there were people everywhere and a queue waiting to pay for purchases. Brigid was, as ever, looking harassed.

"Morning, Brigid,' I said brightly, 'how are you today?'

'My back aches from carrying all these bags down the stairs,' she grumbled 'Veyra is having hysterics and Cyril's just rung to say he can't collect our rags today. What am I going to do? We're running out of space!' I managed to keep a smile pinned to my face, but it wasn't easy. I was beginning to realise that Brigid was the sort of person to see hazards in heaven.

'We'll soon fix all that,' I said, overly cheerful and hoping I sounded more positive than I felt. 'Are Yusuf's repairs all finished?' She brightened a little – just a tad and you had to be quick to catch it.

'He's done us proud,' she said, actually smiling. 'He put in a whole door, not just a window, and we can get out into the yard now. We can sit out when the weather's good, when we get the chance for a break, you know. It hasn't been lately, of course, but we're hopeful.' I smiled, and she went on, encouraged: 'It was an ill wind, when the wall came down.'

What? The wall came down? What wall?

'What? The wall came down? What wall?' I said aloud.

'Well, yes. Didn't I tell you? No, course not, you were too busy for a chat when you called on Friday.' Ouch! That put me firmly in my place, didn't it? 'When Yusuf came to do that window he pulled out the old frame and a huge chunk of wall came with it! The hole was so big he decided he might as well put in a door. It's quite safe, it's got two locks and he even put a security chain on the back so that we could leave it open for a bit for air without any weirdos trying to get in uninvited. Come and look'

I followed her down into the stock room. Brigid showed me Yusuf's handy work and I had to admit, he'd made a good job of it. Not that I'm a builder, mind, but I couldn't see any trace of an RSJ over the door and found my eyes wandering upwards and wondering what was holding up the weight of the other three floors above us. Oh, Lord!

Brigid seemed really pleased though, and the basement was certainly a nicer place to be because of the light and air the door let in. Mind you, everything's relative, isn't it? It was still pretty dismal but it was better than before and Brigid was as cheerful as Brigid was, I guessed, ever likely to be. I made a mental note to ask Yusuf about the apparent lack of an RSJ the next time I saw him. Would that be soon enough? Should I do something sooner?

Admiration all exhausted, one of the volunteers helped me sort out the space problem and we spent the next fifteen minutes re-packing rag bags in the store so that they were neatly stacked instead of randomly and artistically dishevelled. Brother, were some of those bags heavy! Of course, several split open and the contents had to be re-packed. Dirty work, but someone had to do it and, hey, who said life was going to be easy? I'd been a Girl Guide, I was supposed to be prepared for anything, wasn't I? Well, I was prepared. But there's a world of difference between being prepared and actually doing for yourself what you were prepared for! I'd prefer to stay with the preparation, thanks, –the actual doing was bloody hard work!

Then I made sure that the cable from the till wasn't going to bring anyone crashing to the floor or electrocute someone. It meant going up a step ladder to tack it to the wall, which was a bit of a drag. My last excursion up a ladder had resulted in severe shock and the remedial intake of several thousand calories of comfort eating, which hadn't done my dress size any good at all. Brigid seemed quite pleased, in a distracted sort of way, with my efforts, which saw some of her problems resolved. I thought I'd earned back the Brownie points I'd lost by not showing up on Friday.

She introduced me to Veyra who was in charge of the till that morning. Veyra had a nice line in sales chatter, I had to give her credit for that, in a sort of patois of local slang, an accent I couldn't place and a liberal seasoning of words that could only have come from too much time watching continental porn channels on TV. That was one explanation, anyway, and the most innocent. I decide not to venture down any other road on that one, I had no idea what I'd find! I raised an eyebrow at Brigid, who shrugged in an apologetic kind of way, and said, 'I've tried to tell her she should be more careful about what she says on the shop floor, but she learnt her English off the TV mostly, and thinks everything she hears is OK. Mind you, most of the customers here are in the same boat and those that notice don't seem to care.'

I couldn't help thinking that she was probably right. Caroline was a feature that everyone at Broad Barrow seemed to take for granted so Veyra probably seemed quite normal. No-one seemed to turn a hair, as far as I could tell. A really fine example of equal opportunities, this shop.

''Ello, Mrs Manager lady,' Veyra said, shaking my hand so vigorously it rattled my teeth, 'is mighty fine to meet you. This lady here Brigid damn fine lady too, I tell you. Fucking good manager. Bloody good friend. You bin working on that Yusuf man too, I see. Whoreson need someone like you stand on his tail, bloody gangster him.' She turned her attention back to the till and a customer, leaving me with my mouth half open, not knowing quite what to say or do next.

'You find damn fine bargain, lady,' she congratulated the customer with a warm smile and exaggerated facial expressions, folding a rather large, wool coat and reaching for a carrier bag.

'Could be better fine damn bargain,' said the customer. 'You give me discount – bloody hell, I earn it, all damn money I spend here!'

'What?' shrieked Veyra, shock and horror on her face. 'You tink dis bleedin' street market? You get fine wool coat for £10 instead £300 new! What you tink we are – charity?' And the customer handed over a £10 note, glowering crossly, with neither of them recognising the irony of what Veyra had said. I hid a smile. The customer left, muttering under her breath something about heartless people with no generosity in their souls, mixed with a few more expletives.

Veyra looked at me with a pained expression on her face and said, 'We bloody give it away, maybe? Den dey ask for delivery, you bet! Some damn folk never satisfied!'

Phew! I thought. 'I like her!' said the little devil on my shoulder. 'If I needed a new home any time I could make a lot out of that one. Much more rewarding than you.' Oh, go boil your head! I fired back at him.

Just then an idea teased me. Is it just possible, I wondered, that Brigid might be able to handle a tiny bit more originality on top of all this lot? Would she notice one more, when she seemed to have a whole family of odd-balls already?

'Brigid,' I began, hoping she wouldn't notice my slight hesitation. Thoughtfulness, I could have called it, if someone had commented and if I was quick-witted enough. 'Your basement stock room and shortage of volunteers must give you some problems at times, don't they?'

'Oh, yes,' she said, 'I can't be in two places at once and wherever I am I seem to be needed somewhere else. It's very tiring and those stairs are a nightmare.'

'I might just be able to help you,' I said brightly. 'You've heard about Chilton Street, I suppose?'

'Ooooh, yes!' she breathed, all shock and motherly concern. 'Someone could have been killed, you know.' There was a certain relish in her tone of voice. Was she disappointed they weren't, I wondered, or did she think the lorry was an assassination attempt that had failed?

'It's a bit of a mess, I'll grant you,' I said, 'but everyone's fine, thank goodness, no casualties except Gordon's window dummies. Gave the firemen quite a shock, they did, with legs and arms sticking out of the rubble.' Brigid tried to look thoroughly shocked at my attempted levity. 'Well,' I ploughed on anyway, 'Belinda needs to get back to work while we decide what to do at Chilton Street, and you need help. Could you work together, do you think? She could come here on loan, so to speak, if I can persuade HQ.'

Brigid looked stunned. 'She's…' She stopped. 'She's… Gordon's assistant.' I nodded. 'She's... a... she's sort of... strange!' Brigid stopped, confused and anxious, almost wringing her hands. I struggled not to smile. This shop had a collection of odd folks, and Brigid said Belinda was strange? Ah, well, there's no accounting for other people's perceptions, I thought.

'She takes her hobby very seriously, that's true. She also works hard, is very conscientious and you need the extra pair of hands. Think about it, will you, and let me know?'

'Oh, no,' she said, 'that's not necessary really. I'm sure we'll get used to her little ways and you're right, an extra pair of hands would be useful.'

She didn't sound quite convinced somehow, but carried on gamely anyway. 'Shall I phone her about when she can start?' Problem solved, I thought.

'Really?' said the little devil on my shoulder. 'You're putting all your fruits in the same basket, you know, should be interesting to see what happens if a touch of rot sets in and they ferment. Ha, ha!'

Push off! I thought, with the uneasy feeling that he might be right. Still, we'd face that when we came to it. Shona and I agreed a strategy for bringing Belinda in, what her role would be and how the two of them would introduce the changes to the volunteers. All I had to do was think of a way of convincing HQ that hanging on to Belinda at Broad Barrow made economic sense.

Then it was time to move on. My next stop was Canon Row and Kenny Choudhray, a shop I'd had no occasion to visit and a Manager I hadn't even spoken with yet. When I arrived, I found Kenny sitting in an armchair in the stock room, feet up on a donation sack and coffee mug in hand. He greeted me like a long lost friend.

'My goodness, from what the others told me I thought you must have at least two heads!'

Zero for diplomacy, Kenny, I thought, just before it occurred to me to think: good grief, what are they saying about me? Still, I wasn't in this as a popularity test. 'Just as well, really,' said the little devil on my shoulder and I mentally kicked him where I hoped it would hurt.

'Coffee?' said Kenny, rising lazily to his feet. I could see that he thought quite a lot of himself, our Kenny. He was very smartly dressed – too smartly for the physical job he had to do around the shop, really – in pressed black jeans, white shirt and beautifully embroidered satin waistcoat. Unlike Damian's sartorial and expensive elegance, however, Kenny's wardrobe was market, rather than designer, chic.

'Thanks,' I said, 'I take sugar but you can hold the arsenic, thanks.'

He looked startled, then sheepish, then he laughed. I couldn't tell if it was genuine good humour or something else, he wasn't easy to read, our Kenny, but I was sure I'd get the measure of him in time. He made the coffee while I looked around his shop, then we did a tour, which didn't take long since it was quite small. He seemed genuinely proud of the way he'd arranged everything to make the most of the small space, and I had to confess, it was bright, colourful and packed with good stock. It was, however, also chaotic and dirty. There were cobwebs in every corner, the shelves carried the dust of ages (comparisons with Damian and our office came into my head) and the staff kitchen and lavatory were a positive health hazard. I decided that, if I survived this visit, I might be well advised not to have anything to eat or drink at Canon Row in future, much less use the loo.

Kenny told me what a loyal and trustworthy band of volunteers he had. How he never had any difficulty finding enough of the right people to help him. How they worked hard and were always cheerful. Sounded absolutely wonderful and I wondered how he did it till he began introducing me to his crew. Neema was his mother, Lucy was his sister and Sunita and Samir were his cousins, although I gathered that 'cousin' was a loose interpretation of a rather more distant family tie than I would normally use. Kenny proudly told me that his aunts, cousins and sisters were almost all of his volunteer force although there were some neighbours as well. Thirty-seven in total, some of whom only came to work occasionally and some who specialised in filling gaps when others were sick or on holiday. Children were looked after by the non-duty members of the group. It all seemed splendidly well arranged but I felt decidedly uneasy. Eggs and baskets sprang to mind. Supposing Kenny resigned? Would we lose every single volunteer as well?

Still, they were all very welcoming. Kenny opened his weekly sales ledger to me and told me all about his plans for improving the turnover – which was pretty dismal compared with what it had been two years ago, before he'd taken over. His ideas seemed good though, so I made encouraging noises. As we sat in his little office area in an alcove next to the noisome bathroom, he became very serious and sat forward in his chair, hands clasped together on his knees, and frowned into my eyes.

'I have a problem, Gillian,' he said, 'and I hope you can help me.' I braced myself. 'There is a thief.'

Oh, boy, this was so depressing! Less than two weeks into the job, with one member of my team already suspended for 'irregularities' (as they carefully phrased it) in stock handling procedures, and now there might be another awful situation to handle. 'Beam me up, Scotty' I thought and immediately thought of Belinda. She'd be proud of me!

'Go on, Kenny, I'm listening, but please be careful of your words. It's a serious thing, to accuse someone of theft.'

'I know. I've seen him, you know. A small child, he is, no more than high to my waist hardly.' Now I was puzzled, this wasn't quite what I was expecting. 'He prises open the lid of our waste skip, in the yard at the back, climbs inside and throws out everything until he finds something he wants. Then he leaps out and runs away with it! Very quick! There is another child, a small girl, with him. She just stands and watches from a safe distance. Once I caught him but he kicked my ankles and bit my wrist and I let him go in my pain. The girl ran while we struggled and I didn't see where she went. What are we to do, Gillian?' His big, dark eyes looked at me pleading, as though he had the biggest problem in the world to solve and only I had the solution that he'd been searching for.

And then he capped it. 'His mother has written to me. She is going to sue.'

Sue? Who? Why? The world's gone mad, I thought. Kenny handed me a scruffy envelope that looked like something out of a child's writing set, the sort that costs 50p from a street stall. Inside was a piece of lined paper that had been torn from a reporter's ring-bound notebook. It read:

*Dere sir. My kid cum home yisterdy wif a cut hand. It was
bleedin bad. He said your stuff dun it when he wus in your
skip. Its dangerus. He cude have bin hurt bad and its your falt.
My sister says I cude su you and I will, yu'll see.
Lillian Smith*

There was no address. I didn't know whether to laugh or weep.
Kenny was looking at me with a sorrowful, watery-eyed look .

'Any idea where this came from, Kenny?' I asked.

'I have not seen where the little bastard goes,' he said, without
any apparent enmity in his voice at the description, 'but he is a
small child of no more than eight years. He must live close by, you
think?'

'Well, it can't be a million miles, I suppose. Still, I don't think we
need to worry, Kenny, I suspect this isn't going to come to much. It
might be a good idea to see whether we can find him, though. I
think you should keep a close eye on the skip. Have someone
working by the stock room window all the time, or at least as much
as you can, and when you see him again, follow him when he legs
it. He can't be living that far away and if you can get close enough,
you know, a street or a block of flats or something, that would be
helpful. In the meantime I'll get Damain to make up a sign for the
skip. A warning of some kind. It probably won't make a ha'porth
of difference but we have to try.' I glanced at the letter again. 'Not
that it'll do much good here,' I said. 'I doubt whether this little tike
can read!'

'Tike?' said Kenny. 'What is tike?'

'Sorry, Kenny, tike is a northern expression, from Yorkshire, I
think – it means naughty child, roughly anyway.'

'Mmm,' he said thoughtfully, head slightly tilted to one side. 'I
think this one is a stupid little bastard tike.'

'Probably,' I said, 'but we shouldn't say so out loud, Kenny, it's
bad for public relations.' He looked sceptical but kept his own
counsel. He was still doleful when I left but I promised to keep in
touch and told him again to call me as soon as he had some news
to report. I made my way back to the car hoping that a cut hand
would be a good deterrent and that we'd seen the last of Ms Smith's
little boy.

Next stop: Kensington Place and Miles – just in time for lunch. The place was humming, as usual, with several volunteers involved in their Monday routine. Miles initiated me. Every Monday, he told me, he and his crew did a shop-wide sweep starting at the door and working their way around the shop, checking for problems such as loose brackets and wall bars, damaged stock, shortages in their general supplies and stationary and the myriad details that make all the difference between smooth running and chaos. It was also the day when unsold stock was removed from the shelves and rails and brought back into the stock room for disposal.

'What do you do with all this stuff, Miles?' I asked. There seemed to be piles of clothes, and boxes full of books, old vinyl records and assorted bric-a-brac.

'It goes to the ragman,' he said, 'which seems a shame because most of it's in good condition, it just hasn't sold.'

'Have you thought of having a sale rail?' I asked. 'Cut the price of each item in half and have sale day?'

'Well, yes,' he said, 'but Jean said customers would make a beeline for the sale stuff and ignore everything else, so it would be counterproductive. She didn't like us doing it and told us not to. Several of us thought it was a good idea but she can be very... determined.'

'She has a point,' I said hastily. Mustn't split the ranks, I thought, even if one of the ranks has already split to go on holiday, leaving the other one to face the Zulus all alone. 'Still, there are always ways around that. One way is to put the sale stuff right at the back of the shop so your customers have to walk through all the other lovely bargains before they get to it. They might be diverted and tempted to something else on the way, you see. Another is to put out sale goods on only one or two days a week, and on different days. That way customers come in looking for your so-called sale, and when they discover there isn't one, they'll look around the shop anyway and come back again to look for your "sale" another time.'

'It does seem a shame to let good merchandise go to the rag man, it's always grieved me to do that. We'll try a sale for a while and keep an eye on what happens.'

'Let me know, will you, and whether you like the result?' I asked 'You can be the pilot scheme. If it works we'll see if the rest want to adopt the idea.'

'Won't Jean object?' Miles asked, looking sceptical.

'Probably,' I said with more confidence than I felt, 'but leave that to me.'

Over an excellent cup of coffee, ham sandwiches and homemade fruit cake, courtesy of Mabel, I asked Miles if Mrs Woodley had been in touch. She hadn't yet, so I told Miles to let her have the run of the shop to pick out for herself as many items as she wanted to the value of the coat she had lost. If she was unhappy about that I'd have to talk with HQ about paying her some compensation. It was the least we could do after getting the poor lady involved in our problems. After all, if Ginger had done his job properly we'd almost certainly have found the coat and returned it to her. I just hoped she'd be happy with our compensation package. Goods to the value weren't actually her coat, but then she had to accept some responsibility. She'd chucked the thing in the wrong bag to start with so she couldn't really say it was all our fault!

The Ginger business bothered Miles but he didn't seem surprised. He said the stock quality was already beginning to rise, now the best wasn't being creamed off, and that was being reflected in till takings. I was beginning to think today was turning out sort of OK when there was a commotion on the shop floor. We scattered cake crumbs and headed for the door.

Over by the book shelves a small knot of people were gathered and a little man in a pale wind-cheater jacket and brown cords, obviously in some distress, was pleading. 'Send for an ambulance! Oh, Dorothy, oh no, please, somebody, help...'

I could see, through the throng, someone lying on the floor. Miles and I pushed our way through and found an elderly lady lying very still on the floor, her face an unhealthy grey and her eyes closed.

Miles took charge. 'Give me a little room, please,' he said and knelt down next to the prone customer, checking the lady's pulse and respiration. 'Her pulse is very weak but she's breathing.' He looked at the distraught gentleman and smiled at him reassuringly. I made for the phone. Poor Dorothy looked ghastly and an ambulance seemed favourite just now. I found a chair for the chap I took to be her husband and told him an ambulance was on its way. He clung to my hand like Kate Winslet clung to her flotsam life raft in 'Titanic' and I thought he was going to cut off the circulation to my fingers. Someone gave him a cup of tea and he looked at it as though he'd never seen a mug of tea before. Perhaps he hadn't. His dainty little wife looked as though she'd put out the best bone china and lace doilies at the last trump.

After what seemed like an age, an ambulance pulled up outside. They never have difficulty parking, I thought, unlike me, and watched whilst they unloaded a chair thing and joined the little scrum around our casualty. I gave the husband his wife's handbag for safe keeping and made sure he was in the ambulance with her before asking one of the paramedics what, in his opinion, had happened.

'Heart attack, looks like,' she said, 'looks very poorly, she does, but we'll have her in hospital in ten minutes. Ring later, if you want word on her progress.'

'Thanks,' I said, 'I will.'

We watched the ambulance out of sight and everyone drifted back to what they'd been doing before. Brief snatches came my way – 'Poor woman, do you think she'll be alright?'; 'Did you see her husband, poor man…' and similar kinds of stuff. In the stock room little Bianca was standing in a corner with her thumb in her mouth. Mabel put an arm around her shoulder and said, 'Are you alright, dear? Don't be frightened, the lady will be at the hospital soon and they'll look after her. What's the matter?'

Bianca looked at her with eyes full of woe. 'I think I've done something naughty,' she said.

'What have you done, dear?' Mabel asked 'I'm sure it isn't anything bad. Do you want to tell me?'

Bianca looked even more worried and her lip quivered a bit. She brought her hand out from behind the shelter of her back and held out a tiny picture in a thin frame. The whole thing couldn't have been more than ten centimetres square. Mabel took it and Bianca said, 'Look. I made it change colour. Is that bad?'

Mabel tilted the picture slightly to catch the light and then she looked across at me. 'Gillian, Miles,' she said, 'what do you think?'

Miles took the picture and we both saw the bright yellow shine where Bianca had given the frame a polish while our attention had been diverted elsewhere. Miles found a cloth and rubbed a bit more dirt from the frame. It gleamed a rich, glowing honey colour. Then he gently applied to the cloth to the tiny picture. Even though layers of dirt remained, removing surface dust showed us what looked like bright paint underneath. We could see a halo around a blue head scarf. We looked at each other, both thinking the same thing.

'I think we should show this to Lionel,' he said and I nodded. Carefully he wrapped the little picture in an old sheet from the rag bag and took it to his office where he'd keep it under lock and key until he could hand it over to our tame auctioneer and valuer.

A tingle of excitement and anticipation touched my spine. I longed to say that I'd take the picture and show it to an auctioneer, get a quicker valuation and know what we were dealing with much sooner. Patience was never my strong suit. But I resisted. It was Bianca's find, this was her shop and the picture should stay with Miles, where everyone could enjoy a fleeting sense of ownership and anticipation. It was time for me to move on.

Next stop was a new housing development. The homes being built there were a mixture of expensive detached homes – 'executive' type, whatever that meant – and smaller terraces and blocks of flats. Sorry, luxury apartments. What made them 'executive' and 'luxury' was anybody's guess. Perhaps the developer wanted to attract only university-educated city types? Or those with big desks at multi-national corporations? Well, they certainly weren't for me, that I knew for sure! Notices at the entrance roads said that this phase of the new 'village' of 3000 homes was almost complete. My interest wasn't, however, in the homes but in the parade of shops at its heart. An opportunity to start from scratch, perhaps, with a brand new shop we could decorate and equip without worrying if the screws that held up the wall bars and display grids would part company with the 50-year-old plaster at any moment! How a charity shop would go down with the development corporation, I hadn't a clue, but I was a shop down at the moment and had two members of staff to pay without any visible means of income to pay them from.

I sat in the car in the muddy car park, and gazed at the skeleton of breeze blocks and boarded up doorways. The corner property, with entrances on two adjoining sides of its square shape, looked ideal. Plenty of parking, easily seen from the link road that snaked around the whole of the estate – sorry, development – and a bus stop just a few feet away. Notices showed that one of the units was already earmarked by the post office, one by a bookie and another for a doctor's surgery. The big one on the other side would almost certainly be a supermarket. Little short of perfect, I thought. Everything to bring people onto their local parade and to support their local charity shop! But how to convince HQ? How do you put together a convincing business plan for a place that doesn't have any existing shoppers, or even potential ones, on the pavement yet? Doesn't even have a pavement! Ah, well, that should tax my brain and keep me awake for a few nights, I thought, as I turned towards my next stop.

I managed to visit all my shops that day, even though the rest were fleeting visits of no more than a few minutes, before exhaustion sent me heading for home, a hot bath and a G&T. As I got back into my car for the journey home the mobile rang and my heart sank. It was Kenny. He didn't even say hello.

'I got him!' he bellowed down the phone, making me wince. 'He came back! I follow him and found his place where he lives! I watch him go inside then come out again. I caught him on the stairs! He kicked my shin – oh, boy, do I have bruise to show you – and I had to let him go but I know where he lives now and we can fix him, now, yes?'

'We can't fix him, no, Kenny,' I said. 'We do nothing today. It's too late and you're too excited. But well done, that's a fine piece of detective work. I'll call you tomorrow morning and we'll decide what to do then. For now, just make sure everything is doubly secure tonight when you lock up. He might decide that attack is the best defence!'

Home, James, and don't spare the horses, I thought as I turned the key and the engine sprang into life. I had a feeling that the next day was going to be another busy one. Was there any other kind? I figured a peaceful evening would be a good idea and the prospect of a G&T was becoming increasingly tempting.

I'd figured without Greg. It wasn't a business plan for a new shop that kept me awake, or figuring out what to do with a juvenile delinquent. It was Greg. He didn't come home that night.

-9-
Broken Dreams

What an awful night. It was after eleven before I fully realised that Greg was AWOL, so to speak. I tried his mobile but it was either switched off or he was somewhere where there was no signal. He didn't call me. I kept checking the phone in case I'd gone deaf. I put my mobile on charge, just to make sure it didn't run out of juice and switch itself off – even though it was already fully charged.

At half past midnight I put the cat out and went to bed. At one-thirty I got up again and tried to watch a TV programme I'd recorded weeks before. It didn't make a whole lot of sense and, anyway, by this time I was so hyped up and agitated that I made Teletubbies look calm and sensible!

At two-fifteen I made some tea and sat drinking it, watching some woman on TV with a painted smile and dead eyes trying to sell an exceedingly poor imitation of a Gucci watch. I imagined all sorts of things. Was Greg ill somewhere, trapped in a crashed car – *my* car! – in a ditch, or dead? I thought it might be better if he was dead. Then I wouldn't have to kill him.

At 3am I rang the local cop shop and A&E at the hospital. No dead bodies without owners, no car crashes, no arrests for D&D. No Greg. At three-thirty I went to bed. I must have dozed for a while but I was awake at five-fifteen and knew I wouldn't sleep again so I got up to make more tea and let the cat in. She knew it was too early for breakfast but she tried to kid me that she was starved, rubbing around my legs and trying to trip me up every time I lifted a foot to move. I knew her loving attention would stop within 30 seconds, when I fed her, and I craved even this small morsel of loving warmth so I wasn't going to give in to her pleading too soon. I thought I'd curl up in the armchair and turn on the gas fire in the sitting room, where it was at least warm and cosy, so I took my tea and padded across the hall.

The thoughtless slob was asleep on the sofa! He must have crept in during the half hour or so I was dozing, too exhausted to stave off sleep any longer. A red mist descended in front of my eyes. Wrapped in a ball of resentment and rage, I filled a large jug with icy water and flung it over him and the sofa, oblivious of the label that said 'dry clean only' on the covers, which had caused me such agonies of uncertainty when I'd bought the thing just six months before. I had the presence of mind to stand well back to avoid the resulting shower and was quietly gratified at the violence of his reaction. He leapt to his feet, arms flailing, coughing and spluttering and yelling obscenities. Extremely satisfying.

'You daft bat!' he yelled at me when he'd caught his breath. 'What did you do that for? I'm soaked! Look what you've done!'

'Have you any idea what I've been thinking, since about ten o'clock last night?' I asked, trembling with rage but trying to stay calm.

'I never know what you're bloody well thinking!' he yelled, flailing his arms about and trying to sweep water out of his eyes and off his shirt. 'What am I, a mind reader?'

'Obviously not. Nor am I. Where have you been while I've been calling the police and hospitals?'

'Oh, that,' he said, deflating in a heart beat. 'Well, it was just a drink then somebody suggested darts, then a curry and it got late. I didn't want to disturb you by then. I thought you'd be asleep so I didn't call.'

'Till 4am?'

'Why not? I'm back now, what's your problem?' And he glared at me.

I gave up, retreating to the bathroom and not bothering to throw him a towel to dry himself off with. A long, hot shower revived me a bit and I felt half human by the time I was dried and dressed. I was still hopping mad though and by now, a frisson of a different kind of fear was cutting at the back of my mind. Where had he been all night? I no more believed his story than I believed in the tooth fairy! He hated darts and, thinking about it, I'd not detected the scent of curry on his breath while he was shouting at me. Still, chucking cold water over him wasn't perhaps the best way of winning him over or of getting to the bottom of what was happening. He was hardly likely to want to sit down for a friendly chat and tell me about his adventures now, was he? Or infidelities.

Oh, Lord! Was that what he was doing? Having an affair? After all we'd been through together? My anger wilted under the memories of harsh lights in a hospital corridor, a young, exhausted nurse and a doctor who'd seen it all before but still didn't know what to say or do. 'I'm so sorry,' he'd said, 'We did all we could...' Greg had been there, holding me tight to stop me from falling. Holding me again, night after night, as I wept for the little boy who would never smile at me again, never walk, never say 'Mummy, watch me...' from a slide or a swing.

Stop it! I told myself. It was a long time ago. You can't change it. It happened. I took a deep breath and steadied my nerves and tear ducts. Today was a working day and there was no point debating with myself the question of Greg's faithfulness, or lack of it, so I went to work, leaving the shmuck in bed, snoring his silly head off.

It was still really early and the roads were quiet. If I hadn't felt so unsettled and unhappy I'd have enjoyed being out and about so early in a peaceful world of birds and sunrise. Even red traffic lights didn't bother me – no boy racers next to me trying to leave half their tyres on the road when the lights went green. As if there was any triumph or victory in leaving my trusty diesel behind.

The shop and office were in darkness. Chaos hidden in folds of velvet black. Until I tripped over a sales bin in the dark, cracking my ankle painfully. It hadn't been there on Tuesday! Lights on and a entirely new outlook presented itself.

Kylie and her crew had been busy in my absence. Everything had changed. There was a kiddies' playpen full of an enormous pile of soft toys in the corner, wall rails were in different positions with menswear where the book corner had been, ladieswear instead of bric-a-brac shelves and the whole shop cleaned and polished to within an inch of its life. Not only had stock been moved around into new positions but it looked somehow smarter and fresher. I gazed around and realised that there were dozens and dozens of items on display that I was sure hadn't been there a day or so ago. Shoes were shiny, garments were hanging squarely on their hangers instead of slipping drunkenly towards the floor and the changing room curtains had been washed.

I was speechless. Not that that made any difference, of course, since there was no-one to talk to anyway. The whole place looked like a completely different shop. The transformation was stunning. Kylie had channelled her energies into something creative and had learned well from our visit to the 'rival' across the road; I recognised some of their ideas. Perhaps they would too, if they cared to look through our window!

Upstairs I made tea and dug out the biscuit box. I wasn't hungry but it seemed sensible to eat something since, I reasoned, I'd got up so early I must need something even if I didn't actually want it. Besides, sugar was good as an energy source, wasn't it?

I certainly got plenty of energy – almost two packs of biscuits' worth, to be precise! Guilt was added to exhaustion and confusion. Oh, well, I thought, why not? My mind was getting a lot of exercise going through hoops even if my body was too tired to even twitch.

The next thing I knew a chorus of voices was singing in my head.

'Yo, Damian!'

I jerked awake to hear Damian's gentle bellow, my neck stiff from drooping over the desk while I slept.

'Yo, ladies,' he carolled back before he thundered up the stairs. He skidded to a halt on the landing when he saw the kitchen door ajar and his grinning face popped into view.

'Morning, boss lady,' he said, 'what are *you* doing here so early? Man trouble, is it?' My jaw dropped. Was he psychic or what? He laughed at my expression. 'No magic,' he said, 'you were up all *night* or you were *up* all night, if you see what I mean. Nudge, nudge, wink, wink. Still, you don't look as though you *enjoyed* being up all night and that spells *trouble*, see?'

I let it pass for now. My brain wasn't in gear and wasn't agile enough to follow his convolutions.

'Are you always such a smart-aleck this early in the morning?' I said as I rubbed some feeling back into the side of my face that had been squashed on to the hard desk top.

'Well, that's a warm welcome, I *must* say! Haven't you *seen* what's been happening downstairs? It was all hands on *deck* yesterday, I can tell you.' Damian perched his beautifully rounded, gym-toned bottom in its beautifully laundered Paul Smith chinos on the corner of my desk.

'She might be pint-sized but she's a *demon* when she gets going. I was a *slave* to that girl yesterday and I wasn't even supposed to *be* here. Tuesday *isn't* one of my days, in case you'd forgotten. You look like *death* warmed over, you poor cow! Fancy a pick-me-up? Look as though you could do with one.'

'What did you have in mind?' I asked, all prickly suspicion.

'Come with *me*,' he said, 'I'll *show* you.'

Wearily I pulled myself to my feet to follow him downstairs and out into the car park. There was another car sitting next to mine, one I didn't recognise, and a wizened little man in a grubby trilby stood next to it. In his hands he had a clipboard, a small bundle of keys with lots of labels hanging from them and a bulging envelope.

'Ms Morris?' he asked politely.

'That's me,' I said. 'Can I help you?' Even at times of stress and exhaustion I couldn't help being polite and helpful, much to the dismay of the little devil that lived on my shoulder.

'I've brought your new car,' he said, smiling broadly as though he was pretty sure that he was a welcome visitor. I gazed at the gleaming red bodywork, the black, black tyres with tread (*tread!*) and plush, dove-grey upholstery. My brain just stuck. It was like a clock that someone had forgotton to wind.

'A car?' I said. 'For me?' Then I added stupidly, 'Are you sure?'

'Yes, Madam,' he said.

'I'm a madam,' I thought.

'Not yet,' said the little devil on my shoulder, 'but I could show you how, if you're interested.' I ignored him. He was getting used to it.

'We understand you were given the wrong car. This one,' and the man pointed at my beat-up little diesel, 'should have been returned to us but somehow it was allocated to you instead. I've been instructed to apologise and give you this one.'

My brain came unglued at last. 'Wow!' I said and could feel the grin start. 'Nobody told me you were coming! Hey, this is really great! I love it!'

'Should be something more sporty, really,' said the little devil, 'more fitting for a madam. But at least it's red and red's OK. It's cool, I can live with that.'

I meandered around the lovely little car, touching its glossy sides, admiring its sparkling windows, noting the sun roof which was tinted against glare. I pulled open the driver's door and slid into the seat. It was like sitting on a feather bed, only with more support. I adjusted the seat position and squealed when I saw the CD player. Damian and the delivery man watched me patiently, as only men can do when a female admires a new car, with a mixture of patronage and benign superiority that says 'Well she can't possibly fully appreciate the overhead cam, three zillion horsepower, or the double sprocket suspension gee gaws, but she'll know how to vacuum it'. Even Damian, for all his campness, could act the smug male when the mood took him.

Sure, it was another diesel, with about as much street cred as a skateboard compared with… with… well, almost anything really. But it was mine! It was new, it was unblemished and it was all mine. Well, as long as I stayed in the job, anyway. It was enough for me and I was *deeeeeeelighted*!

Damian was beaming as though it was all his doing. *'Thought* you'd be pleased,' he said, 'I saw the little *beauty* pull in as I arrived and *knew* it was for you. That … that…*thing* you're driving has been around since Christ was a boy!'

'Would you check the paperwork, Madam?' asked the little delivery man politely. 'My colleague is waiting to take me back to the depot.'

'Oh, yes. Certainly. Sorry!' I gushed. 'Didn't mean to hold you up. So unexpected. Pleasant surprise.'

'Oh, *do* shut up, Gillian,' said Damian, 'you're *burbling*! Hurry *up* and we can go for a spin. I know *just* the place for breakfast!'

And he did too. A stylish, obviously fashionable watering hole for the man-about-town who wants to meet another man-about-town. There was a long counter with high spindly stools to park yourself on, just big enough for one cheek so the other leg had to hang, showing off its length of knife-edge-pressed, outrageously expensive designer trousers, to the floor with toe elegantly pointing. Polished tables with only two chairs apiece were tucked into narrow spaces between privacy partitions and everywhere there was chrome, stainless steel and pretty cut-glass vases full of flowers. The place was packed. We had to perch on the stools, which wasn't terribly comfortable but at least ensured I was in no position to fall asleep between sips of the absolutely excellent coffee.

'I thought your social circle were all night owls, Damian,' I said. 'What are they all doing out and about at this time of the morning?'

'Breakfast on their *way home* from last night,' he said, as though it was a very silly question.

'Ah,' said I reflectively.

We had the creamiest of scrambled eggs, the lightest of bagels, the most succulent smoked salmon and the most fragrant of coffee. Even though I'd pigged out on biscuits less than an hour ago it was a feast of taste-bud-crashing glory. Who cared about... well, anything, actually, when the senses were being soothed with such superb examples of the chef's art?

Afterwards we took the little red thing up and down the by-pass a couple of times, played with all the gadgets, rolled the sunroof backwards and forwards and gave it a name. Blink. Because if you did you missed it. Sure, it was a diesel but once the turbo cut in it went like a rocket. Most satisfying. Not in the least bit environmentally friendly, sensible or civic-minded. Still, I could be sensible later, after I'd got used to it and the novelty had worn off.

Then it was time to go back to work. I opened the envelope with all the gubbins about the car first, just to make sure everything was in order. Principally the insurance, given last week's events. A little blue envelope fell out of the owner's handbook as I turned it over in my hand. Inside was a small card. Just a classily plain, creamy card with a small picture of a seashell on it. Inside had been written 'Enjoy!' It was as though time had stopped. Why a seashell? .

Oh Lord! The hairs on the back of my neck stood on end and a shiver ran down my spine. I dropped card and envelope in my desk drawer. If Damian saw it he'd never let me hear the end of it. I couldn't pretend that was just a mentor's natural interest, could I?

While we'd been out doing childish things with the car, Kenny had called from Canon Row and left a message on the machine. He wanted to know why I hadn't called about Ms Smith's little boy. That was the last thing I wanted to deal with today but it would, I supposed, be distracting at least and distraction was definitely a good idea today. I called him back.

He told me that the boy had come back to the skip the previous afternoon. He'd been armed with a large stick, freshly torn from one of the sickly trees that lined some of the surrounding streets, and had used it to prise open the skip lid. Even when locked those things were about as boy-proof as a five-bar gate. Anyhow, when Kenny spotted him he was already head first into the open skip. Kenny had, apparently, bellowed at him, catapulted out of the back door and across the yard and had almost caught him by the laces of his dirty Nike trainers as he bolted across the road, almost under the wheels of a Parcel Force delivery van, and disappeared into the jungle-thick garden of the laughingly called local park, with a glass flower vase in his hand. Appropriate, I thought – he could find something in the overgrown garden to put in the vase.

Kenny had picked up the trail again a few yards down the road, when the boy had appeared over the side gate of the house next to the park's perimeter on to the pavement, still clutching the vase in one hand and this time with a few flowers in the other – presumably picked without the garden owner's permission. This time he wasn't in so much of a hurry, assuming, no doubt, that he'd given anyone tailing him the slip. Kenny, however, was pretty street-wise himself and he had followed at a discreet distance.

A couple of streets away from the shop the boy stopped at a bench seat on a scuffed little patch of earth that was trying to masquerade as an urban green space. Sitting on the bench was a tiny girl child, no more than five years old, Kenny said. I pictured pigtails and ribbons, with little feet in white socks and jelly shoes swinging backwards and forwards as she waited. Kenny was too far away to hear normal conversation but he saw what happened next. The girl listened to whatever the boy told her as he held up the vase and flowers for her inspection. Then she stood up on the bench, so that her head was level with his, leaned forwards with both hands on her hips, opened her mouth and yelled at him in a high pitched, infant voice. Kenny heard that alright.

She'd shouted, 'Yer waster! What the fuck do yer fink that fing is? A fuckin' vase! Wot's she gonna do wiv a fuckin' vase!'

My bubble vision of an angelic little girl child with all the pretty trappings popped and disappeared in a shower of rainbow-coloured droplets.

The boy appeared to cringe, then he reached into his pocket, pulled out a Tesco's carrier bag, carefully wrapped the vase and flowers in it, put them down on the pavement close to his feet and stood up again. With both hands he gripped the front of the little girl's scruffy T shirt and lifted her clear of the bench. Kenny said she wriggled and flayed her feet, trying to reach any tender spot of his anatomy she could with her dirty sandals. Kenny didn't hear what he said to her but when he put her down, she quietly climbed down from the bench, put her hand in his and let him lead her away, quiet as you like.

Kenny followed. They led him to a run-down block of flats a couple of streets away. Number 17, Mafeking House.

It was time for action. Also a very good excuse to get away from all the desk stuff, where I was beginning to feel my eyelids droop over the sandy pits where my eyes normally were. I left Damian producing the sales charts for the past four years from his ancient computer and drove over – in my shiny new car – to find Mafeking House.

Having found it, I wished I hadn't. It was a few streets away from Kenny's shop and there was plenty of parking. Probably because it wasn't the sort of street where any car would be safe, or even that it might still be there in half an hour. There was litter everywhere. Several flats in the blocks were boarded up and much of the exposed brick and concrete was covered in graffiti. It was really imaginative, some of it, although you'd need to be a contortionist to reproduce the various positions illustrated, Kama Sutra style, on the walls of a flight of steps. Even with my head tilted to one side and one eye closed to a squint, I couldn't figure out how much of it could be done without serious risk of dislocating some important part of your anatomy. I considered that my education had been pretty liberal but there were obscenities written there that I'd never seen or heard before.

On reflection, I thought it best to leave the car close to the shop and walk back. Having already upset Malcolm severely on more than one occasion, I didn't want to have to explain another mishap to him just yet. Especially in my lovely little new red car.

Mafeking House was a six-storey block of flats with flights of concrete stairs and open walkways. About a third of the flats had at least one boarded up window and. although the doors and window frames had probably been painted once, there wasn't much evidence of it now. Most were rotting and some had the leprous stains of lichen growth on them. Bleak. Very bleak.

I found number 17 on the third floor. Standing in front of the battered door with its peeling paint and blocked up letterbox, I almost chickened out but, having come this far, I thought I'd knock just once, and then leave if there was no answer. No problem. I knocked. Moderately loudly. Well, it might have been just a tad lightly. No answer. Honour satisfied, I was balanced on my toes ready to turn to go when the door opened and I was face to face with the woman I took to be Ms Smith. She was probably about 30 but she looked a lot older. And she was, quite clearly, not in the mood for visitors.

'Yeh?' she barked, glaring at me. 'And 'oo the 'ell are you?'

'My name is Gillian Morris,' I said and hoped she didn't hear the quiver in my voice or notice that I'd taken a tiny step backwards. Oh, alright then, a stride. 'Can you spare me just a moment please, it's quite important?'

'What for? You from the Social? I already told your mates down the office, 'e moved out last week and 'e never even gave me money, anyway.'

The Social? He? Co-habiting stops your benefit, doesn't it? I swallowed and started again.

'No, I'm not from the Social. I work for a charity and one of my shops is on Canon Row. You might know it?'

'What if I do? What's it to you?'

She was suspicious and she folded her arms across her thin chest, shifting her weight onto the other foot as she leaned on the doorframe. I noticed, through a fog of nervousness, that the slippers on her feet didn't match. One was red with blue patterns on it, the other was pink with a chewed looking pom-pom. They were both very old.

'Er... I'm here about your son. You wrote to us about him. You said he'd hurt himself at our shop.'

I had her interest now. She unfolded her arms and looked at me with a speculative glint in her eye.

'Yeh. I did, didn't I? What you going to do about it, then?' She straightened her shoulders and her stance said that she was confident she had the upper hand. After all, I wasn't from the Social and her darling boy had been hurt on our premises.

'Well, I've come to find out if he's OK. A cut from something in a waste skip could easily become infected.'

''E's alright, no thanks to you. Cuts and bruises heal up overnight on 'im, crafty little sod.'

'The thing is,' I plunged on, 'when he does that… you know… goes through the skip like he does, he's taking quite a risk. It's full of all kinds of rubbish and he could really hurt himself quite badly. If he fell in and the lid slammed and locked shut he might not be found for several days, if it was a holiday weekend, for example. Is there… well… anything you can do to stop him?' I finished lamely. I didn't dare mention the girl child, I felt I was in enough hot water already without opening up another battle front.

'Stop 'im? What, 'im? You must be jokin'! I 'aven't bin able to stop 'im since he were three years old! Nah, it's down to you, precious, you fix your skip to keep 'im out, 'cos if he hurts 'isself again, I'll sue you, just see if I don't!' And she slammed the door in my face.

I didn't have the energy to walk all the way back to the car without taking time out for a breather. I was pretty well exhausted by now and reaction from the encounter set in. I sat on a low brick wall on the street to give my knees time to stop shaking.

'Coward!' berated the little devil on my shoulder. 'She was a pussy cat! You should see some of the wasters I have to deal with in my world! She frightened you? Pah! You don't know you're born!' Oh, push off, I thought at him wearily, I'll be a coward if I want to be, go away.

He was right though, I thought as I sat there and pondered the state of my courage. Or lack of it. This wasn't a gang of yobs on a dark street corner, this was just one woman with attitude. What was I thinking of? This problem had to be solved or the boy would plague us until he was sent to a youth offenders' institute! Or caught something nasty from the rubbish and died. Oh Lord! In my weary state alarm took hold. He might, mightn't he? Catch something. Bleed to death. Fall and bang his head and die of concussion! I knew what he was doing, now, and M's Smith was quite right. You can't unknow that kind of thing and the knowledge made me, somehow, responsible. I'd have to do something about the skip

160

before something awful happened. But I knew I had to try again with M's Smith before I felt entitled to give up on her.

With purpose and intent, I strode back up the concrete stairs and marched along the walkway. A faded middle-aged woman stepped aside as I went by and never raised her eyes from the floor. My knuckles rapped on the door again.

'Bloody 'ell, not you agen!' Ms Smith said. This time there was another presence. From behind her skirts a dirty little face peeped out at me. Was this the little girl Kenny had seen? Her eyes were watchful and her chestnut-coloured hair was cut short, almost cropped. I could just make out that she was wearing a rugby shirt at least three sizes too big for her.

'Yes, me again,' I said firmly. 'We need to talk about your son.'

''Is name is Billy,' she said. Had to be. Just had to be. Not just Billy the Kid this time though, but Billy *and* the Kid.

'Billy is risking too much when he steals from our skip, Ms Smith. We can't make it 100 per cent safe and it's not fair of you to expect us to protect your child from harm when you can't even do that yourself! He's only a little boy, even if he is wilful and disobedient and we've got to stop him somehow! Why does he do it, anyway?'

The words just fell over themselves. I'm not sure which of us was more startled by the outburst, her or me. There was a short pause and the girl took the initiative, springing into action from behind her mother's skirt. She launched herself out of the doorway and barrelled into my shins, flailing her arms and kicking out with her bare feet. Fortunately she was small and very light but even so, she caught me a couple of good whacks on the shin that brought tears to my eyes before I caught hold of her and held her at arms' length, still swinging and scratching like a feral cat.

The distraction gave Ms Smith time to recover her cynical tone and she said, not paying the least little bit of attention to her screeching, flailing daughter, 'And just 'ow do you suggest we do that then, Miss Smart Aleck?' and I realised I didn't have a clue 'We're rich, as you can see,' she said, her voice dripping with sarcasm and throwing her hand out wide to take in the darkened interior of her home, ''E does it to bring fings 'ome, yer daft cow, nice fings like teapots and flower vases. 'E does it for me more 'n' 'isself.'

If I hadn't been so preoccupied I might have heard the pride and the pathos in what she said but I was too busy with the cat child. Still, my brain must have been working OK because it came to me in a flash. Eureka! Inspiration!

'Do you have a job, Ms Smith? Do you work outside your home, I mean?'

'Cheeky cow! What's it to you if I do or don't?'

'Well, if you'd be willing to come to the shop, for just a couple of hours at a time on, say, two days a week – as a volunteer, you understand – maybe Billy could come with you when he's not in school. We could find things for him to do on the shop floor...' What was I *saying*? Kids on the shop floor? And what about the cat girl! Jean would have my guts for garters! '...and maybe he'd stop stealing if he could see his mum was involved with the place. No, please, don't say no. You see, even though volunteers aren't paid, there's as much tea and coffee and biscuits as you want while you're there and every volunteer either gets their bus fare paid or gets to pick one item a week to take home.'

I stopped. She looked at me, head tilted slightly, speculating. 'Not much, is it?' she said. 'Workin' for nothing? People do that, do they? What a bloody daft thing to do! Why would I want to do a stupid fing like that then?' She sounded totally disbelieving and very suspicious.

'Loads of people do it! Sometimes they go on to take paid jobs with us. Or even somewhere else. It's good experience and puts you in a much better position for proper job hunting than just living off the Social. It's a new start for a lot of people. You get out more, learn new things, meet people. You'd be amazed. Really you would. This time next year, who knows what you might be doing or even where you might be! Isn't it worth a try, for Billy's sake?'

I was getting breathless now but the cat girl showed no signs of slowing down. Ms Smith leaned over and plucked the child off me, picking her up by one arm and swinging her sideways into the dark room behind her. It didn't stop the struggling. In fact, the girl seemed to re-double her efforts when she realised I would soon be out of her reach altogether. Her Mum held on to her with the ease of long practice.

'I'll think about it,' Ms Smith said and slammed the door in my face again.

162

For a moment I stood there, facing the closed door, feeling the grit of tears behind my eyes. I knew it was exhaustion after a mostly sleepless night, and that the little bit I'd achieved had been quite a victory in its way, but it felt like utter defeat. As a last act of hope I pushed my business card under the door and walked away.

This time I went back to the car and sat for a while, eyes closed and head resting on new, fresh-smelling seat covers until I felt a bit better. I knew I'd have to tell Kenny what had happened and hesitated to report a failure but he had to know that he'd have to guard the skip with his life for a while until I could figure out what else to do.

Back at the shop it didn't take me long to explain the situation to Kenny. He was aghast. A possible volunteer who wasn't in his family! Children, and destructive, foul-mouthed children as well! Still, as I told him, it might not happen. In fact, it probably wouldn't and he'd better look at ways of making his skip even more secure. I suggested a bicycle chain with links as thick as my forearm and a padlock OKd by MI5. He was sceptical but said he'd give it a try.

Desk work was the last thing I needed right then but it was too early to justify going home and, besides, I didn't really want to be there either at the moment. Back at the office I pored over Damian's sales figures. No pretty coloured pie or bar charts here so I had to slog through long columns of figures, by the week, the month and the year, which was a bit of a grind to put it mildly, especially since my eyes felt they had sand in them. It was much too soon in my new career for my presence to have any impact at all on sales but, nevertheless, I was beginning to see where the potential might be in the short term, and where more time and effort might be needed elsewhere for long term improvements. Kylie's efforts downstairs gave me hope, we'd see next week, when the sales figures were totalled up, whether she'd be rewarded with better figures on the balance sheet.

I drafted an ad for the local paper, a kind of catch-all to see if there was anybody out there who might want a part-time temporary job that was hard work and didn't pay much. I needed someone to drive Ginger's van while we were sorting out that little problem and I tagged on a plea for more volunteers to work in the shops. Somehow I couldn't quite bring myself to ask Lawrence to sanction several hundreds of pounds for a paid advert just to find volunteers but the need to advertise for someone to fill a driver's position gave an opportunity. Sitting in their ivory tower, some of our HQ people seemed to think volunteers just fell out of the trees, like leaves in autumn, exactly when you needed them. Still, he couldn't object if an advert had to go in anyway. Could he?

My mind slid back to Ms Smith and Billy. From what Kenny had told me, Billy was a competent, imaginative, experienced little thief. Maybe he'd come back later for another go, just to get his revenge for my stirring things up with his mum. I flipped open the telephone directory and phoned five other charity shops in the area. I learned that all of them had had their skips and bins ransacked and three of them had seen a boy of Billy's description lurking around. None of them had seen him inside the shops though, which suggested that shop-lifting wasn't his thing. Perhaps it was a good sign. Hope springs eternal, so they say. If that's true then I should have been baptised Hope, since it fitted me very well.

'Stupid, though,' echoed the little devil on my shoulder. 'If you'd let me take over I could make sure you'd never have to rely on hope again!'

'Really?' I thought back. 'And how would you do that, then?' I was hoping to surprise him with a little dialogue instead of ignoring him as usual, or telling him to shut up.

'Well, I have friends in high places. I could arrange it.'

'Don't you mean friends in low places? And why should any of them do you that kind of favour?'

'Well…'

'Thought so, you're not as sure as you think you are, are you, when I call your bluff?' Silence. No reply. Victory!

The phone rang. My heart sank. 'Hello, Gillian here,' I said, trying to sound bright. 'How can I help you?'

'Gillian, it's Miles.' It took me a few seconds to register his voice, it sounded so different. He was excited and didn't care who knew it. Not our usual oh-so-controlled Miles at all.

'You sound on top of the world, Miles, what's happened?'

'Well, the more I looked at that little picture yesterday, the more I felt we had something a bit special. I was so convinced that I just couldn't wait and I went over to see Lionel first thing this morning.

Luckily he was in his office and not out at an auction or something. He got very excited and started pulling books off his shelves and riffling through them. He has to check it properly, of course, but he thinks it's a Russian religious icon. It could be worth up to two thousand pounds!'

'Good grief! Two grand?'

Damian snapped to attention in his chair. 'That's *incredible*! I don't believe it!'

'Bloody hell, she sounds like Victor Meldrew now,' said the little devil on my shoulder and, back to my true form, I ignored him. Damian might be gay, but it was still insulting to call him a she.

'When will he know for sure?'

'He said he'll show it to a colleague, who's an expert in Russian art history, early next week and get back to me by Wednesday afternoon. Isn't it wonderful?'

'Absolutely! Whatever comes out of this we should say a big thank you to Bianca. Without her we may never have spotted it. Well done, Miles.'

'What for? I didn't do anything'

'Yes, you did. Without you there'd be no Bianca. You look after her, encouraged your team to accept her and teach her. Without that, there'd be no two grand!'

He was silent for a moment. 'I didn't think of it like that. Bianca's not here today, she's not very well, but I'll make sure there are jammy dodgers in the biscuit box tomorrow, she loves those. Oh, by the way, I rang the hospital this morning about the lady that collapsed. They wouldn't tell me much, of course, not being a relative or anything, but they did say that she's still rather poorly but on the mend. I asked them to tell her husband that I rang.'

'Thanks, Miles, I'm glad she's doing OK.'

'If I hear anything else I'll let you know. Bye, Gillian, I'll call you as soon as Lionel gets back to me.'

'Thanks, Miles. Bye'

Damian was gobsmacked. He paced the floor, threw his elegant hands around and tossed his perfectly arranged hair. Very dramatic.

'Two grand!' he muttered, then '*Two grand*! That's fantastic! Will it go through her till as a *sale*? Just *think* what it would do to the *averages*! We'd meet *targets* that week! We've *never* made targets before! *Never*!'

It exhausted me just watching him. I persuaded him to make us some more tea and breathed a sigh of relief when he took his excitement into the kitchen for a while

Eventually I could hear that he'd calmed down and I went back to mundane number-crunching to come up with next month's sales targets, along with some pre-prepared reasons for HQ why we hadn't reached them. Again.

By the time Damian had made the afternoon cuppa, I was trembling with fatigue and wondering if the matchsticks-under-the-eyelids trick really worked. Eventually I gave up, told Damian I was going home and left. I drove home at a sedate pace, with the radio on and windows open to make sure I stayed awake and alert.

To my surprise Greg's car – my car – was in the drive. I walked around the back of the house and the back door was open slightly. I could hear his voice. He was using the phone and I heard him say, '...in the morning, early' and then there was a pause. 'Don't worry about that. I'm almost ready so it doesn't matter anyway.' Another pause. His voice was different somehow, and I realised with a shock that I hadn't heard him sound like that when he spoke to me, not for a very long time. Kind of soft, like a verbal caress. 'Yes, well, she gave me a hard time but it was worth it. And we'll have a good time tomorrow.' Another pause then 'She doesn't know anything. She's so wrapped up in her bloody job she wouldn't see if it was right under her nose. Nobody could expect me to put up with this any longer, I feel like a stranger in me own home. Don't worry, pet, it'll be alright.'

I went back to the car, started her up and drove away. I wasn't up to that kind of thing, not as exhausted as I was. I thought I heard something break inside me. I drove around for ages, not feeling, not knowing where I was, just on automatic pilot. When I came home again, an hour later, he was gone and, in spite of the tiredness, I sat at the kitchen table for ages, just drinking tea and eating my way through several KitKat Chunkies. Comfort food. Ice cream was better, Ben and Jerry's Cherry Garcia. But there wasn't any left and I was too tired to go to Tesco's.

I've no idea how long I sat but eventually I decided to run a deep, hot bath full of bubbles. A bit of self-pampering often helped.

Not this time though, I still felt as though I was the only person in Pompeii who was still gazing up at Vesuvius, not believing that the smoke meant anything more than a bonfire. Still, I was so shattered that I lay down on the bed and was instantly asleep.

-10-
Spin

I didn't hear Greg come in or feel him get into bed, but I heard him banging about in the kitchen really early next morning. I opened one eye and tried to focus on the clock. *Five-thirty AM!* Good Lord, what on earth was going on? I tried to ignore the noise and turned over, burying my head under the pillow. It didn't work. If he was trying to be quiet and discreet, he was succeeding as well as NHS management.

Eventually I gave up and swung my legs over the edge of the bed, searching with my feet for my Garfield slippers. In the kitchen, Greg was sitting at the table nursing the remnants of a cup of tea. There was an untidy little parcel next to him which looked suspiciously like doorstep sandwiches.

'Going somewhere today?' I asked brightly as I re-filled the kettle, eyeing the package pointedly. For some reason my heart was banging against my ribs like a xylophone hammer. I was surprised he couldn't hear the racket. This didn't feel right, my instincts were at full alert.

'Nowhere special,' he said.

I almost told him he was lying, that I'd heard his conversation on the phone yesterday. More to the point, though, I'd heard the tone of his voice. Cowardice kept me quiet. And good old-fashioned denial of the obvious. This time the little devil on my shoulder didn't taunt me. Perhaps he was still asleep. It was pretty early, after all. Do devils get up early in the morning? Doubtful, I thought, doesn't fit the image somehow.

'We've had a bit of a rough time lately,' I ventured, testing the ground. 'We haven't seem much of each other, or talked, for ages.'

'Whose fault is that then?' Greg said, but without venom, which gave me hope. Silly cow that I was.

'I know. My being away didn't help, did it? All that training all over the place. It was rough on me as well, you know, and you could have come with me sometimes. Even just an overnight with me midweek would have helped. It might have been fun.'

'Yeah, well, that's water under the bridge now,' he said sulkily. 'You never have time for me. Always swaning off somewhere, working till all hours and sometimes not coming home at all. How do you think that makes me feel? Especially since I'm out of work. My mates think you're keeping me! It's demeaning!'

It's also true, I thought, but didn't dare say it. Instead I said 'I'm sorry' and there I was again – in the wrong, all my fault, guilty as charged. He wasn't slow to take advantage.

'I just have to do something for myself every once in a while. I've got my pride, you know. Sometimes I think it's the only thing that keeps me going.' That and my cheque book, I thought. 'So I'm going out for the day with a… a… mate. I'll be really late back. So don't wait up.' And he was gone.

My heart had stopped banging about by this time but it felt bruised. My head was aching and my stomach was churning. For a few moments I indulged in self pity and just sat, where Greg had been a few minutes ago, nursing a cup of rapidly cooling coffee. I'd just convinced myself that my headache was due to too much sleep and my stomach churning was hunger when I realised it was eight-fifteen and I was late. Bloody hell, no breakfast again!

In the office the answerphone was blinking and there was a pile of mail on the desk. I raided the biscuit box again and sat down to pick through the advertising and other junk that was all I seemed to get in the mail both at work and at home. Except not today. The first envelope I opened was from Malcolm. At first I wasn't sure if I was up to Malcolm first thing in the morning but I'd been enough of a coward today already and felt obliged to handle tough stuff with some self-respect now. It was easy after all. Wasn't it?

In his usual pompous style Malcolm gave me some good news. He wrote:

Dear Ms Morris (not Gillian, I noticed, in spite of his personal comments about my clothes. Weird.)

Re: Your recent traffic accident (Mine? Was I the one who shunted an innocent motorist into the car in front without a by-your-leave?)

After carefully examining the files relating to your lease vehicle, I find that you were, after all, fully insured on the company's policy. (Yippee! I thought and realised I'd been more than just a little bit worried about that, after what he'd said.) *I have decided, therefore, that I shall take no further action concerning this incident and shall close the file. Your car will not, however, be repaired. A replacement vehicle has been ordered for you. You should have received a different vehicle when you took up your post but an oversight resulted in the misallocation of a car that was due to be returned to the Fleet Hire company. You will now, however, be allocated a new vehicle, and not one from the existing fleet which is due for re-allocation. This concession has been approved by the Shops Director* (good old Lucas!) *and the vehicle will be delivered shortly.* (It's here already, old son, and it's lovely!) *Please take care of it.*

And he'd signed the letter with an illegible scribble. That's that then, I thought, no hangover from the accident and I had a decent little motor to play with. It's an ill wind, they say. So what was still pecking at the corners of my memory? My brain hurt. Yesterday. Clearing my tissues, windscreen de-icer and half eaten Fry's Turkish Delight from the glove box, handing over the keys to the wizened little man… Oh, Lord! The boot! The sack of bondage gear in the boot! I'd left it there! After a moment of paralysis, a fit of giggles overcame me and I laughed until the tears ran and the hiccups started. Hysteria, probably. Reaction to stress.

It took me ages to calm down and even longer to stop the hiccups but eventually, after a cup of tea and a few more biscuits, I was in a reasonably fit state to pick up the phone and call the vehicle fleet company. A switch board operator put me through to someone she called Mr Summers.

'Andy Summers, how can I help?'

'Mr Summers…'

'Andy, please.'

'Oh. OK. Andy. My name is Gillian Morris and I have a delicate situation you might be able to help me with.'

'Ah!' he said knowingly and my heart sank. 'You're calling about the car we collected from you yesterday?'

'Er... yes. Have you... looked at it... yet? You sound as though you know what I'm going to say.'

'Well, yes actually, if you mean the sack in the boot.' Was he laughing? He was laughing! How humiliating!

'I was rather hoping you might not have found it yet and I could explain before anyone jumped to conclusions or started spreading... stories. Well, OK, gossip. Unfounded, of course. There's a perfectly innocent explanation.'

'Too late, I'm afraid. One of our valeters had a go at the car yesterday. Not a lot of point, really, with the dents and stuff, but we try to do our best, you know. The car's pretty old and bashed up but we're putting several old bangers in for auction tomorrow. He thought he'd see if he could smarten it up a bit first and add it to the auction lot. He was...well, let's say he was... amused and shared his... amusement with the other guys. I wasn't here yesterday and my secretary was more than just a bit concerned so she rang your head office. I believe she spoke to your Shops Director? Chap called Barrington? Would you know him?'

Please, God, I thought, open up the ground now and let me disappear without trace. Or if you can't do that please send the USS Enterprise so that I can beam up and join their next time warp!

Andy was speaking again. 'Hello? Are you still there? We still have your... sack. Er... would you like us to keep it for you? Would you like to collect it?'

What could I say? What *could* I say? If I said yes they'd all be convinced the stuff was mine no matter what else I said. But could I trust them to dispose of it all properly or would it end up as Exhibit A at my trial when I was charged with running a vice ring? What sentence did Cynthia Paine get? Living off immoral earnings? No, not that, I hadn't actually gone into business, had I? It just seemed that way to those with unkind minds.

'I'll collect it,' I said wearily. 'I'm down your way tomorrow, I'll pick it up then. In the meantime, Andy, would you do me a favour?'

'If I can,' he said, very warily indeed, and I couldn't help but smile at what he might be thinking! 'What is it?'

'Tell them the stuff came into one of our shops as a donation and I was trying to find an incinerator for it. I wasn't expecting to return my car to you and, in the surprise, just forgot the sack was in the boot. Can you do that for me please? I doubt if they'll all believe it but some might. It's true, after all.'

Andy chuckled. 'Is that really what happened? It must have caused a bit of a stir in the shop!'

'It did.' And I thought he might be able to hear the smile in my voice too. 'An elderly lady found it and nearly had apoplexy. The other volunteer was male – he had a bit of a twinkle in his eye, I can tell you! Thanks, Andy, see you tomorrow.'

Next I turned my attention to the blinking answerphone. The first message was from Lucas – surprise, surprise. He sounded confused, amused and intrigued all at once. He said, 'I'm sure there's a mundane explanation but I'd love to hear it anyway. Call me please, before the vice squad take you away.'

The second message was from the insurance assessors. They wanted me to meet them at Chilton Street that afternoon, if I could make it please (which meant 'be there or else') for their first brief look at the damage. Then there was a message from Brigid. She sounded anxious, but then she always did. Cryptically she just asked me to call without telling me what it was about. I reached out to pick up the phone to make the first return call but, just as I touched it, it rang and my jangled nerves sent me almost to the ceiling. It was Miles.

'Bad news, Gillian,' he said in hushed and reverential tones. What now? I pleaded with all the powers that be for just a little respite!

'Go on,' I said.

'The lady who collapsed in the shop? You remember her?' How could I forget! 'I'm afraid she died last night.' Just for a moment the world stood still. I felt small and selfish in the face of the grief the customer's husband must be feeling about now. Poor man, he was clearly devoted to her and I couldn't begin to imagine how he'd cope without her. And I didn't even know her name.

'Her husband came in this morning to tell us the news,' Miles continued, 'I think he was still in shock. He brought us a vacuum cleaner.'

Had I heard that right? 'A what?'

'A vacuum cleaner. I know, strange isn't it? Anyway. He came in just after we opened this morning, said he'd just come away from the hospital and was on his way home. He said they'd been out shopping on the day she collapsed and they'd just bought a new vacuum cleaner which has sat in the boot of the car since then. He said he couldn't bear to look at it now, because she'd been so excited he was sure it had brought on her heart attack. She'd never had a vacuum before, apparently. He wanted to know if we could find a use for it. Can we use it in one of the shops? He's adamant that he doesn't want it and he thought it would be a suitable way to thank us for trying to help her. I don't need it – I have two here already. Does anyone on the patch need a new vacuum?'

Yes! I thought, it really is an ill wind and all that, isn't it?

'Yes!' I said. 'Bell Lane does! Mind you, keep it in its box for a while, Miles. You never know, he might change his mind later. Poor chap's in shock and we don't want to take advantage of him. Do we know who he is, by the way?'

'Well, that's the other funny thing. He introduced himself as Donald White.' Why did I know that name? 'Do you remember him,' Miles asked 'or were you too young? He was a music hall comedian, you know, the comedy pair who called themselves Black and White.' Of course I remembered him! My mum had loved them when I was a kid. Couldn't stand them myself, but then I was an arrogant little squirt who thought anything from before 1980 that didn't twang a guitar was totally beyond the pale.

'I remember. Odd, isn't it, how life comes around again when you least expect it?' We both mulled over life and its unexpected twists and turns for a moment before I said, 'By the way, did you think about what we discussed? You know, helping me out with training?'

'Yes,' he said, 'I did. I think I'd like to do it but we need to sort out who's going to help out here before we do anything else.'

The six million dollar question. I took a deep breath. 'How do you get on with Gordon?'

There was an ominous pause. 'Gordon?' he said, then again 'Gordon', thoughtfully.

'Yes,' I said, more to stop him saying Gordon's name again than anything.

'Well, he's very… hard working.'

'And conscientious,' I said, 'and at a loose end at present. He's had a bit of a shock, losing his shop like that, and I think he needs to keep himself busy and take on a new challenge. Not that you're a challenge,' I said hurriedly, 'what I should have said was, something different. Something to broaden his horizons, get him out of the rut...'

'Show him some new ideas in action and keep him out of your hair at the same time, you mean!' Miles was laughing at me!

'Well, yes, if you put it that way,' I said, with a grin. 'Then you will? Take him in, so to speak? At least for a while so we can get our show on the road.'

'Of course I will. He's got a few rough edges, has Gordon, but he's not all bad and we get along alright together. Shall you tell him, or shall I speak with him?'

'It should come from me.' Unfortunately, I thought, remembering my last encounter with Gordon. 'I'll see him later this afternoon. I'm sure he'll call you before close of business today.'

Next I called Lucas.

'Good morning,' he said brightly.

'Good morning,' I said, a bit more warily. There was a pause while I gathered my thoughts. 'It's amazingly easy to earn an undeserved reputation, isn't it?' I started. 'All it takes is a poor memory!'

'Mmm,' he mused. 'Perhaps you should tell me what comes before the poor memory part. Not that it's any of my business, of course, but you can't leave a chap's curiosity unsatisfied, can you?' He was laughing at me too. I seemed to have a talent for amusing people this morning.

'One of the volunteers at Lupin Lane found... it... in a sack of donations on Tuesday. Shona sniffed a lot. Fred, one of the volunteers, said it should fetch a good price and Margaret thought he wanted to test it all first! I signed it out in the book and was planning to find a safe disposal for it. Until my new car arrived yesterday morning, that is, and I completely forgot about it. Thanks for the car, by the way, but it means you have to take some of the responsibility for my embarrassment, you know.'

The words were out before I could stop them. That wasn't the way one spoke to the Shops Director, I was sure, even in jest. I waited for the sky to fall in on my head.

'Touché,' he said and I nearly fell off my chair. 'I thought you might be the sort of person who enjoyed a surprise – the car, I mean – but I guess I should have warned you.'

'That's OK. The surprise was great. Just what I needed, in fact. The last ten days have been a bit of a roller coaster and I think there're still a few loops to go.'

'Yes. And that reminds me. I understand you're meeting the insurance assessors at Chilton Street this afternoon?'

'That's right. It looks pretty bad, Lucas. The fire officer I spoke to, just after it happened, seemed to think the whole of the building front might collapse. They've put jacks underneath it for now but it doesn't look hopeful.'

'Malcolm is on his way to meet you. He'll be at Chilton Street at around 2pm, traffic permitting. You've met him, haven't you?'

'Yes, a few weeks ago at my first HQ briefing.'

'Good, so you'll recognise each other. He'll deal with the insurance people but you should feel free to chip in when they start talking time scales and anything relating to getting trading up and running again. Malcolm is an expert in his field but I need you to be my eyes and ears about future trading. We can't afford to lose any more time than we must on this one. Is that clear?'

'Absolutely.'

'Good. Malcolm will report back to me later today but I shall need your report and proposals when you're here on Monday. It looks like we're in for a busy day.' And he put the phone down. No 'goodbye' or anything. You never know where you are with men, do you? I thought. Such an unpredictable lot.

The phone rang again.

''Ello?' said a voice that managed to sound nervous and bellicose at the same time. 'This is Lillian Smith.' And for the second time that morning I nearly fell off my chair.

'Hello, Lillian. May I call you Lillian?'

'I suppose,' she muttered grudgingly.

'Thank you. And thanks for calling. What can I do for you?'

'Billy's bin in your skip again.' My heart sank. Had he hurt himself? Was he dead?

''E brought me a clock. It's a nice clock, just needed a bit of a clean. I put a battery in it and it works. What's 'e think 'e's doin', your manager, chucking away stuff what works and what 'e could sell?'

'Good question, Lillian. I'll ask him.' I waited. There was more to come, I just knew it and I felt a kind of suspense in the air, over the telephone wires, between us.

'It's OK, your shop,' she said at last, 'but it needs… summat. It needs… well, me. I bin shopping in charity shops for years, even when I was working and 'ad money. Your shop's alright but it needs a woman's touch. There, I said it. Not PC, is it? But that bloke you got runnin' it, he don't see the cobwebs and dust and them women in there, they's all 'is family. They're not going to gee 'im up, are they?'

'What do you suggest, Lillian?' And I held my breath

'You shouldn't judge my place from the outside, yer know,' she said, 'it's like a new pin inside. And my Billy, 'e's not a bad kid, 'e's just wild.' She paused and we both thought about our own definitions of 'wild'. 'If I come to work for you,' she continued, '*if*, mind you, don't you go thinking I've agreed. If I came to work for you, I'd want a free 'and with cleanin' the place up, no matter what yon Kenny says.'

'Agreed.' I'd figure out how to sell that one to Kenny later

'And my Billy gets to choose that thing every week. You know, what you said about choosing summat to take 'ome. Maybe that'll keep 'im out o' skip.'

'Lillian, I think that's an excellent idea. I have a condition or two, though.'

'What?' She was all suspicion.

'You do two separate sessions a week, for not less than two hours each. You make sure Billy knows that you enjoy your work, even if it kills you to do it. You don't let Billy upset the customers, you don't let him use the till or any other equipment and you don't let him sort stock. And you let me talk to Kenny before you do anything else.'

I thought she was going to tell me to get lost after that string of conditions, but after the longest pause she said, 'Done. I'll do Monday and Wednesday and I'll start next week.' With that, she put the phone down before I could say anything more.

I sat back in my chair and allowed myself a quiet moment of

self congratulation. All I had to do now was convince Kenny. No time like the present.

On the way out to the car I found Kylie in her office, feet up on the shelf that was her desk, sipping tea and with her mobile phone tucked between her chin and her shoulder. As I popped my head around the door, she leapt to her feet, looking guilty, spilling tea and dropping her phone.

'Call yer back,' she said, recovering the phone and sweeping tea droplets from her so very short skirt. 'Er... that was Bingo,' she said, blushing furiously. 'We're... sort of... seein' each uvver. Tonight.'

'That's nice for you, Kylie. Have you told him about Charlie yet?'

'Glory, no! 'e knows I got a kid but 'e don't know 'e's the Dad or about... you know... Rupe and that stuff.' She lowered her head a little, letting her hair shield her face for a moment or two.

'How's Charlie?' I asked gently. 'Is he home yet?'

''E's talkin' to me now,' she said in a small voice, 'and says 'e'll come 'ome soon.' She lifted her head ''Es quite bright really, yer know, and me mum says 'e's sleeping OK.'

'That's good.' I touched her arm lightly, smiling. 'Let me know if you need time off when he comes home. Kids are hard work, aren't they?'

'Too right!' she laughed.

'But we only have them for a short while. We should try to enjoy them as much as we can while they're with us.' She tilted her head slightly and looked at me knowingly. Had I given away too much? 'I'll be off, then,' I said, briskly. 'I won't be in the office tomorrow or Monday but I'll certainly be back on Tuesday. See you then.' And I turned on my heels and left.

First stop Canon Row and my best persuasive techniques on Kenny. In spite of everything I felt almost happy as I turned on to the ring road and put my foot down on Blink's accelerator. The sun was shining, the air was soft and the sky was blue. True, my marriage was falling apart, the job was driving me to distraction and I would probably never stop the rumours that I was Miss Whiplash in my spare time but what the hell, I'd come through worse.

'True,' said the little devil on my shoulder, 'but what did that poet chap say about keeping your head when everybody else was losing theirs? Wasn't there something about not understanding the situation?'

Oh, push off, misery, I shot the thought at him, what do you know about feeling good?

'Actually,' he said, 'quite a lot. I could show you…'

Go away!

There was a parking slot across the road from the shop. Why was there always a slot nearby when the weather was fine and nothing within half a mile when it was raining cats and dogs and I'd left my brolly behind? Kenny was behind the counter, dressed to kill as usual, and flirting with a young female customer. He had the grace to look a bit embarrassed when I caught his eye.

'Hello, lady boss,' he said effusively to hide his embarrassment. 'This is a pleasure, I'm sure.' It might be now, I thought, but wait until you hear what I've come to tell you.

'How're things, Kenny? Well done on your detective work, by the way, that was excellent work and I've had some success, thanks to you. Can we go somewhere to talk?'

He lead the way into the stock room, looking conspiratorial, and offered me tea. Remembering his kitchen facilities and my self imposed vow I thanked him and declined.

'You wish to talk about important matters?' he asked, looking curious and self-important at the same time.

'Well, yes, I do. It's about Ms Smith's little boy.'

'Ah!' he said, and pulled his chair closer. 'He has been arrested, perhaps?'

'No, he hasn't been arrested, or hurt, or punished. But I *have* spoken with his mother. I think we've found a way of stopping him. But I need your help. Your co-operation is absolutely vital to establishing some kind of control over his future activities.' First step, make them feel important.

Kenny straightened his back and sat even taller. 'But of course!' he said. 'I can be policeman as well as detective! Of course!'

'I was thinking more in the role of big brother, or uncle, perhaps.'

He looked puzzled but thoughtful. 'Mmm,' he said, 'I have little brothers. Yes, I can do that. But what? What is it I should do?'

'Help his mother find useful things to do around the shop. While she's here as a volunteer.'

For a moment his expression froze. Then it changed, with almost comical speed, through puzzlement, disbelief, amusement (I could almost see his thoughts – 'she's joking, right?'), truculence and then stubbornness.

'You are not serious,' he said. 'You are, I think, pulling my leg, yes?'

'No, Kenny, I'm not. Let me explain. Billy is a determined little thief and he seems to have no sense of danger or regard for consequences. That's about par for the course in a kid like him. Things aren't always what they seem though, because it seems that he's not stealing to feed a habit or breaking into things just to wreck them. He does it to take nice things home to his mum because she's house-proud but they have no money.' I paused and then continued. 'Lillian will come here as a volunteer and we can expect to see Billy here as well when he's not at school. I'll square that with HQ.' But how, I haven't a clue, I thought. 'She lives in walking distance so she'll be able to take home an item a week in lieu of bus fares. Except she'll let Billy choose. I think he won't want to ruin that chance for her or himself.'

I shut up then and let Kenny mull it over. After a while he said cautiously, 'This sounds not good to me. I am unhappy with a stranger volunteer.'

'I know, Kenny, you're used to having people you know around you. Still, look at it this way. It's difficult to ask your relatives to do the menial jobs – you know, like clean the kitchen and stuff.' Not to mention the lavatory, I thought. 'But Lillian is house-proud! Just think, she'll actually enjoy keeping your shop clean! That just has to be a plus, doesn't it?'

Kenny shifted in his seat, desperately trying to think of an objection he thought I'd listen to. 'But the child! What should I do if he is rude or steals from the shop or… or…' He ran out of 'ors'.

'We let them both go and revert to plan B.'

'Plan B?'

'Yes, plan B. I'll tell you about that if we need it.' Providing I can think of one if the time comes, I thought.

He slumped, defeated. 'OK,' he conceded, 'I am not liking this, but OK, I will try. But so must she and her little thief boy – or else!'

I grinned at him and patted his arm. 'Great! I'll let her know and tell her she starts on Monday. We'll speak on Tuesday and you can tell me how it works out on her first day. Thanks, Kenny, you're a real brick.' And I left before he could change his mind.

My euphoria was still with me and I decided to play hooky for an hour. A sandwich bar provided a fresh baguette and a bottle of orange juice and a dusty little park with a brave magnolia tree provided a small oasis of calm. God was in his heaven and all was right with the world. Just for once. And just for a little while. Before I knew it, the time was creeping toward two o' clock and it was time for me to set off to Chilton Street.

Once again there was a parking slot, although this time I could see it was probably because everyone thought the front of the building would fall into it. What the hell, I thought, nothing is going to spoil the way I feel today, and I parked Blink where I could keep an eye on it. Malcolm had beaten me to it. I could see him standing on the pavement, looking at the devastation and shaking his head.

'Hello, Malcolm, good to see you again,' I greeted him, fingers crossed behind my back against the blatant lie.

He turned to face me slowly, and gave me a piercing look. 'Mmm,' he said, and turned back to the building. We gazed together, in companionable silence, until two smartly dressed guys wearing hard hats joined us a few minutes later. They introduced themselves as Matt Butcher and Declan Baker. Butcher and Baker. Sounded like a supermarket chain. Matt and Dec could be a chain of carpet retailers. A grin tugged at my mouth but I controlled myself with some difficulty.

Malcolm drew them to one side, effectively excluding me from their conversation. I rocked gently on my heels and toes, gazing into the darkened interior of the wrecked shop where bits of fabric from the ruined stock stirred in a faint flow of air. Fortunately my sharp hearing allowed me to eavesdrop while they talked of loadings, materials, JCBs, plans and timescales. It was the plans and timescales that interested me most and eventually I sidled over to join the boys club. ''Scuse me,' I said politely, 'but I'd be interested to know how long it's likely to be before we can resume trading.'

All three men looked at me as though I'd suddenly grown two heads. Matt said, 'We have to determine whether we can repair the building or whether we need to demolish and re-build. It'll be a long time before you can begin to think about trading again; several months at least, and perhaps as long as a couple of years. These things take time, you know,' he explained, as though he was talking to a small child.

'Of course,' I said, 'but won't it take about the same length of time whichever option you choose?'

'That depends on whether the landlord's insurance will cover either option or whether he's covered only for repairs,' Dec said impatiently.

'Ah,' I said, 'forgive me, but I was under the impression that we knew that already.' I looked at Matt and Dec in turn. 'Aren't you the landlord's insurance agents?' They glanced at each other, with looks that said I knew nothing about how these things worked and I should really stay out of the way of the big boys.

'Malcolm, may we have a moment please?' I drew him gently to one side. 'I've looked through our lease,' I said and he shifted slightly, which told me he probably hadn't or, if he had, he was uncomfortable that I had, 'and I notice that our lease only has another 18 months to run. I also notice that, in the last two years of this lease, we can quit on three months' notice on payment of a penalty. The penalty is three months rent at market value. This shop is uninhabitable. It has no market value.'

'What are you saying?'

'I'm saying that I have to recommend that we give notice that we are terminating our lease, effective today. It's going to cost us three months' rent and we can walk away from this without wasting any more time. I can look for another retail unit to move to and you can recover loss of trading income from our own insurance policy, can't you?' He nodded. 'Good. I think we can leave Matt and Dec to their own devices, don't you?'

'Mmm,' Malcolm said, but reluctantly. 'Finding and re-fitting a new shop unit is time-consuming. Neither their insurance or ours will cover our time and lost trade for that whereas, if we rebuild here, either their or our insurance will cover almost all our costs.'

"Almost' still leaves a lot of money though, doesn't it? And would our insurance company pay if they knew about an alternative strategy that would minimise their losses? And we have to pay Gordon and Belinda in the meantime or make them redundant.

They've both been with the charity for years and I gather our redundancy terms are generous.'

'Mmm,' he said again. 'I'll need to see your hypothesis worked through with figures to see if it is correct before I could recommend to Mr Barrington that we terminate our lease here and move on. In theory, however, you might have a point.' He re-joined Matt and Dec and, a few minutes later, waved his hand in my general direction and was gone.

Yes! I metaphorically punched the air with an invisible show of triumph. Who wants to wait while insurance companies argue and fuss about when and how and who and stuff? Now all I had to do was find another shop unit. Common sense flies out the window when optimism reigns, but I preferred optimism to the alternative.

In all the excitement, I'd quite forgotten that Gordon was supposed to be here with us. Where the hell was he?

My mobile rang. 'Hello?' I said.

'Hello,' said a voice, 'this is Gordon.'

'Hello, Gordon, you must be psychic, I was just thinking about you. Where are you, are you OK?'

'No, I'm not OK!' A feeling of déja vu spread over me. 'But I will be. I quit. Resign. Retire. Whatever you care to call it, I'm through, had enough, finished!' Boy, did he underline his point!

'Gordon, I'm really sorry to hear that. I've just told HQ that I'm looking for a new shop unit for you.' Well, it was only stretching the truth a bit, wasn't it? I'd told Malcolm and he was from HQ, wasn't he? True, he hadn't actually agreed and I still had to win over Jean. And Lucas. And the Board. Still, it was close enough.

'What?' Gordon said, with a bit less heat and a bit of curiosity.

'We've decided it will take far too long and be far too difficult to re-build. That it would be far more sensible to look for a new place. I was rather hoping you'd take the lead on that, since you have so much more experience than me with the charity. Plus, since that won't take all your time and I know how much you like to keep busy, Miles has asked if you could see your way clear to giving him a hand for a bit because he's pledged himself to another project that will take quite a bit of his time. We were struggling to think of a safe pair of hands and there you were, free just at the right time.' I paused, letting it all sink in.

'Eh?' he said. 'I thought… well, that you'd be wanting to… you know, get rid of us. I have my pride, you know, I wasn't going to wait around to get the push.' I could feel anger rising inside me. Pride. Stupid, childish, ridiculous male pride. How much grief had that caused through history? I squashed down the feeling. After all, the history of the world and my little problems really had nothing to do with Gordon, had they?

'So what do you think?' The last thing I needed right now was to lose Gordon. Difficult though he was, I needed him if my plans to use Miles elsewhere were going to work out. He wouldn't be available to help with my re-launch if there was no-one looking after Kensington Place.

'Well, that puts an entirely different complexion on things,' Gordon said, rather warmly, I thought, much to my surprise. 'If you need me that badly it would be very churlish of me to let you down, wouldn't it? I'll phone Miles now and start with him on Monday. Presumably my salary won't be affected, I hope? Good.' And he rang off.

Phew! But the selfish sod hadn't once mentioned his hapless assistant, Belinda. Men!

It was early, not yet three o'clock, but I'd had enough of all of them for one day. Later, much later, I looked back at that afternoon and wondered if some instinct was casting a caring wrap around me by giving me that brief space, in the soft warmth of a perfect spring afternoon, as a benediction to arm me against what was to happen the next day. Fanciful or what? Still, I played truant and went home. I took out the lawn mower and filled the air with the sweet scent of newly cut grass, then set up a deck chair in the sun, with the cat purring on my lap and an icy G&T in my hand. Bliss!

-11-
Endings and Renewals

I woke with a jerk. Not Greg, not that kind of jerk. It was really early, I could tell because the cat was still asleep across my feet. She'd normally be up and about at least half an hour before I was, patrolling the kitchen waiting for the first person to appear who might know where her breakfast was. I'd forgotten to put her out last night, which I did quite often. I think it was a convenient forgetfulness, really, because I rather liked to feel her weight across my feet when I woke up in the night. It was quite pleasant being alone in the bed, I realised, apart from the cat. I wasn't squashed into a corner by Greg's bulk taking up half the space and the cat taking up most of the rest. I stretched. Maybe Greg was asleep on the sofa.

I knew I'd not go to sleep again so I flicked on the radio and listened to a bit of some farming programme for a while. Bad weather and poor harvest. When was it ever any different in a farmer's world, I wondered, unless you lived in Ambridge, like the Archers? Still, even they had their problems. Eventually I decided to treat myself to breakfast, not a usual occurrence since I was habitually late in the mornings, and face the world with a full stomach.

Greg wasn't on the sofa. There was no sign that he'd been home at all last night. I mulled over the possibilities while I slowly got myself ready for today's meeting with the other area managers, my new colleagues. My thoughts all came back to one thing. My marriage was over, it was just still trying to struggle on because neither Greg nor I could do the necessary thing and knock it on the head for a merciful death.

The meeting wasn't until mid-morning, and it wasn't a long journey, but I'd never been to the place before so it seemed like a good idea to start early and have time for breakfast when I got

184

there. Given my propensity for getting lost it seemed like a sensible thing to do.

My new car was sitting in the drive, gleaming gently in the early morning sun. I stroked its bonnet, feeling shallow but proud. I found a duster and polished windows that were gleaming anyway. Picked a few imaginary specks of fluff from seat covers. Slid into the seat and settled in slowly, savouring the luxury. Well, comparative luxury anyway.

I took a slightly different route than usual, since I wasn't going to the office, and set out across town, glad I'd get clear before the traffic became heavy with the daily school run. I hadn't planned for the jam caused by the bus that had tried to get through too small a gap between a parked white van and a trailer offloading new cars outside a local dealership. We crawled for about half a mile, stuck in a tailback. It would have been quicker to walk. Eventually I could see the cause of the problem and realised that we'd be clear of it in a few minutes, unlike the poor smucks that were coming the other way. They were well and truly stuck for the duration, by the look of it.

Driving clear, the little cheer in my throat died as I recognised my own car, the one Greg was using, idling on the other side of the road, stuck in the traffic that was trying to get around the obstruction in the opposite direction. And he wasn't alone. Sitting next to him was a woman with long dark hair and a laughing face, leaning over towards him with one hand on his chest and the other against his cheek.

They hadn't seen me, of course, they were focused on each other and, besides, I was in a car Greg wouldn't recognise. I drove past in a daze, and all the little clues – and the big ones – of the past few weeks clanged together to make a perfect picture of discovery, painted in glorious colour and backed by surround-sound, that I couldn't deny any longer.

I pulled over into a bus stop and started to shake. I wasn't sure with what. Anger? Yep! Pain? Oh, yes! Disappointment? Certainly! I wanted to kick something, scream, swear, anything. I dug out my mobile to call him and yell abuse at him while she was next to him and, hopefully, listening, but I stopped halfway through retrieving his number from the phone's memory. The little devil on my shoulder was trying to tell me something and this time I listened.

'Hold on! Don't give yourself away, idiot! He doesn't know you know, does he?'

'No,' I answered, on the verge of tears.

'All his stuff is still at home, isn't it, except for the car, that is?'

'Yes,' I answered silently.

'There's his beloved snooker cue, that leather coat he's so proud of and the beer he's brewing in the pantry. His golf clubs, souvenir football programmes, the England shirt from the '66 World Cup?'

'Yes,' I said, this time out loud.

'He'd really miss them, wouldn't he?'

'He sure would!' And a grim light began to dawn.

'It would be a real shock if he couldn't find them. Or, even better, if he found them but...' I didn't give him the chance to finish. I was mad enough to think up my own mayhem!

I started the car again and shot off down a little side road that would take me, in a roundabout fashion, back home avoiding the traffic jam. I headed straight for the garage and the tool box I kept on the bench at the back. My memory hadn't let me down; inside was a blister pack containing a new Yale lock barrel. I'd bought it ages ago for the front door after Greg said he'd lost his keys. He'd found them the next day, in his jacket where he said they weren't, and the new lock had languished ever since. It took less than ten minutes to change the lock on the front door and Part One was completed. Next, the beer barrels. I wasn't sure I could lift them but they weren't that big and anger gave me strength. I hauled them onto the patio in the back garden, opened the bungs and tipped them over. The smell was indescribable! It was like every hop harvest and party room the-morning-after-the-night-before all at once. And it was out of doors! Lord knows what it would have been like in a confined space. Suffocation, probably.

Next, the bedroom. That was quite painful. Had he... here... with her? I shook myself, deliberately refusing to think about that. I found the snooker cue propped up in the corner of the wardrobe and pulled out his leather coat as well. In a chest of drawers I found the England shirt, his Lâcoste sweater and the other stuff he was so proud of, including the silver cuff links that had so mysteriously appeared around the time of his last birthday. Hidden under his socks (original, or what?) I found two letters addressed to him in a hand I didn't recognise. I held them for a moment, then took one of them out of the envelope and slowly unfolded it. I wasn't going to read it but wanted to know who she was, this woman who was crackers enough to want my waster of a chap. The address was across town – I knew it – and the letters were signed 'Jane'. Well, having seen her, I knew she wasn't plain. I wasn't sure if that was a help or not.

I gathered up the collection and took it all downstairs. Everything except the letters went in the car. I put the letters into a sandwich bag, the kind with tie handles on the top, and tied it to the outside of the back door knob. Then I locked and bolted the door from the inside and left by the front door with its new lock guarding it against entry by anyone without a key. Of which I had the only two in existence.

During the drive down to where I was to meet the team, my mood fluctuated between jealousy, self pity, anger and, oddly, relief. We'd had some good times, Greg and me, but there had been some awful ones as well. It occurred to me now that those times were far too many for comfort. I refused to think about them although I could feel them all crowding in on my memory, hammering at the edges of my mind, demanding to be let in. Rage fuelled me.

It was still too early for the meeting when I arrived, so I stuffed Greg's things into an old Tesco carrier bag, tucked the snooker cue under my arm and set off down the High Street. Marc had said that the address I was looking for, our regional office, was behind one of our shops and I found it pretty quickly. I handed the stuff over to the volunteer manning the till, explaining what was in the bag and extracting a promise from her that the value of some of the items inside would be fully exploited and that they wouldn't be sold for peanuts. She thanked me as she took a quick peek. She smiled at me broadly and said they'd be sure to do quite well out of such quality. I hoped she wasn't just humouring me.

I smiled back, left her to it and went to find breakfast. I was suddenly ravenously hungry. Forty minutes later I was back, stuffed with the best full English the local greasy spoon could provide. Why not? I'd felt sick before so I wasn't going to feel any worse. The volunteer I'd spoken to was surprised to see me back and she looked a bit concerned. I think she thought I might have changed my mind and had come to retrieve my donation. I introduced myself and asked if any of the others had arrived.

'Oh, yes!' she said, relieved. 'Sally Bridges is here and Marc Childers has called to say he's in traffic but will be here a soon as possible. Go through, Sally is in the office.'

Sliding around donation bags and stepping over boxes, I found the office next to the kitchen. The hairs on the back of my neck stood on end as I looked at the back of the woman who had her back to me as she looked out of the window on the other side of the room.

'Sarah Wooley!' I breathed. 'Good grief!'

She turned and, after a few seconds of puzzlement and dawning recognition, she cried, 'Gillian! Oh, my God! Is it really you?'

We stared at each other for a few seconds then both spoke at once.

'The last time I saw you…'

'It must be nearly 20 years…'

Then we both stopped and laughed.

'You first,' I said. 'Why "Sally", and how come you're here and not in China or Africa or somewhere?'

'Well, my mother-in-law is Sarah so my husband decided he'd call me Sally to avoid confusion. It just stuck. Now everyone uses it. As to far flung places, I found out that I hate flying, spices in my food and creepy crawlies in my bed. Oh, and I missed my hair dryer. And Chanel Number Five. How shallow is that, then?'

I chuckled. I'd always thought, when we were at school together, that Sarah enjoyed her creature comforts too much – and preferably without crawling creatures since she'd had a phobia about spiders – to be the roving free spirit she said she wanted to be. Sarah had been just as naively inspired by tales of selfless devotion to ghastly duty as most schoolgirls, but the practicalities hadn't occurred to her at the time. We'd both grown up since then.

'What about you?' she asked. 'You were going to travel too, weren't you?'

'Yes,' I said, 'and I did, for a while. I went to South Africa to stay with my brother and then moved on to France. I came back when my mum died.'

'Oh, Gillian, I'm sorry. I didn't know. What happened?' Sarah had known my folks, just as I had hers. Each set of parents had said their darling daughter had been led astray by the other. We'd egged each other on really, doing things that neither of us would have thought of alone but which seemed to spring into our minds almost instantaneously when we were at school. How we'd survived without being killed, or at least expelled, was a mystery. Like the time when… But that was another story.

'She caught measles from the kid next door, it turned to pneumonia and she was gone within the week. Odd, really, she'd nursed all of us through it when we were little and never caught it then.' I remembered Sarah's mum well, a quiet, gentle woman who'd been totally bemused by her bright, vibrant and extrovert daughter.

'That must have been awful.'

'It was at the time, but it was a while ago now. What about your people? Your mum?'

'She's well and just as unworldly as ever. She's still in the same house. My dad died last summer. The big C. Yours?'

'Dad will outlive us all. He's just started a new business and is driving his bank manager wild. He moved house last year and is renovating a Victorian vicarage, would you believe!'

At that moment Marc arrived, muttering to himself and scolding under his breath like an old woman. 'Bloody road works! Damned lights! Not a single set in sync! Unbelievable! We can put men on the moon but we can't even synchronise traffic lights.'

He was amazed when Sarah and I explained how we knew each other, and a little about our history, and was even more spooked when he found out that history had been 100 miles away in a different city. It wasn't as if we'd both gone home after youthful adventures and met up again there; to lose contact then find each other years later and 100 miles from our original home must have been beyond logical probabilities. If there was such a thing as logical probabilities.

We were discussing 'strange co-incidences I have known' when Martin arrived and we had to go over it again for his benefit. He wouldn't be stopped until he'd shared his own 'it's a small world' story and told us about the time he'd knocked down a pedestrian on a dirt track in India, and found it was the manager of his local branch library at home. He did concede, however, that the guy was visiting his home village just a couple of miles away and Martin was in the area only because Ranjit had told him so much about its beauty that Martin had been compelled to make a detour on the journey to join a walking tour through the lower slopes of the Himalayas. Not quite such a coincidence then, given Martin's driving skills, which seemed even more accident-prone than mine.

Then it was down to business. For three hours we talked about sales promotions, targets, budgets, the shortage of volunteers and what to do with all the stuff that people gave us that we weren't allowed to sell. Electricals, huge amounts of kids' toys and household stuff like pillows and cushions, 'over 18' books and videos… the list seemed endless and all because we couldn't satisfy all sorts of regulations. The time flew by and ideas were tossed around the table till my head hurt with the speed of it. They asked me about Chilton Street's demolition, about Shona's pet stalker and what the plan was for Ginger. I listened to hair-raising tales of shop-lifters, a manager who failed to enforce the 'no dogs' rule and had to separate fighting terriers among the clothes stands, and other assorted tales of everyday life in charity shops. The coffee cups stacked up and the biscuit plates emptied until Martin said, 'Enough! That's enough. It's time to call time and find a pub somewhere. Who's for a little R&R?'

We all nodded and verbally agreed in various terms:

'About time…'

'Thought you'd never ask…'

'It's your shout…'

Marc looked across at me and said, 'How're you fixed for a late night, Gillian? We don't see each other that often, especially without Management hanging around, so we thought we might make a night of it. Should have warned you, I suppose, sorry, just forgot you didn't know the routine. What would your old man say if you didn't get home till the small hours? Can you call him to let him know?'

I'd almost forgotten the traumas of the past few days in the distractions of the morning. Marc's question brought it all flooding back and I was lost for words. I felt a lump rising in my throat and, before I knew what was happening, to the consternation of everyone else and to my horror, the tears were streaming down my cheeks.

They all leapt out of their seats. Sarah put her arms around me, Marc started patting my hand and Martin paced about behind my chair muttering, 'Oh, dear. This is dreadful. You poor girl. What is it?' and similar sort of stuff that comes out of the male of the species when he's completely at sea in a woman's tears. Eventually I calmed down enough to tell them what had happened and there were more sympathetic choruses.

'What a rat...'

'I'd have trashed everything he owned and taken it round to her place in bin bags.' (This from Sarah).

'...and you'd no idea? The bastard!'

I had to smile, in spite of it all. None of us was perfect and I couldn't imagine that any of us was lily white as far as a little sin was concerned.

'Too right,' said the little devil on my shoulder, 'remind me to tell you about that one over there one day...', which left me wondering which of the three of them he meant. Still, it made me feel better to know that they were trying hard to look after me and make me feel better.

Eventually I calmed down and repaired my face with a little judicious war-paint while the others decided where to go. Within half an hour, we were in a local café bar called Caprio's. Pretentious place but the prices weren't too exorbitant and, anyway, everybody seemed to assume that I was in need of copious amounts of good cheer and I didn't buy a round until about nine-thirty. By this time we were all plenty cheerful and in need of something to soak up the liquid. We discussed the various merits of Indian food, Chinese food, Mongolian food and a few others I instantly forgot, until we finally settled on Italian.

I have no memory of what any of us ate but the Chianti was good. I called my neighbour at some time and managed to be coherent enough to ask her to feed the cat before I realised that I'd locked her out of the house as well as Greg. I explained, in a rather garbled fashion, that there was a new lock on the door and she said not to worry, she'd put a saucer outside by the back door where Sammy could find it, and invite him in when he turned up. She said he spent as much time at her place as he did at mine anyway, so was sure to be quite OK about it.

She didn't ask me about the lock, maybe out of politeness or maybe because she already knew the gist of what was going on – or both. But she said she'd seen Greg at the house earlier in the evening. What with the high fence around the back garden she couldn't see what he was doing but she'd heard a lot of banging and swearing for a while before he'd slammed his car door (*my* car door!) and driven away in a cloud of exhaust fumes and screeching tyres. For some reason I thought that was hysterically funny and told the gang. They all saw the funny side of it too and for about ten minutes, we were all in the grip of manic hysteria. The waiters thought we'd all gone bonkers and kept asking us if everything was alright. All in all it was a good night.

Next morning was a different matter. I woke up in a strange bed for the second time in two weeks. This time the sun was streaming directly onto my face and when I turned over to try to ease my aching head on to a cooler part of the pillow, I made eye contact with large, limpid brown eyes. Startled, I leapt backwards, yelled, fell off the edge of the bad and ended up in a crumpled heap in the small gap between the bed and the radiator, my right elbow and left knee having somehow made painful contact with something hard on the way.

I pulled myself up and peered over the edge of the bed, rubbing the injured bits of me gingerly. The eyes were still there, looking at me, unblinking, from the far side. I could see the top of an impossibly blond head, long silky ears, huge brown eyes and a wet, shiny black nose.

'I see you've met my seven-stone blonde bombshell,' said a voice, and I looked up to meet Marc's amused gaze. 'Did she startle you? She's just curious. One of her tricks is opening doors so nowhere in the house is very private, I'm afraid.'

I realised I was in my underwear – at least I wasn't naked this time – so stayed where I was, in the shelter of the bed.

'Fancy breakfast?' he asked. 'I need something to take the fur off my tongue, I don't know about you. Orange juice suit you?' And the dog followed him as he turned to go down to the kitchen.

Having found my clothes and the bathroom, I joined him there ten minutes later. There was a large tumbler of juice on a mat on the table and the wonderful smell of fresh coffee and warm bread wafted across from the kitchen worktop. Marc put the coffee pot and a large dish of warm breakfast rolls on the table next to a jar of honey.

'Did we... last night?' I asked, waving my hand in the air vaguely, hoping he would understand without my having to say what I meant. Not remembering was quite humiliating enough.

'I don't think so,' he said, 'we were both rather... er... tired.' He grinned and I smiled back, carefully so as not to cause my face to wrinkle too much. That would be painful since my skin felt especially sensitive this morning.

'You mean we were legless.'

'Absolutely rat-arsed!' And we both laughed, then cringed from the pain it caused. 'I couldn't have raised a finger let alone anything else,' Marc said, 'so your maidenly virtue was quite safe.'

'Probably just as well,' I said, 'shouldn't mix business with pleasure and we are working colleagues, after all.'

'Rubbish.'

'Quite. Don't usually say such pompous stuff. Need time to get used to being footloose and fancy free again, I suppose.'

'As long as that's all it is. Now, tuck in, you need something to put you back together before you drive home – and plenty of strong black coffee.'

Home. Oh, Lord!

It was late afternoon by the time I got there. There was no point in tempting fate or the traffic police by leaving before the night's excesses had worked their way through my system. Beside, I wasn't sure what was waiting at home, apart from a hungry cat, so I was in no real hurry.

The house looked quiet and innocent when I arrived and there was no sign of Greg or my car. No broken windows, no trampled flower beds. Just a pale, sunny Saturday with a few of the neighbours' kids out on their bikes or roller blades and the odd sparrow coughing in the elderberry bushes. I made a dash for the front door, key in hand, just in case.

There was a little mail on the mat, the usual circulars and bills plus a more interesting letter from an old friend who still kept in touch from the safe distance of some overpaid, tax-free haven halfway around the world. There was also a large, foolscap page, folded into four, addressed to me on the outside in Greg's bold hand. Coward that I was I decided to shower, get changed and have a cuppa before reading it. Likewise I dodged the winking answerphone.

It's amazing how long you can stand under the shower, gradually getting pinker and pinker and steaming up everything till water rains off windows, tiles and the loo cistern, when there's something unpleasant waiting for you when you get out. Still, there's only so much water the skin can take before it starts to look like a prune and only so much hot water in the tank anyway. Eventually I was forced out, by cold water and wrinkled skin, to face the world again.

Towelled dry, I wandered around in my bathrobe for a while, telling myself that my skin was too delicate, after all that soaking, and would rub off if I tried to slide into clothes too soon. Tosh, of course, but it was all I could think of as an excuse to avoid the inevitable. Eventually I was completely dry, dressed and the kettle had boiled. Pencil in hand and paper close by, I pushed the 'message' button on the answerphone. It bleeped and stopped. Bleeped again. And again. Three calls, no words. This was even more ominous.

'Hello, Titch, this is Colin, how are you?' I breathed again as my brother's cheery voice boomed around the room. 'I'm passing through your way next Friday, are you around? I might even buy you a drink this time! Give me a call when you've got a minute. Byeeee!'

Another bleep and nothing. Then Greg's voice.

'I know you're there, Gillian, this is childish.' Childish! Me! Cheek! 'Pick up, will you, we need to talk.' Yeh, right, like an Eskimo needs more snow. 'Oh, be sulky then, we have to talk sometime you know!' The closing bleep told me he'd put the phone down.

So far, so good. No obscenities, no yelling. It occurred to me that the Bitch (my new name for the not-so-plain Jane) might have been listening and he'd restrained himself because he hadn't wanted her to get a bad impression. I sat down on my comfy sofa, feet tucked underneath me, cuppa in one hand and Greg's note in the other. I took a deep breath and unfolded it.

'Called around this morning to collect my stuff. No-one at home. Will come back.' And that was it. What an anti-climax! Stuff the tea, I

thought, I need a G&T! Fortunately I'd replenished the stocks just a few days before and now, trembling with adrenalin-fuelled reaction that had nowhere to go, I poured a large-ish measure. Wrapped around the warming glow of alcohol, my trepidation seemed a bit cowardly and, after a second, I began to wonder if I'd misjudged Greg. Maybe he wasn't such a shit after all and we could talk about what happened next like two sensible adults. I looked at the phone and pondered. I poured a second G&T and looked at the bluish tinge of Dutch courage in the glass, the only sort I'm really familiar with but better than nothing.

Eventually I picked up the phone and dialled his mobile. He answered right away and caught me off-guard. 'So what's new?' said the little devil on my shoulder.

'I wondered how long you'd be able to resist calling me,' Greg said and I suppressed an urge to say something cutting. Probably because I couldn't think of anything suitable that wouldn't make matters worse than they already were. He sounded smug and I regretted the thoughts I'd had about being adult and him maybe not being so bad.

'It was a bit childish to change the lock,' he said, 'and to dump my beer was just unbelievable. I'll come round now to pack up the rest so you'd better be in this time.'

A pinkish mist began to creep into the edges of my vision. I held my cool. I thought I could hear music in the background, like a movie score, then realised it was in my head. High Noon. Yes, that was it, High Noon. Then a little bit of the theme from Jaws.

'Are you still there?' he said, sounding angry now.

'Yes,' I said in what I hoped was a conciliatory, breathless sort of way. 'I'm here. Look, I know this is going to sound like I'm being awkward but it isn't that, it's just that I'd find it really hard to have you here, moving around the house, packing up and everything. Can't you understand what that would be like for me?' I was quite chuffed at the little tremor in my voice. Lost and kind of vulnerable. Hopefully it was mostly an act. I didn't dare look at it too closely, just in case it was real and I fell apart at the crucial moment. Besides, the last thing I wanted was him prowling around the house looking for all his precious souvenirs. Which weren't here, of course.

'I could pack your stuff for you and bring it round. Well, bring it wherever you'd like me to. It would be quicker and I probably know better than you where all your stuff is.' After all, I thought, I'm the one that washed and ironed everything and put it away. You couldn't even find a clean pair of socks!

'Well,' he said, sounding reluctant and thoughtful, 'I'm not sure about that.' There was a pause, then: 'I suppose it would be easier' For you, I thought, you lazy sod.

'It would,' I agreed

'When could you do it?' he asked

'This evening? About eight?'

'That would be OK,' he said, 'you can bring it to John's place. We're... I'm there now.' John was a friend of ours. Well, more of Greg's really, but it hurt to think that mutual friends had probably known what was going on while I'd been kept in the dark.

As I put down the phone, with the untouched G&T next to it, I realised I was rocking backwards and forwards in my chair, very gently. Like a caged animal or a traumatised child. Good grief! I shook myself. This is no good! Snap out of it! Wallowing won't help.

'No,' said the little devil on my shoulder gleefully, 'but I can show you something that will. How about a little more mayhem?' I ignored him and went upstairs to begin.

By early evening all Greg's stuff was carefully packed and the bags were neatly stacked at the foot of the stairs while I phoned for a taxi. I put the spare set of keys to my car in my pocket and was glad I'd had only the one G&T. It wouldn't do to get pulled up by the local plods before I'd got clear. I knew John's house. His drive would be full of bits of cars as usual, with no room for Greg to park. He'd have left his car – my car – on the street close by. A rescue mission was afoot!

The bags sat there, innocently hiding what was inside. Every button, every zip removed, every hem let down, every pocket with its stitching neatly cut. Nothing damaged. Well, sort of not damaged. Just completely unwearable, except for the sweaters and T shirts. The satisfaction was huge. I hugged it to me like a lifebelt in a storm at sea. The taxi arrived and the driver, of course, watched from the comfort of his front seat while I lugged the bags down the drive and into the back seat alongside me.

Fifteen minutes later I paid off the taxi outside John's place and stood there on the pavement, like little orphan Annie with bags around my feet. A curtain twitched. I touched the car keys in my coat pocket and spotted my little blue Golf about three places down on the other side of the road. Close enough? Turning slightly so my left side was hidden from any peepers at the window, I pointed the key and pressed the button. The car lights blinked and the locks released. All set for a quick getaway!

I lugged the bags to the front door and pushed the bell, heart thumping wildly. There's something to be said for this adrenaline stuff, I thought, it gives your heart a really good workout if nothing else.

John opened the door. I didn't know whether to be relieved or disappointed.

'Hello, Gillian,' he said, 'look, I'm really sorry about all this.' He was clearly very uncomfortable and uncertain what he was supposed to say. My heart didn't exactly bleed for him.

'You should be,' I said, cuttingly I hoped, indulging in some quick-shot soul-salving. 'I thought we were friends.'

'We are!'

'You think so? Well, let's just say then that your idea of friendship is different from mine.' I wafted my hands vaguely in the direction of the bags on the doorstep. 'It's all here. Every single last item.' That was left in the house, I thought. 'Clothes, CDs, bathroom stuff, everything. Even the odd trainer.' John raised an eyebrow. I wasn't about to enlighten him about the night Greg had thrown a shoe out of the bedroom window at a howling dog, only to see the hound pick it up and run off with it. I'd been convulsed, he'd been peevish and had threatened the hound with a painful castration when he caught it. Which he didn't. Which left an odd trainer behind.

I saw a curtain twitch again and I made to move away.

'I'll give you a call soon,' said John. I made eye contact and he had the grace to blush before adding, 'Well, maybe not then.' And he watched me walk down the drive. At the gate I glanced back to see him passing Greg's bags inside and, behind him in the shadowed hall, another figure taking each one from him. I legged it fast down the road to my car.

Within a minute I was inside, key in ignition, engine firing into life (thank heavens), off down the road to the corner and away. Two streets away I had to pull over and stop. I was bawling my eyes out.

I couldn't face the house again that night. I went for a walk by the river for a while and then to the pub by the bridge where I propped up the bar, nursing a glass of orange juice. I was driven out after an hour or so when a group of three couples came in and I could see they were celebrating an engagement. That was the last thing I needed.

At home the answerphone was blinking. I made myself some beans on toast, more for something to do than because I was hungry, then attacked the gin bottle again and pushed the button on the machine to hear what he had to say. Except it wasn't Greg, it was my niece, Leila.

'Hi, Auntie Gillian,' she breezed, 'I'm down your way tomorrow for a wine-tasting thing at that winery we went to last year. How about joining us? There'll be about 20 of us altogether and we could have dinner. Call me! I'm at home tonight. Bye!'

I smiled. Lovely girl, Leila. Pity her mum had been a fan of Derek and the Dominos. The last thing our Leila was was a rock-chick! Clever, beautiful and going places. Sometimes you can really hate the ones you love!

The next call was from my friend Jan, who'd said when we were at college that she was never going to marry or have kids and had kept her promise until last year when in the space of four months, she'd met the man of her wildest dreams, married him and got pregnant. Two months ago she'd delivered a beautiful boy and called him Gilbert. Well, she was always a little odd.

'Hello, Gillian, how are you? You haven't called me for ages and it was your turn! Are you OK? You seemed a bit tense the last time we gossiped. Listen, we've decided to have Gil baptised…' That really did make me sit up and take notice. As far as I knew Jan only went to church for weddings and funerals '…and we'd like you to be his godmother. Call me, will you?'

I was crying again, but this time it was different. Life goes on. I rang Leila and we gossiped. She said she'd introduce me to a handsome Italian wine importer she knew. I asked her if he was married and how old he was and she said he wasn't and he was 27.

I said 27 was a bit young for me and she said, 'Don't be daft, it's perfect for therapy.' We agreed to meet at the winery at noon the next day and she told me to wear the red jacket she loved so much. She said it was brash and bold and just the sort of mood I should cultivate.

Next I called Jan. Gil was bawling in the background and Jan said he'd just thrown up over her new cashmere skirt. I asked why was she holding the baby while wearing cashmere and she said friends were over for dinner and Gil was supposed to be asleep. She still had a lot to learn about babies and planning a social life. I told her about Greg and she called him a two-timing shit. I agreed.

Oddly, I slept well that night. Talking with Jan and Leila had been a little like germoline on a gunshot wound but somehow it had worked a kind of magic and soothed some of the pain.

The answerphone was blinking again in the morning but I enjoyed a leisurely breakfast and caught up on my own neglected desk, paying the inevitable bills, before turning to the phone again. It struck me as funny really that when you first meet someone and you're waiting for them to call, you're desperate when they don't. When you just want them to go away you're desperate when they do. There's nowt so queer as folk, as my Grandad used to say.

There were two more calls from Greg on the machine. Oh, Lord, was he angry! He went ballistic! He used words I didn't even know existed and I'd had a pretty liberal adolescence! Boy, oh boy was he livid! He was so cross in the first call that he couldn't get out all the words he wanted to use so he'd had a second try! Who cares, I thought, and went to get myself ready for an afternoon of wine-tasting, solace, fun and anarchy.

-12-
Past Forward

Monday morning again. My third in the job and my first as a young, free and single female. Well, youngish, free-ish and... OK, not exactly single either but close enough for now. There was too much to do today to brood on just how much, and what, but I was most certainly female. Oh yes! That I did know for certain. Paint on a glowing face this morning – gently rosy blusher to disguise the pallid cheeks, soft blue eye shadow, a generous coating of mascara and a shiny, pearly pink smile – put on a decent suit cut to show off the figure and an outrageously impractical pair of sexy shoes. Not exactly Manolo Blahnik, since my plastic doesn't run to that kind of expenses, nor too girly and frivolous, but designed to lift my spirits and make a good impression on what is a serious day. Investigations into unacceptable goings-on with white vans and garages. Alleged goings-on, anyway.

When I was very young I use to think that grown-ups knew everything, were all powerful and would do the right thing in every situation. Naïve. Very naïve. Sometimes it made me a bit sad, thinking about the faith of childhood, lost forever along with little white ankle socks and Clarke's sandals. Where had all the certainty gone?

'Same place as all your other useless illusions,' growled the little devil on my shoulder, 'but I can show you how to stack the odds a bit more in your favour, if you like?'

'Oh... push off,' I said out loud, confusing the cat into thinking she was in trouble. I couldn't help but smile though, in spite of the lump in my chest where my heart was aching; at least my little devil always had a humorous, if risqué, alternative to offer even as he brought me back to earth. Hair clean and tidy? OK. Teeth brushed? Check. Shoes polished? Well, last week, anyway. I gave them a quick going over with a duster. Check in the mirror and off out. House locked? OK. My car safe in garage and garage locked? Done. I'd decide what to do with it later but for now, I was a two-car family of one!

I needed to call at my office to collect all the papers on the Ginger business before heading off down the motorway to HQ, so I turned my shiny new motor into the traffic on the bypass. There was a bus directly ahead of me and I gazed idly at the graffiti scrawled in the dirt on its rear end, as you do when you're in traffic with nowhere else to go and nothing more interesting to look at as you bowl along at almost zero miles an hour. 'I'm blue under here,' said one effort, while 'Dyslexia rules, KO?' said another. Something drew my eyes upwards to the rear window and I realised with a jolt that the head attached to the body that was bobbing about on the back seat belonged to Greg! Oh, boy, I thought, he's having to use the bus! He doesn't believe in public transport, he says it's just for plebs! I could imagine his reaction to having to wait at a bus stop, perhaps in the rain... Well, it certainly wouldn't have improved his temper at all!

I let a couple of cars overtake mine and slid back a bit in the queue as we reached the traffic lights. He didn't know about my new company car and I didn't want him to, not for a while anyway. The risk of his turning around and catching sight of me was probably non-existent, but I wasn't prepared to take it. His not knowing gave me a sort of confidence, the thought that he wasn't going to spot me as long as I could see him and take avoiding action was hugely liberating. I wasn't up to facing him just yet, even at a distance.

It was a bit too early for the shop staff to be in so I let myself into the shop and invaded Mabel's kitchen. She was getting used to me helping myself and had scolded me only three times last week for being untidy. She could spot a speck of dust at ten paces and a watermark on her shiny surfaces at double that. Eyes like radar and a tongue as sharp as my mum's dressmaking shears. Mind you, I'd been out of the office a good bit so she hadn't had me under her feet very much. I treated myself to a cup of hot chocolate – the real kind, mind you, not that watery low-cal stuff – and two chocolate chip cookies.

While I was reviewing priorities for the week, and collecting the papers I needed for that day's meeting, I heard people arriving downstairs, voices shouting greetings and general banging and clattering noises as the volunteers began the day. No-one came upstairs and, from the safety of distance, I felt a sort of affection for them all. They were getting on with their lives and jobs, and doing their bit to benefit others, even thought they had big parcels of troubles of their own, some of them.

Eventually, just as I was ready to leave, I heard the usual chorus of 'Yo, Damian!' and Damian's voice calling back, 'Yo ladies! How are my beauties today?'

Kylie's voice trilled "Aven't a clue, Damian, yer never shows us ladies them fings!' and a burst of female cackling followed him as he clattered up the stairs laughing. I stuck a cup of chocolate in his hand almost before he'd stepped through the door.

'What, ho, boss!' he said with a grin, looking at the steaming cup and raising a beautifully plucked and combed eyebrow. 'You need a favour, then?'

'Not really, Damian, and good morning to you too. I'm out all day today, if you remember?'

'Ah, yes,' he said thoughtfully, tilting his head slightly to one side. 'Nervous?'

'Not really,' I replied, 'not yet anyway. Probably will be later though. No, it's just that there are a few things I'd like you to do for me today, if you will please. The list is on your desk. If you can't get through them all, it's the top three that are the most important.' I paused a moment, not quite sure how far to go. 'Then there's the personal stuff.'

'Oh yes?' he said, a question mark raising the tone of his voice. I explained, as briefly and dispassionately as I could, about the domestic difficulties of my weekend and briefed him on what he should do if Greg took it into his head to call me at work. Damian looked suitable sorrowful and sympathetic.

'Can't trust 'em, you know,' he said sorrowfully when I'd finished, and stroked my arm with a feather light touch. 'They *break* your heart every time.' The gentleness in his voice made my eyes sting with gritty salt. 'Never mind, lovey,' he said more cheerfully, 'when you're ready I'll find you a *smashing* dike to take your mind off your troubles.' He patted my arm again, but more briskly this time, and grinned before turning to check out the list on his desk.

I escaped downstairs, smiling in spite of myself. I popped my head around the door of the office where Kylie was scratching her head over her weekly accounts sheet for last week, trying to follow the same routine I'd shown her. The pencil was between her teeth and I could see that she'd already chewed off the eraser. Her hair was on end where she'd run her hands through it so many times. She looked up at me with a slightly hunted look in her eyes.

'It's alright, Kylie,' I said, 'I'm not here to check up on you, I didn't expect to see you this morning, anyway. How's Charlie doing?'

She relaxed and slumped her shoulders. ''E's OK, I s'pose', she said, ''e's still wiv me mum but 'e came out wiv me yesterday and we 'ad a good time at the park. 'E likes the swings and fings and I bought 'im an ice cream. At least 'e's talking to me now.'

'I'm glad, Kylie. It'll get better, believe me. Be patient. Don't beat yourself up, Charlie needs you to be upbeat and positive, as well as kind. Listen, I'm out all day so Damian will man the office, so to speak.' We both grinned at the thought of Damian being a macho chap. 'But if anyone telephones and asks to talk to me, or come here in person, I'm not contactable today, you don't know when I'll be back but you can take a message. If it gets awkward, call Damian down. Not everyone knows he's a coward and he's bigger than you, so it might help. Is that OK?'

'Ooooooo, our Gillian!' she said, brighter in an instant and with a trill of thrill in her voice. 'You bein' secretive, int yer?' Then she tilted her head to one side and said softly, 'Yer got trouble too?' and surprised me all over again at how perceptive she could be.

'Yes,' I admitted, 'I have.' And she touched my arm in the same gesture of sympathy that Damian had used, nearly bringing the tears to my eyes again. I smiled a watery smile and said I'd see her the next day.

Most of the early morning work traffic had gone to wherever it was going by the time I left the office, and the local school run was over. On such a bright and sunny morning it was quite pleasant being out on the road, away from the tyranny of the Monday morning round of telephone calls, with complaints about rude customers, too much stock/too little stock, too few volunteers, unrealistic sales targets and so on. I had the radio for company and tried not to think about anything much, recognising that the day ahead had the potential to be stressful enough without allowing the problems of my personal life to add to it.

The normally busy roads were clear for once, and I enjoyed the long drive, arriving at HQ in plenty of time without having lost my way even once! Joy of joys, I even managed to find an empty space in the car park next door to the office building! In spite of everything, I began to feel just the teensiest bit of optimism flicking gently at my psyche, trying to get in.

They were expecting me at reception and asked me to wait while someone came down to meet me. The building was a large one, of around 20 floors, in which the charity had three floors for its national HQ. The reception hall had all the trappings of the large, corporate organisation that owned the building, including security guards, a big shiny desk and bland reproductions of some of the most over-used art masterpieces in the world. I wandered around, trying to feign an interest in the prints of 'Girl with a Pearl Earring' and 'Sunflowers'. Eventually the lift doors opened and a woman with a curly cloud of jet black hair, wearing a Chinese embroidered silk shirt, black Thirties-style wide leg trousers and spike-heeled shoes, strode over the vinyl floor towards me. What was it about charities that attracted life's eccentrics?

'Gillian?' she said and I nodded. 'Good morning. Please follow me. Lucas is just finishing off a briefing to some visitors but he'll be with you in about 20 minutes.'

The lift moved upwards noiselessly and without a tremor. We stepped out onto the eleventh floor and into a cramped reception area where a couple of chairs shared the floor with a delivery of stacked boxes of stationary. My guide invited me to sit and asked if I'd like some coffee. I asked for tea, which made her twitch a bit, but she said she's see what she could do. I twiddled my thumbs for a while, sipping the weak, lukewarm tea she'd provided and made small talk with an elderly lady who told me she was the volunteer who manned the switchboard on Mondays. She kept cutting off callers instead of transferring their calls to their destinations and seemed blissfully unaware of the chaos she was causing.

After a while my escort came back and asked me to follow her down a corridor of acoustic panels, arranged around small islands of desks where earnest looking people bent over computers, to an open door at the far end. She motioned me in and left me to it.

As I entered the room the man behind the desk came slowly to his feet, unhooked a large and very knobbly stick from the back of his chair and limped around the desk towards me. Recognition flowered like dawn on a misty morning. Time stopped. Sounds faded into silence. I was stunned and speechless. He held himself upright, with a straight back thanks to the help of the height of the stick and what was obviously long practice, and his face was absolutely still. He was watching me closely, gauging my reaction. My knees went weak and I couldn't feel my fingers. A tingle spread up and down my spine and I could smell ozone and the scent of seaweed on the low tide from memories made long ago.

'Leo,' I whispered.

He stopped and looked at me, head slightly tilted to one side. 'Gemma,' he said, softly. 'I told myself it couldn't be you. But it is, isn't it?'

We stood, locked in space but in a time years before. It was like watching a movie with him and me as the stars. Ten years disappeared and I was 23 again, driving to Hove to stay with an aunt for a few days while I made up my mind whether I should marry Greg or not. It hadn't occurred to me then that if the decision was a difficult one, it might be better not to make it at all but to wait for whatever inspiration might have illuminated the situation and helped me to see my feelings more clearly. It was early in the morning and I'd taken a wrong turn off the M23 ending up on Brighton sea front instead of being 11 miles away on the other side of Hove.

It had been such a beautiful morning and I couldn't bear to miss the experience of soft, warm air and sunlight streaming over the millpond sea. There were few people around and the pearly light of misty sun across the promenade was enchanting. Brighton's pebble beach was empty and the sound of slow waves across the shingle was hypnotic. I'd stopped for tea and toast at a pavement café, not far from the derelict pier, and had been gazing out into the haze of the English channel when a voice had said, 'Do you mind if I join you?' I'd looked around to see every other table completely empty and then up, into the sun, to see a neat head surrounded by a halo of sunshine.

The silliness of it made me giggle. 'It is a bit crowded, isn't it?' I'd said. 'Please, feel free.'

He'd sat down and stretched out his long legs. 'Well, I should confess,' he'd said, then stopped.

'Already?' I'd asked. 'But we've only just met!' And it was his turn to laugh.

'It's my birthday today and I'd rather not spend it all on my own. Not all day, anyway. Can I buy you another cup of tea? Will you take pity on a poor soldier, home on leave, with no-one to talk to?'

'You're a Leo,' I'd said, 'if it's your birthday today. I'm a Gemini.'

'Hi, Gemma,' he'd said. 'Pleased to meet you.'

'Hi, Leo, happy birthday.'

We'd spent a magical day together. He told me he was in the Royal Marines and had come home for an unplanned weekend leave only to find that his wife and daughter had gone to Scotland to visit her parents. He said he was leaving for the Middle East the next day and would be away for several months, that he'd been devastated when he'd realised that his family wasn't at home and angry with himself for taking it for granted that they'd be there. He talked about his love of mountains, his passion for trees and about his ambitions for the future. We'd walked, then lain on warm grass in the park, under the shifting shade of a chestnut tree, and laughed at the antics of a tiny, laughing, toddler chasing a butterfly. We'd eaten candy floss and strolled along the promenade. We'd had lunch in a tapas bar and paddled at the edge of the sea. I'd told him about college, my two years in South Africa and nine months in France. He made me speak to him in French, and I told him I thought he was beautiful and sexy and that I wanted to go to bed with him. I had no idea whether he could understand what I'd said. He just grinned and said French was only the second most musical language in the world. I asked him what was the first and he said Russian.

He'd spoken to me in Russian and I hadn't understood a word. I'd said I didn't think it was particularly musical and he'd said that it depended on what you were saying. He wouldn't translate and I never did learn what he'd said. I hadn't told him that he'd made my toes curl just from the sound of his voice on the words.

In the sunset, with a sea wind tumbling my hair about my face and his open shirt whipping around his body, we said goodbye. He'd cupped his hand around the back of my head and pulled me towards him, kissing me hard and driving all thoughts of his wife and child, and my dilemma over Greg, from my mind. I kissed him back and my world shrank to the size and shape and taste of his mouth.

We walked away from each other, with just one backward glance and outstretched palms in salute. We hadn't told each other our real names, or where we lived or anything that would have allowed us to find each other again. It had been like a day out of time. Unreal. Unconnected. I'd married Greg three months later and put the memory of that day into a small and quiet place in my mind. Never forgotten, and never explored. Just in case.

I blinked and was back in his office, and it was today again. I realised my eyes were on the stick and was angry with myself for staring. He hadn't had it when we met at Brighton and I wondered what had happened.

I appraised him again, closing the gap of the years. He was striking rather than handsome, a little under six foot tall with dark hair, touched by grey at the sides, that hugged the perfect shape of his head; large hazel eyes and a warm smile that displayed perfect teeth. He was just as I remembered, except for the grey in his hair and the creases around his eyes. In the pictures in my mind I hadn't remembered him as older than me. Now I saw that he was by quite a few years. But still beautiful to my eyes.

'But it is you, isn't it?' he said again 'What a very small world it is. I never dreamed...' His voice tailed off.

He held out his free hand and shook mine, like newly introduced people. His was warm, dry and had an easy, comfortable grip that lasted just the right length of time. He motioned to a small group of two easy chairs and a low table.

'Let's be comfortable,' he said, in a businesslike tone but with that warm honey voice I knew from my memory and our recent telephone conversations. Another little shiver went down my spine. He said, 'I think we should keep this businesslike, don't you? We have a lot to get through today.' I nodded, nervous of what my voice would do if I allowed myself to speak. Squeak, probably. 'Have you had coffee?' he asked and I nodded, unable to say I'd had tea instead. 'Good. We'll have a break in about an hour. I promised you a full day and that's what we have. You'll be with me for the next hour, then I'll pass you over to the HR department until lunch. After lunch there'll be an interview with Molly Chambers. She's our legal advisor and she'll want to go over your statement about the driver and ask you questions about it. Then I shall need to talk with you and Malcolm about Chilton Street to decide what needs to be done there. That's a full day for you, what with your journey and everything. Is it OK? Not too much in one day?'

'No, that's fine,' I said, relieved that my voice didn't squeak too much and that my tongue, which had been stuck to the roof of my mouth, seemed to work OK. I opened my briefcase to take out my smart, black leather conference folder, with its equally smart, chrome, roller ball pen and legal sized writing block. I sat to attention and smiled to show I was ready, tension in every line of my body.

For the next hour he was all business, which was exactly what I'd expected but which I still found disappointing for some daft reason only my psyche could understand. Anyway, he ran through the charity's business plan, spending targets, priorities and the myriad of fundraising initiatives they had. All part of my induction into the job that Jean would have told me, had she been here. He set a cracking pace and had me struggling to keep up with him in the note-taking department.

After about 45 minutes his phone rang and I found myself watching closely the way he moved back to his desk. The limp was on the left side. I wondered again how he had come by it. Was it something to do with his service in the Marines? Had he been wounded in Ireland? In the Middle East? Somewhere else? He spoke, abruptly but not unkindly, to the dippy receptionist I'd chatted with while I was waiting. She'd managed to find his telephone extension so she must be improving with practice, I thought.

'I asked you to hold my calls, is it urgent?' There was a long pause. 'I see. Tell her I'll call back in about 15 minutes.' He replaced the phone and came back to his seat. 'Apologies,' he said, and shook his head in a gesture of some irritation, 'that was my daughter's school.' He settled himself in the chair again and smiled. It hit my soul like seeing the sun rise over the clouds when you're sitting next to the window of a jet flying over the Alps. If I'd been wearing socks it would have blown them off. Fortunately I was sitting down so everything else stayed in place. 'She's 15 now and giving her teachers the runaround. Do you have children?' he asked

'No,' I said. His question caught me off guard and I felt the familiar, painful spasm deep down inside. It must have shown.

'Was that the wrong thing to say?' he said. 'I'm sorry, I shouldn't have asked. I said we should concentrate on business and here I am, breaking my own pledge.'

'I don't mind you asking,' I said, 'it's the answer that's tough.' I took a breath to steady myself. 'My son died and I wasn't brave enough to risk it again.' I hurried on before he had the chance to say any of the useless, vapid things people generally did when I told them. 'But now it's my turn. How did you come by the limp? You didn't have it the last time we met.'

'Boy, you're certainly direct!' he chuckled. 'Not many people just come out and ask like that, they mostly tie themselves in knots trying not to be too obvious about their interest.' He paused for a moment and then continued. 'A climbing accident. I was on exercise with the Marines. The bone was badly broken and it took a couple of days for them to get me off the mountain, which didn't help. It mended eventually but not very well.'

'Now we're even,' I said, 'shall we stop before we embarrass each other?' He raised an eyebrow. 'Or do you need to call the school?' I added, hastily. He laughed and my knees went weak again.

'We've made good time,' he said, 'I'll take you over to HR. They'll have sandwiches and things there for a working lunch and fill you in on how we handle disciplinary matters such as the one you're involved in at present. Molly will bring you back here at about two-thirty.'

The next hour and a half were tedious, tedious, tedious. We covered all sorts of things that were without a doubt extremely important but dull, dull, dull. All delivered in tones that were loaded with doom and filled with predictions of the direst of consequences should we be hauled up in front of the ogres who inhabit the depths of the employment tribunal system. It occurred to me that I might have found it quite interesting if only I hadn't been so overloaded with emotional stimuli that even the last trump would have seemed pretty mundane. By the time we were through I was beginning to think everything I did as a manager was bound to end in disaster and they, the HR experts, would magnanimously fly to my rescue and pluck me from the mire into which I had dropped my caring employer. If I asked them very nicely. And was willing to say it was all my fault anyway. And promise to do penance for the rest of my life.

When Molly came to fetch me, after her minions had finished with me, I was glad to escape. That was before. Before she put me through the third degree. Boy, was she thorough. And totally without humour or a speck of human warmth. She asked about why I'd followed Ginger that day, how I'd come to think he might be doing something irregular, who had advised me on the action I'd taken and why I'd taken photographs. She wanted to know if I'd visited Ginger's house and made me repeat, again and again, what I'd said to him and to his wife in person and on the phone. When she'd finished, I felt like piece of chewed string.

'Well,' she said, 'it could be worse. You seem to be able to stick with your version of events quite well.' My version? Cheek! I was telling it as it was! Patronising… Words failed me, which was probably just as well.

'I could let you have a few good ones, if you need them,' whispered my little devil. I ignored him and he disappeared in a huff.

'We will arrange a disciplinary hearing as soon as possible. If, and I say if, we move to dismiss this man, we have to be prepared for the fact that he may take us to an employment tribunal for wrongful dismissal. However, if the evidence is clear and unequivocal, he may see that there is no possibility of success and decide it wouldn't be a sensible thing to do. Unfortunately, common sense doesn't always have the allure of compensation. We'll be in touch.' And with that she swept out of the room and I had to almost run to keep up with her.

Lucas was waiting for me, looking cool and unruffled. 'Malcolm will join us in a few minutes,' he said. 'How're you doing so far?'

'My head is spinning a bit. Molly the rottweiler has just chewed me up and spat me out.'

He grinned. 'I don't remember you being so direct. Is this new or has my memory let me down?'

'Defence mechanism. It's been a busy day and full of surprises, to put it mildly.'

'I know, I'm sorry to put you through all this at once. It's unfortunate that Jean is away and you've been thrown in the deep end.'

'I'm not. Sorry, that is,' I said. 'If she'd been here it could have been months, if at all, before we'd have spoken or met.' I paused. I wasn't sure if I should be the one to mention the unsaid things lying between us, but plunged on anyway. 'I haven't thought about that day in Brighton very often. I haven't...' I stopped, not knowing how to say the feeling.

'Wanted to?' he suggested, his voice quiet and hesitant.

'Not that.'

'What, then?' The silence lengthened

'Dared to, I suppose.' We looked at each other. Just looked. Then there was a knock at the door and Malcolm walked in without waiting for a response, breaking the spell. He looked at me with that way he had, like I was a vaguely interesting specimen but he couldn't quite figure out whether I was worthy of extended study.

'That suit is more suitable than the outfit you wore on Wednesday', he said. 'More business like'

Lucas masked an expression that could have been irritation or amusement, I couldn't decide which, and gestured us both to chairs. For more than an hour we talked about options, insurances, costs and comparisons for Chilton Street, as well as my embryonic plans for the patch, till my head felt as though it was in overdrive. I explained about the administrative nightmare I'd found around the shops, that I believed a concentrated effort on sales training and volunteer recruiting was crucial and that Miles was the perfect person to take that programme forward. I said that he could only do that if he had someone to help him at Kensington Place and Gordon was a good choice to do that. I said I'd placed Belinda at Broad Barrow, in the short term, to help Brigid pull Broad Barrow around.

Lucas smiled and sat back in his chair at that point, hands locked under his chin and elbows resting on the arms of his chair. His eyes twinkled. 'She's one of a kind, our Belinda, isn't she?'

I was surprised that he was so well informed about Belinda. 'She's very knowledgeable about her hobby,' I said innocently, 'but the rest of her seems to be... well... relatively normal.'

Malcolm sniffed. Lucas barked with laughter. 'I met her at an open day, here at HQ last year,' he said, 'she button-holed me for half an hour on the value of uniforms as a way of promoting team spirit and suggested that we give each of our volunteers a T shirt and a pair of jogging bottoms to work in. Actually, she argued her case quite well although I disappointed her on the issue of expense, I think. And the strap line. She wanted 'Live long and prosper'.'

'Mmm,' I said. 'I can just see Caroline in a T shirt and jogging bottoms, he'd look like the incredible hulk on a bad day.' Lucas barked his laugh again and even Malcolm smiled, although he tried to hide it behind his hand. He took up the story from there, before I could pick up my thread again. I was shattered by this time, and could feel my brain slowing down and begging for a rest. I hadn't made it work so hard for longer than it could remember.

Malcolm reprised the briefing he'd given to Lucas the day before. He ended by saying '...so I've decided to recommend that we give notice to terminate the lease at Chilton Street and look for a new shop unit as soon as possible.' I felt my jaw drop. That was *my* idea! Where the hell did he get off, stealing my idea and the whole point of my strategy? So what if everything had happened backwards, with things falling into place almost on their own? It was still my idea, wasn't it? Malcolm shifted in his seat. He avoided looking at me and I could feel the colour rising to my face as I tried not to leap across the coffee table to throttle him. I felt, rather than saw, Lucas looking from one of us to the other and back again.

The woman who came through the door at that minute, waving a piece of paper in her hand, saved me from an uncontrolled outburst of murder. She handed the paper to Lucas who glanced at it and said, 'Well, that's it then!' and looked at me. 'Ginger has just phoned in his resignation. There'll be no investigation.'

I was speechless. Again. But a huge sense of relief flooded through me. Malcolm made his escape while my attention was diverted. I think I said something suitably astringent, but very controlled, as he left. Lucas certainly raised an eyebrow, although he didn't say anything.

'That message was from Ginger's wife,' Lucas said when we were alone. 'She says Ginger had planned to resign if it went as far as a disciplinary hearing and that he had only done so because he felt he was being victimised. We find that's a standard response, unfortunately. It allows a quick path to a tribunal for constructive dismissal. When Molly spoke with Ginger about an hour ago he threatened to do just that. His wife also had her say but she said, that he's decided not to go for a tribunal after all, although she didn't say why.' He sounded a bit puzzled and I felt the expression on my face change. He narrowed his eyes as he looked at me for a moment and I could see that he was calculating what might have happened to make Ginger take the low road before he said, 'Did you have a hand in that? You said you'd talked with his wife. What did you say to her?'

'I think you'd rather not know,' I said. 'It might be best that way.'

He was suddenly all alertness, all business and more than just a bit daunting. I could see the power that came from his training in command of Marines 'I think you should explain,' he warned, so I told him what Ginger's wife and I had said to each other and about my assurances that he would not face a prosecution.

'But we don't prosecute anyway,' he said, 'although we're reviewing that policy now, partly in the light of this incident. Why did what you said make the difference?'

'I told her that we don't prosecute,' I said, 'because I thought she probably knew that already, since Ginger's been around for some time. Then I said that something as systematic and long lasting as what he'd been doing would cause a policy review. I said that if a review recommended changing the policy, and it was officially changed before the disciplinary hearing, who could say whether Ginger wouldn't be caught squarely in the middle and face prosecution under the new policy?'

'But you didn't know that we were reviewing that policy. We decided only yesterday afternoon.'

'I didn't. I was bluffing.'

'My God!' he said. 'You're absolutely priceless!' I wasn't sure if he meant that entirely as a compliment but I decided to accept it as one and was basking in the warm glow of his appreciation when my own mobile warbled at me. It was Miles.

'Gillian,' he said, 'I'm so sorry to disturb you but I just couldn't wait any longer. You're not driving or anything are you?'

'No, Miles, I'm quite stationary. What can I do for you?'

'It's the picture. We've just been told that it's a Sixteenth Century Russian icon and we should put a reserve on it of at least eight K at auction!' I was speechless. Again. It was a day for losing the use of my vocal cords, obviously.

I took a deep breath. 'I don't quite know what to say, Miles. That's just the most incredible thing I've heard in a long time. In fact, it's almost too good to be true. I think we'd better be a bit cautious, though, because it seems unlikely that anyone would deliberately give away that kind of valuable item, no matter how much they supported a cause. It could be an accident.'

'Yes, I suppose you're right,' he said, calmer now. 'Should we check, do you think?'

'I think we should, yes. Tomorrow I'll stop by and we'll decide what to do. In the meantime, would you do something for me?'

'What's that?'

'Buy Bianca the biggest box of jammy dodgers you can find and treat the rest of the staff to custard doughnuts. On me.'

'I will,' he laughed. 'See you tomorrow.'

I just sat for a moment, stunned by the implications of what Miles had said. If no-one claimed the icon after we had exhausted efforts to trace an owner, and the police didn't have it on their stolen goods list, auctioning it would be a tremendous coup. Such a find would generate stories in the local press – maybe even the nationals if there weren't enough disasters and political banana skins to fill the columns that day. The publicity could be just what we needed to launch us into a surge of prosperity. I put my phone away, took another deep breath, and told Lucas.

He was just as stunned as I was.

'I thought that sort of thing was just urban myth,' he said. 'Your Bianca has probably just made history. I think we should celebrate,' he said and then paused for the longest time before he said, 'Will you have dinner with me this evening?'

An attack of the tingles hit my toes and I breathed 'Yes'. He grinned.

The little devil on my shoulder rustled in my ear 'Now this is interesting. Want some tips?' and I shrugged him away.

We agreed to meet a little later at a local bistro that Lucas suggested. I walked out of the office feeling like… well, like I hadn't felt for long time. If ever. I did some shopping while he finished his day in the office and was waiting for him in the bistro at a tiny table where a deep red candle, stuck into a wax encrusted bottle, flickered. I'd bought a new dress and had found a hairdressing salon with a gap in their schedule, where they'd washed and dried my hair into a shining glory. I knew I looked good, and that anticipation had put colour in my cheeks. The food was good and the service unobtrusive.

We talked. And talked. At first it was about work, the job, being new and thrown in the deep end. He had a fund of anecdotes that made me smile, laugh and then left me with aching sides.

Lucas asked me why I was working for a charity. I told him about Dominic and how I'd thought I would never function again, after he had died. Told him about struggling to make sense of it all and wanting to do something to stop it happening to other people and to try to solve the mystery of unexplained infant deaths. Then finding that I couldn't work in that field because it was just too raw and too closely linked with the source of the pain but desperate to find a way to live a life that seemed to have no real meaning left in it. Of opening the paper one day to find the advert for this job staring me in the face, like divine providence. I'd reasoned that if I couldn't help directly, then I'd raise the money to pay the people who could.

When I finished the story I realised that his hand was resting lightly over mine on the table. He didn't move it when he saw me watching. For a while we just sat, then I moved my hand gently away and said calmly, 'Tell me about your daughter. She and your wife were away that day we met, weren't they? Your daughter must have been just a baby then.'

He sat back in his chair, the remnants of the meal between us on the table, the wine bottle empty and the candle guttering down.

He twirled his wine glass around by the stem and I could see him thinking.

'Jenny and I met at university,' he said at last. 'We separated for a while after we graduated, she went to Edinburgh to join a legal firm and I joined the Marines. We met again about five years later. I was stationed in Plymouth at the time and she was in Brighton, setting up a new office for her company. We were married when I came back from the Falklands. Lots of us did that. It was a kind of fierceness. An affirmation of life in the teeth of death. Psychologists will tell you it's a common phenomenon. She was already pregnant when we got married and she had a tough time. The birth was difficult and Lauren wasn't an easy child. Still isn't,' he said ruefully.

'It changed us both, those two years. It was easy to ignore the problems we had, and that Jenny had raising Lauren, because I was away a lot. When Lauren was old enough for a nursery Jenny picked up her career and, even when I was home, we didn't see much of each other. That's where we were that day in Brighton. In limbo, really. Then I fell off the mountain. My career collapsed and Jenny didn't know how to cope with me at home all the time. Nor did I, if truth be known.' He paused. 'We're still friends though, and there was nothing acrimonious about the divorce. We're still Lauren's parents, after all. We don't see much of each other but we're in touch often.'

We looked at each other over the candle flame.

'What about you?' he asked. 'You wear a wedding ring, I see.'

'I'm married too,' I said, 'but I was more married than he was. I think I knew that for ages but we were glued together for a long time by losing Dominic. That was seven years ago. We're separated now. It's over.'

'You sound sad.'

'Yes, I am, but there's no going back and there's more to life than moaning about what might have been.'

He smiled. 'True. Coffee?'

'It's late and I have to drive home.'

There was a pause. A long, expectant pause.

'Do you?' he asked finally. 'I'd like you to stay. Please. I keep remembering that kiss.' His voice was soft, gentle, with something…

an edge of… longing, perhaps? Lust? What? 'Is that going too fast? ' he asked and I could hear my own heart beat.

'It's been ten years,' I said, 'I don't think that's too fast. After all, I asked you before.'

'You did, didn't you? In French, if I remember.'

'You knew! You never said!'

'Yes, I knew. And I said yes. In Russian. With a bit more for effect. Just think, if you'd been more of a linguist our lives could have been completely different.' And he grinned.

Twenty minutes later I turned my car into the drive of a small, but elegant house on the outskirts of the town, following where he led in his BMW. A security light came on as we parked and I could see a neat garden with laurel hedges, and roses and huge, luscious fuchsias in flower beds. He opened the door into a large, cool hall decorated in shades of barley and cream with heavy drapes the colour of port wine. I followed him through to a sitting room with big, squashy cream sofas and long velvet drapes that he closed against the night.

'This is my place,' he said, 'I hope you like it.'

'This is crazy,' I said, panicking a little after the bravado show in the bistro. 'We only met this morning. You could be a mad axeman for all I know!'

He glanced around the room and said, with a wry smile, 'Not quite compatible with pale furniture. You'd be able to see the stains.' I couldn't help but smile. He grinned back at me, curling my toes again.

'Good. Now, come into the kitchen and I'll find the brandy and coffee.' He made some awful coffee, which I found reassuring, and poured us both a generous measure of very fine brandy. Then he told me more stories of his days in the Marines. I drank the coffee anyway, washed away the taste with his brandy and told him about my own erratic career path.

Just before midnight he took my hand and lead me upstairs. On the landing I pulled back a little and he stopped.

'This is still crazy. We work together. Well, sort of. You know what they say about work relationships.'

'Do you want to stop now?' he asked and we looked at each other in silence. Tonight was full of pauses, I thought, but no sign of the little devil on my shoulder. Maybe he thought I was doing alright on my own this time.

'No. No, I don't,' I said and opened the door behind me. 'Is this your bedroom?'

'Right on!' said the little devil on my shoulder. 'Well done!'

-13-
Epilogue

I didn't stay with Lucas that night. I couldn't explain why to myself, let alone to him, but he smiled wryly as I stuttered and rambled about nothing in particular, making no sense at all for several minutes. Eventually he took my face in his hands, tilted it upwards slightly and kissed me full on the mouth. That shut me up. I didn't want him to let go and I put my arms around him, feeling the warmth of him through the thin cotton of the shirt he'd shrugged into when I left his bed and began to gather my clothes together. I felt awkward, embarrassed, slightly ashamed and I didn't understand why. I wanted to delay the moment that I had to let go of him, but still couldn't wait to get out of his house.

He was quite clearly puzzled and I thought I saw hurt in his eyes, but I could no more stay than I could fly to the moon just at that moment. How could I explain how I felt when I had absolutely no idea myself? I saw him, through the rear-view mirror, watching me drive away. At risk of life and limb I watched his image in the rear view mirror as I turned onto the road. Thankfully there was precious little traffic at this time of night – or was it morning? – and I managed it safely. The light in the hallway shone from behind him, out into the quiet darkness, and I saw it shining steadily until I turned the corner out of his sight, long after I would have expected him to close the door.

It was quite a long drive home, and after three in the morning, but I was wide awake. There was no risk that I'd fall asleep at the wheel, there was too much activity going on in my brain. I couldn't seem to get my head around the fact that we'd met again after ten years. Or that I'd leapt into bed with a perfect stranger. One day ten years ago didn't constitute a relationship, after all, and we were different people than we'd been then in any case. But it had felt... it felt... Oh, Lord, it felt good!

So why had I run away? Because that's exactly what I'd done, scampered like a scared ninny. Was it all about running away from my unhappy marriage and grasping at straws? Had the rosy glow of Brighton beach in the sunset, ten years ago and amplified by time, tinted everything with an impossibly glorious technicolour vision? Worse, had I let the first fella that made a pass at me make a fool of me? Part of me didn't give a damn. Part of me was too disillusioned to know truth from deception. Not that I was any good at spotting deception. Greg would attest to that, the rat!

Halfway home it began to rain. Music on the radio merged with the swish of the windscreen wipers. He loves me, he loves me not; he loves me, he…

I started to giggle. After about 20 minutes, as I drove, I felt my mood start to lift a little and I began to hum along to the music on the radio. Out of nowhere my memory clicked back to a time even before Brighton beach. Perhaps a tune on the radio, from years ago, had flipped me back in time.

I remembered a so-called fortune teller, consulted in a mad moment during a weekend of student hilarity, when I'd gone with a crowd of friends to a dingy house on a council estate. The guy had seen us, each in turn, in his kitchen, while his wife sat in frosty disapproval watching Coronation Street next door. Not an auspicious setting and I treated it with humorous distain.

Until he'd asked, 'Who is Geoffrey? Spelt with a G, not a J.'

I sat up and took notice then. 'My brother,' I said, curiosity piqued.

'And Simon?'

Now I was wary. 'My… my first boyfriend,' I sort of whispered.

'And what does the name Greave mean to you?'

By this time I was well and truly spooked. My voice had a strange quiver in it. 'It's the name of the road where my junior school was.'

For a time he just looked at me. Oddly, I didn't feel uncomfortable in his gaze and after a while, the turmoil in my mind quietened. He put his hand gently on mine, where it lay on the formica of his scruffy kitchen table, and it was warm. My hand became warm underneath his and the warmth spread gently to my wrist and forearm. He smiled then, just a faint lifting of the corners of his mouth and a relaxation of the rather harsh planes of his face.

'You have a gift, you know. You can use it, if you wish. Trust yourself. Not your heart, not your head, all of yourself. Oh, and by the way, you think too much.' He emphasised the word 'think'. He paused and watched me. I was afraid. Dabbling in the black arts was dangerous, my school teacher had shouted at us – Kelly, Lucy and me – when she'd caught us hiding in a disused hay loft in the school orchard during a drizzly lunch break, with a Ouija board. We'd just finished scaring ourselves so when she shouted about the board and seemed completely to overlook the fact that we were seriously out of bounds, we knew she was deeply shocked. We'd pretended a blasé nonchalance, but we only talked about the board after that, we never used it again.

I said, rather shakily, 'I can't.'

He sensed my fear. His expression changed again. 'Go, then. You're wasting my time. You and your friends came here for the wrong reasons and I've had enough of you.' And with that he stood up and turned his back to me. I was appalled. And angry.

For weeks I clung to that anger and blamed him for being a fraud and, somehow, a trickster. One of my friends had set us up and told him stuff. They must have. And I spent hours, when I should have been studying, trying to figure out who it might be. Then I forgot all about it, as you do with stuff that tires you out for no purpose, especially when you're young.

Except that Greg had said something, years later, that brought it all back again. He'd said, in a quarrel, 'You could bloody well think for the Olympics!' It stopped me in my tracks and I asked him what he meant, forgetting that we were supposed to be disagreeing about something. 'You never just take things for what they are,' he'd tried to explain, 'you always have to tear it all to bits and examine every little piece. It drives me crackers. Why can't you just stop trying to figure everything out and just… just… I don't know.' He'd tousled his hair in frustration. 'Just stop thinking. Sometimes you don't have to think. It just gets in the way. You let it get in the way.'

Very profound, for Greg. I was astonished. He wasn't usually one for philosophy, although he had a good enough brain. As witnessed by his ability to mentally calculate his winnings on a treble yankee for a £5.25 bet. Or whatever.

It made me think, though. Was that what I did? Analyse, ponder, examine things from too many angles? It was like the loop that Excel won't let you do, the circular calculation or whatever it was called.

So what about Leo? Or Lucas, as I now knew him. Had I lost what I'd found again simply because I couldn't stop thinking and analysing too much? Why had I run away? What did any of it matter in the scheme of the cosmos, anyway? Oh, Lord, here I was, doing it again!

By this time I was almost home. It was after four in the morning and the only things moving on the street were a solitary cat and the milkman. I'd no idea he did his rounds so early. On impulse, I stopped the car next to his float, as he trotted down a garden path from my neighbour's door, and I asked him for a small carton of milk. He grinned at me and winked as I opened the carton and took a deep draught of the cool, sweet white stuff.

'Thirsty night, love?'

I grinned back. 'You could say that!' And I handed him back the empty carton, winking at him jauntily.

The house was quiet and the cat looked up at me from her basket, blinked sleepily a couple of times, then put her head down on her paws again as I shrugged off my coat and stood in the moonlight that came through the uncurtained window. I could almost hear the world breathe.

I hesitated only a moment, then walked over to the phone. It rang only once at the other end before he said, 'Hello, you.'

He must have been waiting.